EARLY EXIT TO THE VOID

EARLY EXIT TO THE VOID

JACK B.S. NORTH

Dedicated to the Seekers Among Us

Contents

Author Presence

ADDITIONAL TITLE BY JACK B.S. NORTH

Simon's Death

ONLINE PRESENCE

Twitter @JackBSNorth
jacknorth.ca

Author's Note

Computer terms pepper this novel. I considered defining them. But I faced two problems.

One: if you're not a computer programmer or have a bent toward understanding machine language, you probably wouldn't understand the definitions unless I tried to explain them at length, which would bore most silly. And if you are, you'd probably object to any definition I gave.

Two: the computer terms are a metaphor. I asked myself: if I define the terms, if that would fence in your, the reader's, imagination? I don't want to limit your mental-scape, your imagery of what void.NullTime is or what David.admin would look like, or your ideation of EnergyMind class, as examples.

Way, way back my English professor taught us that when we use unfamiliar diction to place it in a context such that the reader could guess what the word(s) meant. So, for example, when I used WORM, I defined it literally, but I also used it as a metaphorical representation in Ev's self-image. I tried to define other computer terms or phrases such as "throw statement" by giving it understandable context or straight-out definition within the scene.

Immersing yourself in Ev's mental-scape will, I hope, make the unfamiliarity fade into the background and let her story take you on her journey.

I

Early Exit

A point of light. Prismatic white. Luminescing in the vast void of black non-light. A speck in the distance of NullTime. The white point expanded toward her eyes until it filled her front view and surrounded her, extending above and below, around her to enclose her from behind, or so Ev assumed. She wasn't sure exactly where the white ended. She stepped forward, and the heel of her shoe connected with the white surface below her, bending it and sending it in regular ripples back toward the infinity from whence the white had come. Ev watched the ripples, each one slightly shorter than the one in front of it until the last ripple, barely a bulge up from the luminous surface, waved smoothly away from her until it became one with the original pixel that grew the white.

Ev sent her eyes around this box of white, yet not a box. The sides seemed to have dimensions, yet they seeped outward. She sensed depthless depth. As she stared at the wall to her right, notes of cream appeared in the whiteness. The cream turned the wall milky. Ev lifted her face up and stretched her eyelids so that she could take in as much of the ceiling as she could. It was like the sky. Close yet far. Vast yet every pixel seemingly visible. Its whiteness pricked her pupils, yet she couldn't stop looking at it; as she looked through her wide-open eyes, shadings of the subtlest dove grey emerged and outlined clouds. She raised her right hand. She pointed to each grey edge as if she were with her grade-school friend when they had lain side by side on the scraggly grass of the school playground, pointing out the clouds sailing past their vision, calling out their shapes, and competing over who could spot the silliest animal. Ev smiled in memory retrieval, and the dove grey darkened ever so slightly so that the shapes read back into her consciousness appeared in her vision.

Ev retrieved her hand quickly and drew down her brows. *Was that supposed to happen?*

"Yes," a voice said near at hand, startling her. Ev jumped yet stayed at the apex of her trajectory, floating yet stationary. She carefully searched for the source of that voice.

"Over here," the voice said. "No, look to your left. Now, look down."

Ev blinked. Below her, to her left, was a white desk with a white computer display atop it, behind which sat a white chair in which sat a man...woman? She wasn't sure. *A person.* She nodded to herself.

"We don't have gender," the voice said. "But we've retained our names. We're of the EnergyMind class. You're of the EnergyHuman class. So you can call me EnergyMind David.admin."

Puzzlement like a dive weight sank Ev down until she was standing in front of the white desk that seemed to meld into the surface below. But as she scanned it, foamy green began to froth at its edges, and she saw it was like an old metal desk from the 1950s. *Or was that the 60s?* She wasn't sure. *It was from before she was born. Maybe the 70s.*

"The sixties," EnergyMind David.admin said. *It not he*, thought Ev, as she scanned its whitish lips barely discernible in its whitish face, its irises a white-grey infinitesimally darker than its skin.

"Oh," Ev whispered, her whisper filling the space.

"Void.NullTime," EnergyMind David.admin corrected, its half-transparent whitish hair melding partially into the air.

"Oh," Ev whispered again, the sound waves of her whisper appearing...in the air?

"No air. We don't need air or oxygen here. But you do, so we've pumped some in for you. You can call it air."

Oh, Ev thought, keeping her eyes firmly ahead of her to see if her thoughts produced waves of steam or mist or whatever that was that the sound waves had become. But she saw nothing, just the last wisps of her whisper's sound waves drifting apart at the edges, still travelling away from her to become one with the walls for lack of a better term for the white sides with their creamy intrusions.

"Why are you here?" its calm, matter-of-fact voice interrupted her gazing. Ev's eyes sharpened as she flicked her eyeballs back from the walls to its face. She couldn't really perceive its face though. *Shouldn't its skin be something other than white? Weren't only corpses white? Or were they grey?* She didn't know. She'd never seen a dead person. Anxiety fluttered her heart. She tried to suppress the cough. She inhaled as quietly as she could so as not to disappear into the white below surface. To her relief, she didn't move, and EnergyMind David.admin's eyes remained on her, its features motionless, waiting, its demeanour not judging as if it didn't matter to him how long she took to answer his question. *Or was that its question? Is 'it' the way to address a genderless human? Was it a human?* Suddenly she couldn't remember.

"EnergyMind class," he said. "Character object David. Function admin. You won't remember."

"Oh," Ev replied, wondering why it said she wouldn't remember. She didn't forget anything. She remembered her second birthday; she remembered the last thing her mother had said to her; she remembered the last day of university, every detail of it; she always remembered every line of her code. Her eyes fixed on David.admin's eyes. She felt drawn into their grey depths. Grey not white. Sparkles like diamonds winked deep inside their pupils, and she became hypnotized. It flicked its gaze away, breaking her hypnotic trance. She swallowed. "Um," she said as she suddenly realized that she didn't remember its character object.

David.admin returned its patient gaze upon her and waited for her to continue her utterance.

She sucked in breath. *No, she must focus on why she entered void.Null-Time. This was where game play began, here and with her question, the one she'd been thinking about for the last eighteen years. But now that the time had come to ask she felt unnerved. This was so unlike her, being forward, asking for something, but she needed to ask. She didn't want to ask. She felt unready. Yet an urge entered her, pushing her to ask, giving her desire wings to speak.* She breathed out. "I want an early exit."

"An early exit?" he queried, its brow wrinkling, sending off sparks of pink.

She followed one of the pink sparks, fascinated at the randomization. EnergyMind David.admin sat forward, sending the sparks swirling through the air, flashing lighter and lighter pink until they became white and vanished into the walls and the above surface, a sky or ceiling she still wasn't sure. She thought: *sky. But was there a sky in void.Null-Time?* She couldn't remember. A second detail forgotten. Ev shrugged away her internal observation, for she had more pressing problems: her heart was fluttering and her breath had begun to rasp in this fragrant air, fragrant with...white? EnergyMind David.admin's hands had disappeared on the other side of the display, and she could hear it typing yet could not see a keyboard nor its fingers. The sound waves from the keys banging down, one rapidly after the other, shot out scents of unknown flowers. How she knew the pleasant scents came from flowers she didn't know. The pleasant scents built and built; they clashed and overpowered her nose. Her nostrils squeezed themselves shut against the onslaught.

"Ah," it exclaimed. The coordinated staccato on the keys stopped all at once. The silence hummed calmly against her ears and cheeks. The silence caressed her facial skin, and she felt her forehead and cheeks glow as if love had accepted her request. It leaned down, retrieved something from its side of the desk on the right side, and lifted up a sheaf of papers. It extended its right hand toward her, offering her the sheets. "Your application for an early exit," it stated matter-of-factly. "I'm not an 'it.' But you'll come to know as you fill out the application, hear your bots, and connect with those you need to meet."

Ev wrinkled her brow. She hesitated. She looked into EnergyMind David.admin's eyes. She forgot his statement about "it." She sank into its eyes' pupils, not wondering how she could see through a pinhole. She searched for the diamond sparkles, and they sprang into being. They emitted waves of truth, of something overwhelming. She yearned to be what it was. *But was this what she really wanted?* She'd been planning for an early exit since she was fifteen years old. Certainty over her goal filled her days and comforted her nights. But strangely, now that she was here in void.NullTime, being told she could have an early exit if she filled in the application form, uncertainty fluttered out from her heart into her skin and sprang her fine hairs to attention. Why was she hesitating? She no longer sought others' approval or cared if anyone did approve.

At one time, she'd told others in her coding community about her idea. They had laughed at her, told her no girl could do it. It was okay when she was learning from them, playing their games, creating first-person shooter games like theirs, mimicking their aggression, but when she dared to speak out her question, expecting answers of curiosity or accepting even if not agreeing...

She skirted from the memory. The problem with never forgetting was never forgetting the bad stuff. She had left the community. No one had noticed enough to ask where she had gone. She'd left home, her parents both psychiatrists approving of her independence and both suggesting that as an adult child it was good to have less contact with them. "Adults aren't dependent and needy," mother had said. "Adults need to find their own way," father had said. Ev had quickly found her own expertise: designing websites that gave the owners and users exactly what they wanted. She began to name her own price. That left her free to work on *Early Exit To The Void*, her question hanging in her mind like fruit just out of reach. Being able to restart thinking and coding an answer settled her mind.

Ev had started coding an answer to her question long before she'd moved out. One night in her bedroom, on one of the many nights the house was still and she was alone, only the sound of her breathing filling the space, she'd fallen asleep and dreamt of void.NullTime. She'd awoken, startled, and began thinking about a virtual reality program to exit early. After she'd moved out and had earned enough not to code for ten hours a day then drum up new business for eight, she allowed herself downtime. Thoughts of how to exit early had filled that downtime. Every minute down, she'd thought about her program *Early Exit To The Void*. And now its fulfillment was here. The early exit she'd dreamt of that night long past.

Ev lifted her right hand and stretched her fingers out toward the sheaf. Her fingertips touched the paper, and suddenly David.admin, of EnergyMind class, the white surfaces, all of it vanished.

Ev is staring into the darkness of a black (empty) screen.

Slowly, Ev pulls off her VR gloves that allow her to sense by touch virtual reality. She pulls them off one finger at a time. She tosses them without thinking. They land on the far left edge of her desk. She lifts her left hand and removes her glossy white VR helmet. She'd had the helmet made to protect her head during her extended play times in some of her error-prone early incarnations. The built-in headphones slip upward from her ears as she shakes her head free. She sighs and lays the helmet down on her smooth maple desk tabletop. How much time was she in there? Is it late morning or early morning?

Japanese Robot wheels silently up to her. She senses him on her right. "Welcome back, Ev. It's six o'clock and fifty-five minutes. What is that you have?" he asks her.

Ev turns her head to query her robot.

"In your hand," he elucidates.

She becomes aware of her right hand, blood pulsing heat through it, nerves sending signals of texture against her fingers. They feel like they're grasping something. She glances down. Her fingers are holding papers. *The sheaf?* Her brow wrinkles; thin wavy rows form on her forehead. She raises her hand to stare at the papers.

Three sheets.

White.

Blank.

In her head, a voice whispers as if from a distance, as if from void.NullTime: "Your application."

2

Email Waits

Ev flings her fingers open. The sheets float onto her desk. They stare blankly up at her.

"That's paper," Japanese Robot says.

Ev doesn't answer. She cannot rip her eyes away from the three sheets.

"I am fully charged. Call me when you need me." Japanese Robot wheels backward to rest in his charging station.

Ev hears but doesn't move. Slowly, slowly, her brain sends signals to her muscles to come back to life. With her fingertips, she pushes the top sheet sideways until her arm stretches so far that her muscle fibres protest. Her body leans way over. The three white papers sit askew of each other at the far-right edge of her wide tabletop desk. Sighing out her pent-up breath, she wheels her high-backed chair out from the desk and sits down, her back leaning against the ventilated back of the chair, her head erect in front of its rest, her weight sinking the chair comfortably into position. She slides her feet into her clogs on the footrest underneath the desk and angles it toward herself. She rolls herself forward until the edge of the desk brushes her stomach. She grabs her mouse authoritatively. Her working display that sits midway between herself and the wall springs to life. Her high-resolution ceiling-height, desk-wide display affixed on the wall flicks on to reveal a white background with bots sitting in their waiting stations, awaiting her commands. She settles into her website work, the tall windows on either side of her desk blinded, the wall with its bookshelf wallpaper shadowed into an amorphous brown.

Who was first on deck? she muses to herself. Her email program whooshes the *Star Trek* door sound effect, letting her know that Jeerah has emailed her. Ev twists her lips up to the right. Jeerah Mutti. Spiritual and busy. Every other one of her emails invites Ev to meet her. Ev says no automatically. Every time. She doesn't meet clients in person. Her primary rule. She asks little of her clients in terms of effort. She asks them many questions, though. She can create their websites beyond their satisfaction and maintain them regularly and without prompting. She knows what those who declare themselves technically challenged want—and charges them hefty fees for them to leave their website design up to Ev, to be free of thinking about their internet presences. For Ev to lift that burden off them, they swiftly agree to what they say are reasonable costs. Then declare the costs against their income on their tax returns. They tell Ev, it's win-win.

She's become so good at it, that it takes her less and less time each year to code websites, freeing up more and more downtime for her to code E3, what she's now calling her "Early Exit Engine," the engine she'd created to create her virtual reality program *Early Exit To The Void*.

Ev frowns. She feels the three sheets pressing toward her. She hunches her right shoulder against them and leans forward into her work, glancing upward to activate her eye-tracking bot then downward to her email program's icon for her bot to open the program then over to wake up her reading bot. But she welcomes Jeerah's email for once and decides to read it herself. She moves her eyes over reading bot to give him the halt command. He disappears back into his station. She moves her mouse over the email subject line and clicks to open it.

"HI!"

Always HI and in capital letters, Ev sighs.

"HI!" Jeerah greets Ev. "How's it coming? I know I only hired you a week ago but I"M SO EXCITED! I"VE NEVER HAD A WEBSITE before!!!!!!"

Ev counts the exclamation marks automatically and instantly.

Six.

Her lips form a moue. Even numbers. Even numbers ripple her spine. Odd numbers drop her shoulders. *Five or seven exclamation marks would've been better.* She continues reading, absorbing each word so that the papers over to her right will stop bothering her with their real presence. They shouldn't be real, they should be—

She shakes her head violently, her spiky brown hair flying into chaos. She hunches her shoulders higher. She returns to the email, squinting, leaning closer in to her twenty-five-inch display, the one she uses for her websites, small enough to mimic the displays of her clients, although she wonders if maybe their displays are older and smaller given some of their complaints. She shrugs away her uncharacteristic wandering thoughts and frowns at Jeerah's words: "SOOOOO... are you done? I thought authenticity would be baked into the website more if we met. I REALLLY LIKE TO MEET THE PEOPLE I meet in person. It's so much better to touch each other's spirits, YOU KNOW? I can FEEL You're a good person." Ev rolls her eyes.

Good. Bad. What do those words mean? She doesn't know. She has spent years on E3, wondering if the physics of her engine should include good and bad variables for the characters but unable to define them. They felt nebulous to her, even while ConsciousnessMind filled her inside world. ConsciousnessMind, the base class, constructor, and object that inhabited void.NullTime at Level 1 of *Early Exit to Void*, was bold, strong, enduring.

Ev squeezes her eyes shut and re-opens them. "Can we meet?" she reads.

Ev clicks on Reply. She types, "No." She clicks Send.

She launches Firefox. Today, she feels like using WordPress in the browser with the fox wrapped around the world. Chrome treats WordPress better, but she thinks she saw an animal out of the corner of her eye in all that whiteness in void.NullTime, or maybe it was the dove grey that made her think: bird, prey, predator, fox.

No, Ev admonishes herself, *best not to think about that strange time in her E3-created virtual reality*. It hadn't behaved like her program is supposed to. She had coded every source file herself. She had created blueprints to use in E3, but she'd preferred to manually code in C++. C++ gives her more control. *Yet it had escaped her control*, she thinks. Energy-Mind class had instantiated a character object David with function admin that she hadn't coded for. She doesn't remember coding him. *Her, it?* She shakes her head. Gender doesn't exist in void.NullTime. She herself had determined that. *So why's she having difficulty understanding even that? It's not remembering coding David.admin. That's what's unnerving her.* She feels lost, uncertain. She refocuses her gaze on WordPress. Its familiar behaviour calms her. So simple, so easy for her to customize WordPress for her clients with CSS. She'll work on Jeerah's. She doesn't really understand spiritual—

Whoosh.

Jeerah must have been waiting for her reply to send another email so quickly. Ev sends her eyes sideways to activate her eye tracking bot. Her bot picks up her movement, opens Jeerah's email, and triggers reading bot to appear and read Jeerah's email out loud in a monotone. Ev doesn't like nuances and inflection and had deliberately coded reading bot to read that way. Nuances and inflections get in the way of her understanding. Monotones are effective. Simple.

Reading bot speaks: "I'm SOOOO disappointed."

Ev frowns. *Why did her bot read Jeerah's capitals as if they were capitals with emphasis instead of the monotone she'd programmed?* She dislikes how her coding is coding itself as if it's coming to life. *No*, she shakes her head silently. *She's making things up. She creates code to create virtual reality, not real reality.*

She clicks her mouse, and reading bot stops. Ev reads the email to herself silently. "The Saviour told Mary that he who had a mind to understand, hear. I feel you have that mind. I KNOW IT. I KNOW you understand the Saviour's peace." Ev has no idea what Jeerah is talking about. She keeps reading. "I can see it in the websites you program for us technology-phobes. I have to feel your spirit. I have to feel YOUR SPIRIT trapped in your flesh to know that you understand the authenticity I'm after. Please, meet with me?"

Ev sighs. This client's worse than those sheets of paper. Paper. She turns her head slightly away from where the papers lie. She wants so badly to ignore those physical papers that came out of her virtual reality.

It isn't possible.

She knows it isn't possible.

She'd heard of coders losing themselves in their programs. Is she losing herself into *Early Exit into the Void*? She grimaces. She must find out. No, she doesn't need to, she suddenly scolds herself. She's doing her day job, and this client is more bothering than the usual sort. That's her real trouble. Spiritual, authenticity, these words are foreign to her. But it doesn't matter. She can code anyone's website. She can code Jeerah Mutti's website. Jeerah hasn't answered all her questions, she recalls. Maybe re-asking her will stave her off.

She types rapidly: "You haven't answered all my questions. Please answer them." She clicks Send.

Ev clicks on the WordPress tab in Firefox to return to Jeerah's website. *Spiritual theme*, she thinks. *What would a spiritual theme be like?* Hmmm. She pulls up Google maps and searches for street views of churches. She has a vague idea that they represent spiritual. Jeerah's Saviour and spirit talk mystifies her, but maybe some church facade will elucidate. She stops moving her mouse through the virtual street she was moving down on Toronto's Google Street View of King Street. She concentrates internally. *Her standard questions don't cover spirit dimensions*, she thinks. *She should ask about that.*

Ev switches to her personal email program she calls E3Here and clicks on Jeerah's name. She rapidly types out her question, "What is spiritual to you? What is authenticity? Please describe their colours and shapes." She clicks Send and Alt-Tabs back to her virtual drive down King Street, searching for a church. The street blurs into streaks of greys and blacks with reds and pinks through them before coalescing into the road and cars. Tall brick buildings with walls at street level appear in the foreground but in the distance a green and yellowish structure with a spire rises.

A church.

Satisfied, she moves toward it until it fills the left side of Google Street View. She inspects it, using the mouse to face it, move alongside it, scan its pillars that jut out along its length, home in on the clock that sits high up in its spire, and examine the stone arches that stagger toward its front doors. Spiritual seems to be yellow stone, juts, and cones that disappear into the sky. *How would that translate?* She stares at the corner of her display where her email icon awaits new mail. *What's taking Jeerah so long? She'd replied to her so quickly before. Why no quick reply to her simple questions?* She razzes her lips and sucks them in.

Whoosh.

Her eye tracking bot opens her email. Her reading bot springs into action and speaks: "I'm soooo sorry. I forgot all about your questions. I was soooo excited about having you work on my website. I heard such great things about you and couldn't believe you agreed to take on my little authentic work. I'm soooo excited. I'll get on the rest of those questions right away. I promise. I don't know what colour spirituality is. Whatever colour you want it to be. You have such a great eye, I know you'll do great work, even better if we could meet. Souls meeting tells us so much more about each other, don't you think? If we meet up, you'd know me and know my authenticity, the work I do. And I'd know you even MORE! I really REALLY want to meet you?! How about tomorrow."

Reading bot falls silent. Ev draws her eyebrows painfully down. This woman doesn't give up. Ev doesn't want to meet her. She never meets her clients. Ever. She doesn't have to. They answer her questions. She designs their websites. They pay her. She returns to E3 until she needs another client.

Ev sighs. She sits up straight to reply with another, firmer "No," when her hand reaching for her mouse feels something against its edge.

She glances down. The three white blank sheets fan out near her, near her mouse's back end. Ev blinks, swallows. Her heart beats.

Virtual reality is not real.

Not real.

How can an application form from it be real? And why is it blank? How can she fill in a form that has no questions?

Hesitantly, she touches the top sheet. It feels real, rough like thick paper. Linen paper, maybe. She doesn't know how she knew it was linen. Or maybe flax, not ordinary paper, she knows, like the kind everyone uses in their printers. Neuropeptides emerge, move in the depths of her neurons; she reads back from her WORM memory—write once, read many times memory—a letter she'd found in the chest of her parents' attic when she was three years, four months, five days, and seven hours old. It had had the same feel. The date's year at the top of the paper had read "1777" and the short line under it had begun: "Dear." That had been all she'd seen and read carefully before her mother had called her name in reprimand from right behind her and snatched the letter from her.

Flax paper.

With her forefinger tip, she slowly pushes the top sheet off of the other two. Fear making her hand shake slightly, she touches the second sheet. This one feels tougher. This one is hemp. She pushes it gingerly off the bottom sheet and gently touches the revealed one. Softer. Cotton.

Ev stares at her forefinger resting near the bottom of the bottom sheet. She rubs the bottom sheet, pushing her forefinger to the right, barely touching the paper yet detecting every fibre of it. Her signature appears, its appearance following the left side of her forefinger.

Ev recoils her hand as she pushes the balls of her clogged feet against the footrest and flies her chair backward, far from the desk and that bottom cotton sheet with her signature plainly scrawled in lavender fountain-pen ink. **Ev Fleming**.

3

Google The Analyst

Is she losing her mind? Ev wonders. Did she stay inside E3 and somehow it has created a virtual reality within a virtual reality? How would she know she's out in the real world and not still inside E3-created reality? Ev scans her code in her mind. She searches the classes, the sub-programs, the if/then statements. She cannot see how E3 could have created a reality within a reality. She must be outside, but then she must be hallucinating. Yet the papers are real. She touched them. That signature—her signature—is hers. It's real. It appeared. Her finger joints tense, her upper arm tenses, her shoulder tenses; they set themselves up for movement toward the signature, to feel the ink mark that scrawls across the bottom of the bottom sheet as if she had signed it herself. Yet she hadn't. She doesn't remember signing any form in virtual reality or here on Earth. Her heart flips. She's signed a form that hasn't been filled out, almost as if she has to commit before she knows what she's committing to.

Ev closes her eyes. She breathes in, releases the tension. She's not going to indulge this fantasy of her brain. She remembers her parents discussing brain states in which memory loss lead to their patients' brains making stuff up. That was how, in her early programming state of organic growth, she'd interpreted what her parents were talking about, using their big words that belonged to their field, their professional lives, the lives that were lived outside of her small universe. Their patients made stuff up because otherwise they'd live in a blank world. That's when she'd realized she needed to create and nurture her own concurrent versioning system to monitor her programming, to record each change, each version, so that if someone introduced a germ, a bug, a parasite to eat at her thinking and mental imagery, she could roll back her own programming to a stable version that had kept her sane. She called it "Lapis," for that colour soothed her in its strength.

She'd thought about that idea, of living in a blank world. She'd called such a world, "Null.Void." That was back in her early computer days when she was teaching herself the old computer database programs. Oracle. DOS. Basic. Somehow learning how to code in those old programs made her feel like she'd entered her parents' world since they rarely entered hers. She thinks, *void.NullTime.*

Ev slowly lifts her eyelids. She stares straight ahead at her computer monitor. Its screen is black, in energy-saving mode. Slowly, she shifts her focus from the monitor to the wall display. It has stayed on. She registers in a subset of her thoughts that she must adjust its energy-saving settings. Her heart beginning to ramp up its beats, her breathing shortening, she slowly drops her eyes down to her desk. Three sheets of paper. Her signature remains on the bottom one.

Her arm shaking from sudden tension carried along every muscle fibre into her fingers, she reaches forward and touches her signature with all four of her fingers. Her nerves carry the message back to her brain.

Ink, thick, slightly raised on soft cotton pressed into paper form.

Ev stands up abruptly. Using the flats of her hands, she presses down on her desk, its surface, its edges, its corners. Her palms feel each surface, their nerve endings sending their sensory input to her brain. This is real. This is real. This is real. Ev drops down onto her haunches and presses her hands down against the floor. She launches herself back upright and takes the few steps to her left-sided triple-paned blinded window. She releases the blind upward so that she can lean against the glass, feel its cold slow-liquid surfaces. *How many people know glass is a liquid not a solid*, Ev wonders. Knowledge reassures her. It's safe; it's familiar. She stares down at heads bobbing along the sidewalk below her. The messiness, the cacophony of the cars jerking forward, angling around others too slow for their impatience, reassures her. She had deliberately excluded such vehicles, such drivers from E3.

She's on Earth. In reality.

So she must be hallucinating.

Ev returns to her chair. She contemplates unseeingly her wall display. No, she's not hallucinating. Nothing has changed in her mental framework. It's something else.

She needs help to find out what.

Suddenly, Ev sends her eyes up to the top left corner of her wall display, automatically triggering eye tracking bot to move to where she looks. Search bot sits up there, a smile affixed to his little square face. She doesn't know how that smile appeared. She doesn't recall coding it in, but there it sits. And as always, when her eye tracking bot wakes up her search bot, search bot's smile widens, showing two rows of teeth, grinning, and he sings out "Good morning!" as he draws a line for her to type her search command on. Ev doesn't like to speak. She likes the absence of human voice, the satisfying clicking of keys. As she types, search bot mimicks the search command on her working screen. Yet again, she registers in the recesses of her mind that "Good morning!" hadn't been part of his coding either. How did he discover and incorporate that?

She types, "analyst of the mind."

Search bot, as is his custom, corrects her search term to "psychiatrist, psychoanalyst Toronto immediate availability." Ev's eyes crinkle slightly in their outer corners watching him add specific geographic parameters. She likes her search bot. He's efficient and doesn't need her to know the exact keywords to arrive at the best search. Despite his independence of coding, he's a good little bot.

A Google search page pops open. Lines and lines of results flash into being on her wall display and onto her working display. Search bot highlights in green the relevant ones on the first page and opens each one up in separate windows once it's analyzed them for viruses and malicious coding. It doesn't take a second. While she begins to read each web page on each of the psychiatrists and psychoanalysts search bot has found, search bot launches the College of Physicians and Surgeons of Ontario's website and searches for and loads the results for each of the psychiatrists she reviews for more than five seconds.

Search bot retreats to his waiting station.

Ev Alt-Tabs between each web page she likes and the matching college page. She narrows her field down to two. She sends her eyes to search bot where he sits blinking in his top left corner. He stretches out a new line for her to type onto. She types, "contrast." Search bot searches the web and finds several different parameters. Search bot launches Notepad and lists them in a plain text document, each on their own line. Ev considers the parameters. She isn't sure which parameters are the most important, other than geographically. She doesn't like to go outside. She prefers to stay close to home. *She wonders at her instant, unthinking reaction to those—*

Ev shudders. Ev blocks out the memory of virtual reality in her space. Why is she going to see a psychiatrist? She'd left two of them behind her. She never speaks to them; they don't speak to her. Yet...

A mental image of her father sitting at the kitchen table holding his broadsheet newspaper with both hands, saying, "Here, Evelyn, here's an article that may focus your attention on what matters, your studies. This'll help you. Let me read it to you."

Ev blinks against her moist eyes and picks male and geographically nearby.

Search bot types the answer out onto his search line.

Dr. Frock.

Ev inspects his credentials. He works in an executive health clinic a block away. It demands a $1,500 fee upfront to access services. Ev shrugs. Not an obstacle for her. She signs up on their public secure signup web page then hacks into their private servers for clinic employees only and moves her money into their deposit account then makes an appointment for herself that day by moving a CEO out of his slot and filling in her name for an hour hence for Dr. Frock. Search bot suggests she secure three hours of his time. She complies. She's forgotten that psychiatrists don't usually book that big a block of time for one patient.

Ev enters the clinic promptly at one minute to the hour.

She strides up to stand in front of the receptionist's desk. The receptionist smiles up at her. "May I help you?"

"Dr. Frock."

The receptionist's smile doesn't falter as she turns her attention to her computer while touching her headset and asking the person who they'd like to speak to. "Evelyn Fleming?" she asks.

Ev nods as she automatically says: "Ev."

"One moment."

Ev stands unmoving in place. A voice to her right draws her eyes around. "Evelyn Fleming?"

"Ev." Ev walks toward the statuesque woman in her snug fitting jacket and skirt with its black-and-white checked pattern. She follows the woman's silent black stilettos across the carpeted floor and to a discreet elevator with faux wood doors and black buttons on the grey silk-covered walls. The woman presses the up button, and the doors slide open soundlessly. Ev follows the woman into the small box with its black mirrored walls.

As she presses the fourth-floor button, the woman says: "Dr. Frock is on our top floor." The doors slide shut as a pleasant computer voice intones, "Fourth floor" and then counts each floor as they pass by it, ending with, "We have arrived at the fourth floor. Have a pleasant day."

As they walk single file through a small alcove with a pink noise machine filling the air with a calming hum, past two wing chairs covered in deep browns with a pattern on pattern deeper brown check on either side of a round coffee table, Ev registers the computer voice and connects it to how search bot had gathered and incorporated social pleasantries. She wonders if search bot had found this computer voice, liked it, and added its coding to his coding.

The intelligence both intrigues and disturbs her.

Ev returns to the present as the woman pushes down a highly polished brass handle and pulls open a solid mahogany door with inlaid ebony trim that outlines its panels. "Here you are," she says.

Ev enters a smallish room with an angled ceiling, its lower end two meters high and peaking over an arched window. A man stands up from an armchair, stretching out his right arm toward her as the door clicks discreetly shut behind her. Ev spies a chair similar to hers standing in front of a heavy oak desk that faces the arched window opposite to the door. She walks across the room, past a table, past the man, and sits down.

Dr. Frock, a benign smile lifting the edges of his closed lips without wrinkling his crow's feet on either side of his deep blue and green striped eyes, turns around and says with a melodious vibration in his deep voice: "I'm afraid you're sitting in my office chair. That is where you sit." He points with his tweed-jacket clad arm to a two-seater sofa dressed in brown chenille with a throw cushion at each end in a brocade pattern of antelopes, beige on beige.

Ev stands up without a word, skirts around the rectangular mahogany table that sits low to the carpeted floor. The walls behind the sofa and his desk are clad in burnished wallpaper the colour of milk chocolate. Ev sits in the middle of the sofa-wide cushion. Dr. Frock hitches up his neatly pressed tweed trousers, revealing chocolate brown socks and light brown brogues, and sits back down across from the sofa in his brown velvet-covered armchair with gold piping. The chair and sofa are perpendicular to the door. Dr. Frock sinks down into the velvet-clad cushion of his chair. He unbuttons his tweed jacket, revealing a vest of matching tweed neatly buttoned up with the gold chain of a pocket watch sagging exactly ten centimeters down from the pocket the watch sits in. He reaches into his pocket, removes the watch, flips open its finely engraved lid, and checks the time.

"You're very prompt," he says approvingly.

Ev nods. Being exact, being precise, is important to coding.

She waits for him to take the lead as he awaits her first words. He steeples his fingers, and the lids of his eyes lower black lashes to slightly obscure his blue-green eyes. Ev processes him. He's not like mother and father who spoke first and taught her not to interrupt their thinking or conversation with each other. Psychiatrists are busy, they'd taught her. She had all their time when they were at home, and so she could wait for them to be free for them to listen to her.

As she waits for Dr. Frock to indicate he's free to listen, Ev's eyes and ears take in her surroundings, her WORM laying down data onto her neuropeptides, recording minute details in her brain's molecular structure, transferring the most usable reality details to her dynamic array to add them to *Early Exit To The Void* for when she returns to her computer. Ev records and sorts data like this automatically whenever she leaves her studio, her home. *Are his features suitable for character building*, she unconsciously queries herself as her eyes roam from the top of his European-fair cast, his precisely clipped fringe of white and black hair over his groomed eyebrows and aquiline nose to his male lips just the right shape to hold his neatly trimmed mustache and goatee, down his neck with its horizontal lines revealing age, and ending in his open-collared, slightly askew white shirt. Ev halts her processing. This note of casual in such precision strikes strange.

Dr. Frock speaks: "Why don't we get started?"

Ev returns her gaze to his eyes and waits.

Dr. Frock stands up and takes four long strides to his desk. He picks up a pinkish snake-leather looking notepad with fresh lined notepaper inside it and a black Mont Blanc fountain pen and then strides back to his armchair.

As he sits, Ev scans the skin of the notepad, riffling at neuron speed through her WORM. Swampeel. Not usually used by humans.

Dr. Frock says: "I was surprised to see my usual clients had all cancelled at once and you being slotted in. But I was informed that the office computer had said that this was so." He smiles at her and stretches his neck forward slightly.

Ev waits.

He waits.

She says nothing.

He waits.

It's as if oxygen molecules hiss the minutes by in the carpeted room.

He clears his throat, leans into the generous back cushion of his chair, and begins: "I like to begin my assessment with the essentials. Name, age, date of birth, that sort of thing. I know the computer has all that information in it, and they say the computer never lies. But I prefer to gather it independently." His smile widens, revealing small even white teeth.

Ev staccatos: "Ev Fleming. Thirty-three. Fourteenth May—"

Dr. Frock interrupts, holding up his right hand, his pen threaded through his fingers. "Let me write that down before you continue," he instructs as she finishes reciting her birth date. He drops his hand, smiles, his eyes narrowing into lakes of blue. He repeats: "Let me write that down. Now your name is Evelyn Fleming." He scrawls midnight blue letters onto the top of the top sheet of notepaper. Ev automatically reads the wiggly letters upside down while saying "Ev." He looks up. "Birth date?" She answers. He asks his standard information questions in order, and she answers each question briefly. He ends with asking her what brought her to his office.

She answers: "My feet."

He smiles, wrinkling his crow's feet for the first time. "I meant, why do you want to see me?"

"Search bot showed me you were the best choice."

Dr. Frock's smile loses their crow's feet but not the lift of his lips. His eyebrows wrinkle. He tries again. "What happened that made you want to see a psychoanalyst?"

"Analysts are the best to analyze a situation or event, a function of an object that went awry, in this case a character."

Puzzlement openly wreathes Dr. Frock's face. He latches on to the words he knows. "What was the situation?"

"E3 created an unknown result."

"I see," Dr. Frock says carefully, not seeing at all. He calls up into his memory the Diagnostic and Statistical Manual. He begins to review its fifth edition internally as he struggles again to ascertain why she's come to see him. "What event happened that made you want to have my help analyzing it?"

"The three sheets in my hand."

Dr. Frock struggles to understand sheets. Was she talking about her bedding? "Do you have trouble making up your bed?"

Ev stares at him. She had clearly answered his questions. Why is he talking about her bed? Japanese Robot, the robot she'd acquired a year ago and had added her coding to his, made up her bed for her. She'd acquired a prototype advanced AI Japanese Robot through her network of coders, who, like her, preferred no social chit chat. Code, troubleshoot code, don't talk too revealingly about one's own coding, end chat. After she'd acquired and improved on his coding, she'd no longer had to think about sheets and blankets except when Japanese Robot told her that her weekly laundry was due to be put outside of her door for the laundry service she'd contracted with when she'd first bought her studio. The service deposited her clean laundry in the neat Rubbermaid box outside her door and picked up the previous week's box of dirty laundry.

Dr. Frock clears his throat in the face of her steady brown eyes. He's used to waiting five, ten minutes for a client to speak. The minutes begin to add up, ticking painfully loudly in his head, and he can no longer hold her gaze as fifteen minutes arrives and departs. The tiny muscles around his eyes tense. He finds thoughts have exited his mind. He struggles to connect to something familiar, comforting.

He shifts his eyes to his desk.

He shifts them again, down to the solid table beside him with its closed drawer neatly containing his well-thumbed copy of the Diagnostic and Statistical Manual, fifth edition. His eyes relax. Thoughts return. He reviews what he knows so far and seeks to tie it to a DSM-5 category. His internal scroll of DSM-5 lands on Social (Pragmatic) Communication Disorder. Usually seen in childhood, his memory coughs up, but seemingly arrested in this young woman. Perhaps she had had an isolated childhood, neglected by parents who hadn't taught her communication skills. He's seeing more and more of this in the adolescent children his executive patients bring to their sessions, asking him to fix them. He'd initially tried to refer them to a separate psychiatrist, but executives don't take being denied their will well. So he counsels their adolescents, teaching them the basics of communication that their parents had neglected in favour of relegating them to the distorted lens of social media: Facebook and Instagram. But he'd rarely seen such issues as the one presenting in front of him.

Dr. Frock restarts: "We seem to be having difficulties in communicating. Do you normally have such difficulties with others?"

Ev replies: "My clients tell me what they want, and I design it for them."

"How are they when they speak to you? Do they understand you?"

"Of course. I ask them my standard questions. They reply. If they skip any, I ask again."

"I see," Dr. Frock responds, not quite seeing. "And how do you ask them again?"

"I resend them."

"Resend?"

"Yes."

Dr. Frock contemplates her with the blue stripes in his eyes narrowing as the green ones widen. Suddenly, comprehension enters his mind. "You email them?"

"Yes."

"Don't you talk to them? Meet them in person?"

"No."

"Why not?"

"I don't need to, to code their websites. I maintain them, too. Search bot helps me personalize their sites based on similar sites, and I've coded my questions to ensure I receive all the information that I need. My clients like my work, and I charge appropriately."

"I see."

Dr. Frock writes words on his notepaper, but Ev cannot see his notepad at that precise instant because he's crossed his right leg over his left and angled the notepad up to face him. He uncrosses his legs as he removes his pocket watch to glance at its face. The notepad flattens. Ev reads upside down: "Deficits—"

Dr. Frock speaks, interrupting her reading. "I believe we're almost out of time. But I have a working diagnosis. It's not the usual kind in your kind of individual. But we must remain open to all possibilities. Let me read these traits out to you." Dr. Frock caps his fountain pen, places his notepad on the table beside him and his pen at a forty-five-degree angle across the centre of the top page. He leans forward to open the drawer of the small table on the side of his armchair. He retrieves a brick of a small book, three of its edges thick with many, many white pages, its cover a plain purple. He flips back its cover and riffles through it quickly to the relevant pages. He scans and lifts the corners of his lips slightly as he finds what he wants. He shuts the book, places it back in its drawer, and pushes the wooden drawer silently shut with a soft thump as it blends its edges in with the table's sides. He leans back, steepling his fingers and says: "I believe you have Social Pragmatic Communication Disorder." He pauses.

Ev watches his face, waiting for him to tell her the answer.

"You have deficits in communication purposes such as greeting. For example, you didn't shake my hand or say hello, as would be usual in social situations such as this. I haven't followed your answers, not for lack of trying." He smiles with his closed lips. "You've been unable to rephrase your statements so that I can understand the situation or event that upset you. You're unable to follow nonverbal cues for answering my questions. And you need me to explicitly state what I'm saying for you to understand. This is not a difficult situation. It will be challenging, but I have had plenty of experience in helping patients learn to communicate effectively and socially appropriately. I'm sure that five daily sessions over this week and next will be all that you need and entirely productive. Once you've relearnt how to communicate, you will find the situation or event that brought you here resolvable." He stands up and says: "For now, our session is up."

Ev blinks up at him, thinking, *It's only been an hour and a half*. But his flow of words don't allow interruption. "I will see you tomorrow at the same time and will ask them to adjust my schedule accordingly. I be-lieve you're an intelligent woman and will pick up on what I'll teach you fairly quickly. And I can see you're one who likes to get things done." He remains standing until Ev stands up. He stretches his right arm out to-ward her, his palm open. "Shake my hand." Ev reaches toward him hesi-tantly with her right hand, and he grasps it in his large warm, dry palm, his long fingers wrapping themselves around her hand. Her own dry, cool palm shakes; her fingers don't return his grasp. He smiles kindly down upon her, the green stripes in his eyes overtaking the blue. He lets go of her hand and leads her to his door. He opens the door and speaks toward the silent alcove. "This nonverbal gesture means it's time for you to leave. But I want to see you again, same time tomorrow. Believe me when I say it was a pleasure to meet you, Evelyn." He glances down at her then back toward the alcove.

Ev hears him and stores his comment about "pleasure to meet her" in her WORM—her organic write-once, read-many memory embedded in her brain's molecular structure—to retrieve later and review. She fol-lows where he'd walked and passes on through the door and out.

4

E3

Ev returns to her studio, her feet rapidly covering the concrete sidewalk, her head down with her eyes aiming her perception into her head, her thoughts focusing on E3, her Early Exit Engine, the one she'd designed to turn the desire she'd had at fifteen into a virtual reality game.

How else to make her desire real? At fifteen, with her logical brain that saw life as if/then statements, preprogrammed consequences flowing from actions, she'd had no other idea how to turn desire into reality.

Ev had begun coding bits and pieces of her desire with engines used to develop first-person shooter games then role-playing games, but after she'd hit her third limitation that had flummoxed all ideas of how to turn her ideas into actionable code, she'd begun creating her own engine.

And that's when she'd left the community.

Frustration had driven Ev to begin designing her own engine, but once she'd begun in secret, the urge to talk about it grew in her heart until one day in chat she'd spilled. Lower back rounded, head forward like a Canada Goose on a mission, eyes rivetted on her monitor, fingers tapping so rapidly the keys had almost sounded like one being tapped over and over with the vibrational bounce of the space bar interrupting the taps, she'd spilled about her desire to create a way to escape Earth, about what she wanted to create in virtual reality. The boys had mocked her; the one other girl in chat had chimed in. Ev had shrugged off the mocking; sarcasm, name calling zinged the air around her in school and in chat. It was their way. And she couldn't stop sharing. The need to talk, the need for others to hear her and be as enthusiastic as she was, dominated her hands. She'd shared that the popular engines were not working for her. They'd scoffed that she could need more power and derided the idea that she could create an engine with more power than what the longstanding coders had created.

Uncertainty hesitated her fingers. Maybe she was being too public with her thoughts, her desire. Her closest allies would understand, the ones who'd worked on games with her and played games with her for hours when her parents were away at one of their conferences. Ev had gone into a private room to talk to these ones she considered allies, the closest she came to friends. All boys, some younger than her. A couple of men who acted as mentors to the rest of them. She'd asked them for advice about how to create her own engine. They'd laughed, not taking her seriously.

Memories ping-pong through her neurons, memories of "Hahaha-haha!" "Oh Ev, really? You?" "Bwahahaha, she thinks she's better than us!" "Uh-uh." She blinks. She shies away from the rest of the memories of their degenerating comments. She'd left the private chat room, checked every window and door was locked, checked again, showered and show-ered again. She'd returned to her computer and swiftly, decisively closed her developer accounts, used her father's credit card to buy the newest, most powerful computer she could find, and had begun teaching herself how to create a virtual reality engine. She wasn't angry. Just as she'd shut down her connection to her allies, she'd shut down her brain's emotion centres. And sent her mental power into goals, projects, tasks, think-ing, learning, creating logic streams to make this engine worked. Ev had named it E3 for Early Exit Engine. Not far into the process, she'd coded bots to do the drudge work like searching and reading.

One day as she was pulling on her coat after another routine day at school, a high school classmate she barely knew had asked her to create a website, something about girl power. Ev hadn't cared why she'd asked, only the ten and twenty bills she'd held out as a down payment. Ev had taken the money and said in few words. she'd work on it. The classmate had shot her phone her number for Ev to text her the link. Once inside her parents' front door, she'd dropped her knapsack, run up the stairs to her bedroom, slammed her door shut, and had sunk into her computer chair, folding into her accustomed C shape, fingers falling into place on her keyboard. She'd put her usual deep focus into the work, desiring to make every detail harmonize and serve this classmate's need. By midnight, she'd finished and texted her classmate the link. Her classmate had been so surprised and thrilled, she'd praised Ev for days. Ev's ears had encoded the new phrases into her changing identity. Her heart had thrilled to her classmate's words. But the girl hadn't stopped there. She'd told her friends, and her classmates' parents had overheard. Her mother had requested she redesign her one-person business website. Ev had complied, wanting to hear more of these strange praises and liking how the money let her fund the creation of E3.

The one smudge in this new time of growth was that she'd had to re-enter the developer world to keep learning in order to grow E3. Ev had created a male persona to do so, entered the coder arena only for when and for as long as she needed, keeping her chat to a minimum. Once E3 was stable, her life had flowed out of this early work into a wide, pre-dictable river of website work she chose that funded her coding of *Early Exit To The Void* with tweaking of E3.

An errant thought spikes into her contemplation of E3 and adding newly acquired details to it. *She has a communication disorder. What does that mean? What else had Dr. Frock said?* She grows still as she tries to understand the words that replay in her internal hearing. She cannot. But she thinks, *It doesn't matter if his words lack computational approach.* He'd stated that he'd treat her, and in five business days she'll be better. And the sheets will disappear. Once she's better, she will no longer see the sheets, for the papers are neither hallucinations nor reality.

Ev pulls her lips to the right and puffs her right cheek out. Dr. Frock hadn't seemed to understand her, either. *How will he explain these sheets and get rid of them?* She shrugs away the intrusive thought. He will.

Ev pulls on the heavy brass front door of her building. She enters and walks past the security manning the Art Deco booth toward the elevator, letting her feet take her in the right direction. The men watch her without saying a word to her. They know the drill. She presses the elevator's worn-smooth brass up button. It dings softly. She steps into the small box with its brass walls and maple rail encircling it at hand height. The elevator raises her up smoothly and silently to the top floor, which her studio inhabits. She exits into a small foyer with a single door across from the single elevator that goes to her floor. A hidden door in the wall is to her right for the fire stairs. It's locked on the inside of the stairwell, and only the fire department has the key. She steps across the foyer toward her steel front door, places her hand around the Art Deco handle of brass, and closes her fingers in a particular spread pattern. Click. The door swings outward, toward her. Safer for swift egress in case of fire. She squeezes her eyes shut against the thought and enters her studio filled with the hum of her powerful computer. She checks her internal calendar: is it time to clean the fans? No. The computers sound so loud because her studio is so quiet after the noise of car engines accelerating, tires rubbing their surfaces at high speed over asphalt. Her triple-glazed windows muffle the traffic sounds almost completely; what filters through is a kind of white noise. She kicks off her outdoor shoes. She unzips her jacket, shakes her arms free of the sleeves, and lets it slide to the floor as she walks to her computer, knowing Japanese Robot will pick it up and hang it on her coat tree.

She remembers how search bot, who'd helped her search for more intricate code to customize Japanese Robot for her needs, had wanted her to name him. And when she'd not thought about it but kept using her moniker for Japanese Robot, search bot had found a name. Ev hadn't liked it. Search bot had insisted on using the name and had tried to insert it into the code she'd sent wirelessly to the robot as she'd programmed him to collect her laundry, put it into a box to place outside for her laundry service, pick up the Rubbermaid of clean laundry, make her bed, clean her dishes, monitor the Roombas so that they vacuumed and mopped her dark-stained wide-plank floors whenever she was out, put them back home when he knew she was returning so that their heavy sounds wouldn't annoy her, maintained himself to keep away any squeaks, and started up her computer so that it would be ready to use upon her return or waking up in the morning. She'd deleted search bot's name for it and deleted any reference to it in her bot.

Japanese Robot whispers on his wheels toward her coat and hangs it up on the coat rack next to the door. Ev has already sunk into her air chair and slipped her feet into the clogs. She pulls her keyboard into a more comfortable position. She places her hand on her mouse and clicks on her E3 engine icon. She sits back and waits for the engine to load. *It always takes too long*, she thinks, *for her massive E3 to load.* How can she shorten the loading time? She shakes her head and arches her neck to stare at the ceiling and consider classes.

Out of the bottom of her vision, she spots the engine window open and populate the screen with black windows, multi-hued icons, the viewport for void.NullTime, menus, lines of code in letters of multi-hues denoting the parts of its language, and the blueprints she'd created. She straightens her neck and stares at void.NullTime. How has it developed all those hues of white, she asks herself, not moving her lips, remembering when she'd first created it.

Ev had called the first iteration of her early exit place, "Heaven." She'd heard of Heaven during the nightly interminable dinner with her parents when, after they had interrogated her about her day, had conversed about their work and their patients, ignoring her presence. They'd talked about how their patients kept bringing up a place where only good people went and good things happened. Her parents had called it myth making of the delusional variety. Heaven. Ev had liked the sound of "Heaven" and thought, *If her parents looked down on it, it must be good.* She'd used that name for her first virtual reality game when she'd been using the standard engine, but when she'd created her own...

Memories swirl up.

She stares at the static display of what she had first envisioned as Heaven: solid white 3D with the back in the distance and the foreground open to her view so that she is looking into a box. She had put away her childish idea when she'd turned eighteen. She'd become an adult, had left home, and had decided that it was time to think like an adult. She had renamed her barely nascent virtual reality from *Early Exit To Heaven* to *Early Exit To The Void*.

Ev refocuses her eyes to bring the viewport back into consciousness. She ponders her strange, last experience in her virtual reality. It had had no dimension. It had looked 3D yet had felt as if there were other dimensions.

And then there was the odd way it had loaded, beginning as a pixel in endless black and then exploding and expanding into the dimensionless or multi-dimensional area that filled her view. It was supposed to flash on immediately.

But, she thinks, *she likes the expanding effect. Perhaps that's how void.NullTime looks? Somehow her randomization code she had put into each level of her* Early Exit To The Void *had "fixed" things?*

Ev frowns and leans forward to stare intently at the colours she'd chosen. She clicks on random areas and inspects the RBG code. All 255 255 255 in the white areas, 0 0 0 in the black. No creams, no subtle pinks, no dove greys anywhere. She shivers. How did E3 introduce those colour elements?

Unsettled, Ev turns her mind away from colours with artificial intelligence and switches to considering the characters. She clicks on the first one, the first character class she had created. She inspects its member functions, the tasks that are specific to it. Then she inspects the objects she'd created from that character class. She always forgot to give the instantiated objects of the characters names. Search bot, her first and favourite bot, would recommend names whenever she began searching for object ideas, but in this case, she hadn't gotten around to adding names. The greeter had been a primitive when she'd first put him in Heaven way back...Ev frowns. She cannot remember when she had placed him. She has such a precise, infinite WORM memory.

Every detail inhabits its neuropeptide structure, available whenever and wherever she wants to retrieve it. Yet this detail escapes her.

Unsettling.

Ev's back muscles contract as her skin goosebumps.

Another puzzle.

She knows that she hadn't given him a name because search bot had been nascent when she'd first created him, when it was still Heaven and not the void. *Had she even given him a gender attribute?* Ev bites down on her bottom lip. She cannot remember.

Ev doesn't like all this uncertainty. *Of course, she'd given him a gender attribute*, she assures herself. Back then, she'd believed gender attributes are basic in character object creation in E3. All persons have to have gender; gender is central to humanity. Her heart flips in her chest, troubled by two details forgotten. She clicks on the C++ tab of E3 and scrolls through her *.cpp files. Her fingers stop. *What is she doing? She needs to search her *.h files, her header files.* Her stomach squeezes in on itself, and she hunches in her chair. She is losing her certainty in these lines of code, the only place she feels at home. The place she knows intrinsically and understands down into subconscious levels. The only place she is free.

Japanese Robot suddenly appears on her right. She flings her head back and looks up at him. *She hadn't called him, had she?*

He speaks: "We recommend a moment of meditation. See my display. Follow the breathing pattern."

Ev's eyes widen. When had she coded him to lead her in her breathing? Search bot?

"Breathe," commands Japanese Robot.

She releases her breath. Of course, she had added breathing instructions to his coding last night after a particularly difficult interaction with a client. The client hadn't liked his website; she'd had to step him through each page and, while controlling his computer, show him its interactive elements. He'd been pleased at the end and had filled his email with the praises that she'd worked so hard to achieve. But she'd been shaking afterward. Search bot had found deep breathing as an acceptable meditation practice for her, and she'd coded it in to Japanese Robot.

How come he hadn't executed his new code this morning when breath had escaped her?

Another puzzle.

Pounding deafens her from inside her neck.

Ev blinks rapidly. She lowers her eyes to the display on Japanese Robot's chest. She'd switched out his original display for the high-resolution one from an iPad. The female avatar on the display, breathing in and out rhythmically, pulls her in to her own breathing. Her stomach lets go; her heart disappears from her ears.

The display switches off; Japanese Robot wheels silently back to his port; and Ev returns to E3.

She considers her levels first. Level 0 is like Earth, at the same level as Earth. The player—only she will play it—moves horizontally into Level 0, space.Time, when she puts on the VR headset and starts *Early Exit To The Void*. Going up levels from 0 to 1 to 2 is like going backward in time yet forward, too. Like returning to the womb but in a different state. The player is matter in Level 0 like on Earth, energy in Level 1. Ev distorts her lips into a disgusted moue as her brain rewinds her thoughts back ten seconds. Not womb. Crucible. The crucible of creation. Her brain snaps her disgust into the round bin where it belongs. Wombs are natural; they are crucibles of creation. It's why she'd named the class that produces the objects Level 0 and 1 Placenta, the outflow of Level 2's class, Zygote, which also produces the ConsciousnessMind class. The point of *Early Exit To The Void* was to return to the beginning point, to Level 2 and above. Above Level 2 must be a void, a void above void.NullTime.

Ev stalls on that idea of no time, null time.

She'd devoured all the texts out there on theoretical physics, texts written by Hawking and Einstein, Higgs and Mayer, Strickland and Curie. But again she asks herself, *Does the physics of E3 hold up on Earth? Does it matter?* Exiting means from Earth and to the unknown. Early means before she's designated to be destructed on Earth. Once she's destructed, she'll be constructed to find what she's seeking elsewhere, to learn why she is—

Ev drives her upper eyelids into her lower ones. Her lashes prick each other.

She must work while she has time, while Jeerah's slowness gives her space.

She is ready to review her classes.

ConsciousnessMind is class, object, and constructor all in one. ConsciousnessMind exists in void.NullTime object of Placenta class. Both Placenta and ConsciousnessMind classes are in and are Level 1 of *Early Exit To The Void*. Both classes are derived from the base class at Level 2, Zygote class.

Zygote is mystery.

What or who had created the creator? She hadn't known where to stop in her backward exploration of who created what she'd first called "Heaven." Zygote is base. It creates two classes, one as creator of characters—that is, ConsciousnessMind—and one as environment creator—that is Placenta. ConsciousnessMind exists in void.NullTime, the object of Placenta class, alone in Level 1.

ConsciousnessMind needs community.

Void has no dimensions, no finite boundaries to incubate the needed—*the desired?* Ev briefly wonders—community of character objects.

But they can't be created out of a void, out of nothing. This is where space is added and Level 0 exists. Space, with its limitations and finite edges delineated by time, is where instantiated objects grow into their coding. But with infinite instantiations, the objects in space.Time must be destructed, otherwise Level 0's limited space will exceed its storage capacity. Executing the destructor code—activating exit—is the only way to level up, to return to Level 1, and enter the void where infinity defies dimensional understanding and community can be whatever number ConsciousnessMind needs and desires.

That thought satisfies Ev. Her nerves relax her muscles into a comforting release of her stress.

In E3, Ev has ConsciousnessMind construct from itself the derived Energy class in Level 1 in void.NullTime, and out from the Energy class comes every derived class for every creature and vegetation she'd found on Google. She'd placed these derived classes in Placenta space.Time, Level 0. But only EnergyHuman class derived from Energy class has the public access specifier—only EnergyHuman can access every member function of ConsciousnessMind. All the rest of the derived classes, named after the flora and fauna she'd found through Google, cannot.

Ev reminds herself:

ConsciousnessMind is the base class. Energy is its first derived class.

She'd sensed a year ago that ConsciousnessMind is not an "it" but neither is it male nor female. More like both. She'd known then that gender doesn't exist in Level 1. She'd called David.admin "it." But perhaps "they" is the best pronoun for ConsciousnessMind and Energy-Mind instantiated characters. Search bot had recently discovered for her that "them," "their," and "they" are the newest neutral pronouns in English for a single entity. Also, she isn't sure ConsciousnessMind is single as humanity thinks of single. More like one of many. She goes back into her parameters for that class, and changes the pronoun to they.

Energy is the first derived class, she reminds herself again, and dives into its derived classes to see where David.admin had come from. Energy class has many derived classes, but she's interested only in EnergyHuman derived classes as they exist in Level 0 in space.Time. As she rests her fingers on the smooth surfaces of her keyboard's keys, she dives deeper into EnergyHuman's derived classes and reviews them: Faith, Language, Prophecy, Knowledge, Interpretation, Healing, Distinguishing Between MagneticFields, MagneticFieldPowers, and Unity.

Unity is rare.

She had built into these nine derived classes rudimentary artificial intelligence and randomization code to add in random and maturing behaviours. MagneticFields are the dynamic memories that exist outside but connected to each instantiated character object from each of these classes. The template of each class populates each of its character objects with its coding, and as the coding executes itself, moves every instance of the character's virtual experience into the dynamic memory of MagneticField. She has coded it so that no memory in the dynamic memory heap is destroyed. Ev reconsiders the wisdom of that decision. The longer *Early Exit To The Void* runs, the more character instantiations, the more environments it creates, the more it expands its memory requirements. She reaffirms her decision; she has heaps of boxes of memory chips. Plenty left to plug new ones in any time memory begins to fill up and slow down E3.

Ev dismisses Unity as possibly having created an object called "David." Ev grows as still as her fingers as she contemplates each derived class in turn. *No, an administrator wouldn't come from Wisdom. Knowledge? No. Definitely not Faith or Healing.* Her lips suck in as she thinks, *Dr. Frock would come from Healing.* She nods to herself. *Healing Frock with attributes male, grey hair, blue-green eyes, 1.7 meters height, 80 kg weight. But how would that end up as Frock.psychiatrist like that character object David.admin?* She returns to her perusal of EnergyHuman's derived classes in Level 0 space.Time. Interpretation. That seems most likely. David.admin had interpreted her request and handed her the three sheets.

So involved is Ev in reviewing her classes that she forgets how creeped out she was by the three sheets appearing in her physical hand and moves her eyes left then right, searching for the sheets. There they are, slightly hidden behind her working display, piled up neatly so that they look like one sheet of flax paper. She frowns. *How had they piled themselves up neatly?* Her brow lifts. Of course, Japanese Robot had stacked them. She'd coded him to keep things neat. Anything she disarrays, he'll array again and place each variable in its place in the array.

Ev thinks about Level 1. *Of course!* she reprimands herself. *Those in Level 1 enter it by exiting from Level 0, space.Time. They have to be destructed to do that. She must review her Destructor coding to find David.admin.* Ev scans the derived classes again and feels certain he'd have been Interpretation.David in Level 0. His MagneticField, his dynamic memory, would have stored his complete existence on Level 0, every execution of coding, every artificial intelligence learning of his. Upon execution of EnergyHuman's special member function of Destructor, Energy-

Human's coding would have deleted the instantiated character object David in Level 0, activated the EnergyMind class in Level 1 to instantiate a new character object with the same name, and created a pointer from the Level 0 character object's MagneticField to its EnergyMind equivalent. The instantiated objects of EnergyMind were the destructed ones' exits from Level 0 to Level 1, from space.Time to void.NullTime. The new character objects exist in community with ConsciousnessMind in Level 1 and grow that community one instantiated character object at a time in void.NullTime.

Some error niggles at the edges of her brain. *Something is wrong with her concept*, she thinks, as the memory of the whites returns to her consciousness. *No.* She shakes her head. *She must stay on track, follow her thoughts to their endpoint. She must remain focused on David.*

So, Ev continues in her silent review, *EnergyMind David had taken on the function of admin. He's a member of the community ConsciousnessMind is creating.*

But how to move on to Level 2? Ev queries herself.

Level 2 remains hidden until all in Level 0, space.Time, have exited to Level 1, void.NullTime, and the community has successfully been constructed in full. She reviews her names again for the umpteenth time. She hadn't known how else to call that class that holds only two objects: void and space. One with no time, the other with time. She knows Environment isn't quite right, but after a decade of trying different names and coding and recoding, she'd settled on Placenta. It was, after all, the crucible of creation, where characters are recreated with advanced dynamic functions and objects of type. She'd modelled their creation on the humans around her, skipping the childhood and adolescent phases. She thinks of them as the same, though located in different environments. An adult in one is like an adult in the other, each with their own function. David's is admin type. Frock psychiatrist.

She nods to herself. All clear.

She saves and closes E3 and *Early Exit To The Void*'s C++ files. She subconsciously pushes the stack of three sheets further toward the back of her desk, hiding them in the rear shadow of her working display. She rolls her chair back with her feet, stands up, and heads for her bedroom.

Japanese Robot silently comes alongside her and reminds her: "The fridge contains your required Thursday-night nourishment of green beans, your starch for this evening of fifty grams of potatoes, and curried tofu." Ev whirls and walks across her studio to the fridge in her kitchen.

5

Finding The Saviour

Whoosh.

Ev automatically looks down at E3Here's icon minimized in the Windows taskbar. Eye-tracking bot expands her email, and directs reading bot to read it.

Jeerah.

Ev sags back in her chair, its back leaning, leaning until Ev is staring at her high ceiling with its regularly arranged LED-bulb light fixtures of flat panels with their frosted lenses throwing a soft light behind and over her. Reading bot reads the email out loud in his restored monotone. As the email continues, the monotone grows louder and louder; as it grows louder, inflections appear. Ev presses her lips together. Search bot has gotten into reading bot's coding again. She'll have to go back into reading bot and edit them out. Again. Search bot is getting too uppity. She knows what she wants in her bots and codes.

She hadn't been listening, she realizes. Her brows wrinkle because she always listens, always hears every word. First something had nibbled on a few molecules of her WORM, now it's interfering with her focus. What's happening? She straightens up, her chair seat slapping back to horizontal. She scans her working display until she spots Jeerah's email.

Eye-tracking bot asks: "Do you want reading bot to read it again?"

Thankfully she had included this throw command in case of this error, although when she'd put it in, she hadn't thought it a realistic error. She types "yes," on the command line eye-tracking bot had drawn on the screen. Reading bot restarts, inflecting every word:

"Hi, Evelyn, Jeerah here! But you knew that!!! It says so in my email address, right?!! I can't wait to see what you're designing for me, but hey, I think I really need to meet with you. I want my website to be authentic, for you to be authentic in designing it. It's super important to me. I want people to be inspired, to WANT TO MEET the Saviour, to want TO HEAR the Gospels. The Saviour says, whoever has ears to hear, hear, and whoever has a mind to UNDERSTAND, understands! This is so exciting because our spirits CAN UNDERSTAND. His spirit calls to our spirits! I want my website to inspire people to BELIEVE that they CAN because the SAVIOUR IS WITH THEM!!!!

"I really want to meet up with you. Can we? I know you're SUPER BUSY. But everyone needs a time out, right? And I know coders like to hang out in coffee shops, and I know a sweet one, just the right one, where WE CAN MEET! It'll be so great to meet in person..."

Ev's eyes involuntarily close, and she groans. She leans back in her chair again, way, way back. She opens her eyes to count her flat panel lights, the rhythm of counting soothing her neurons screeching, "No. No. No!" at the thought of meeting a stranger in a coffee shop full of other humans. Ev counts the boards that lay diagonally across her ceiling, no longer listening as reading bot speaks out then yells out Jeerah's email to her.

Gospels!

Saviour!

Foreign words jangling their insistence at drilling into her brain.

She feels the opposite of inspired. E3 excites her; Saviour deadens her. What is a Saviour? The question protrudes into her counting. She doesn't understand this at all.

She sits up again. She sends her eyes toward search bot's holding place, sending eye-tracking bot to wake up search bot. Woken up, search bot moves seamlessly to the middle of her wall display and draws out a line for her to type in a search, except she doesn't know the terms and parameters of her search. Saviour? Gospels? Maybe if she typed in both, search bot will find it for her. That's why she'd coded the most artificial intelligence, AI, into him.

Ev had begun with rudimentary AI, chat bot level AI, but it was insufficient. She'd needed a smart bot that knew how to interpret her search commands, independently analyze her code, and determine what she needed and went searching for it, to present the results to her at the time she needed it. Search bot's habit of coding reading bot with regular human speech patterns is an irritant she can live with to have him give her what she wants when she doesn't know what she wants, though she wishes he'd stop coding.

And so she's confident search bot will know how to find the meanings of these incomprehensible terms. She types these words, and search bot blinks. His smile straightens. It's his thinking visage. His eyes become downcast. Oh-oh, her error catch code is about to be initiated. Search bot sends out a new command line preceded with the question: "Please elucidate." Search bot stills.

Ev stares. How is he unable to search? She seeks answers in that part of her WORM that stores his AI coding. *Oh.* She exhales as she realizes her mistake. She'd focused his knowledge parameters on coding, computers, websites, but not one piece of code on spiritual matters. She hadn't coded him to do simple keyword searches, but semantic searches. He doesn't know how to search semantically on a topic she hasn't coded into him. She cannot code into him what she doesn't know, either.

Ev sighs. In her disappointment and uncertainty, her eyes land in the darkness behind her working display. She sees a white corner of one of the sheets. She pulls all three toward her. Their unmoving existence has lulled her fear into abeyance. The top sheet remains blank. Flax. She rubs it absently, wondering: does flax mean something? It's the object paper with attribute flax. Why flax? How would this fit in to void.Null-Time? No, it's here in space.Time, and paper is an object from Energy class that has led to derived class Natural that has led to plants and then to flax. Each of these papers come from a different derived class. Flax paper comes from the derived class of—

Weariness slows Ev's neuronal transmissions. These papers aren't supposed to exist. She doesn't want to try to understand their existence anymore. They aren't supposed to exist. Not this one—she pushes the top one off the other two—nor this one, the hemp paper, the middle one, which is blank also. She grasps its edge and lifts it up. The bottom one is blank except for her signature. The lavender ink glows and bleeds into the air. Hurriedly, she drops the hemp paper, grabs the top sheet, and uses it to cover the other two. She shoves them back into the space behind her working display. Not far enough. She pushes them to the right, as far to the rear of her tabletop desk as possible without them slipping between the back edge of the desk and her wall.

Should she listen to the rest of Jeerah's email? She isn't sure. She usually reads and listens to everything her clients send. She feasts on details. Details matter. Like each symbol, each letter in her coding, details from her client's brain outputs let her customize websites precisely and beyond what her clients expect. Her searching out of details they didn't even know and didn't know their websites needed to distinguish her work earns her the praises that create light in her chest.

But how to search for this Saviour, for authentic, for spirit, for to believe?

Should she meet with Jeerah? Again, the foreign thought wanders in. She doesn't push it away, and it wends its way through her neurons, burning her head, and sending heat into her face.

No! She shakes her head hard, fast. She doesn't meet with clients. Her rule. She must stick to her protocol. It's the only way she's succeeded. What worked in the past, works in the present, creates a future of equal reward.

Through her half-closed eyes, Ev looks again at the command line that search bot has drawn, sets her shoulders back, and reminds herself: details. Details about the Saviour and...Ev re-listens in her head to what reading bot had read out. The corners of her lips lift a little, as the relevant line of Jeerah's email writes itself into the front of her consciousness: "want TO HEAR the Gospels." She sees Jeerah's capital letters scream across her internal vision. "Inspired" as well forms itself into her consciousness. She'd searched for the golden letters of "inspired" before. And though she hadn't thought of using "hear" in any of her websites, it too was a common word. "Hear" looks like fans of blue paint that originate midnight blue-black and fade upward into faint sky blue off the edge of a website's background. She thinks, *Saviour sounds human.* She types into search bot's command line, "What does the saviour look like?"

Search bot opens his eyes; his smile reappears as he begins the search on her parameters. It refines the search until images and paintings and drawings of saviours pepper her wall display. Ev snuggles up to her desk until its edge presses warmly against her abdomen. She begins picking out images using eye-tracking bot to find and save them to her image server. Ev settles into a hum of working with her bots. She doesn't need to meet with Jeerah for Jeerah to give her the inspiration she'd yelled for so excitedly. She'll give Jeerah her desired authentic website with the Saviour without breaking her rules.

6

In The VR

Having found all she needed about the Saviour to give Jeerah her desired website, Ev turns to what matters to her. She picks up her VR helmet, settles the built-in headphones over her ears until they're comfortable, and launches E3 into virtual reality. She prefers coding through the 3D space her VR helmet provides her rather than the flat dimensions of either one of her displays.

Ev zooms in ConsciousnessMind class. She talks to herself in her head as she inspects this large class in Level 1. Class, constructor, and object all in one. ConsciousnessMind, existing in void.NullTime derived from Zygote class, becoming the base class for Energy class and Energy class's derived class of EnergyHuman. She cocks her head, and the coding keeps itself level. She asks herself: can she describe how void.NullTime came to be? Other than it came from Placenta class, the second and only other derived class from Zygote class? She shakes her head negatively, and her VR helmet slips a little. She tightens the straps until it's resituated comfortably and resumes inspecting her code. She needs connecting code. She needs a way for ConsciousnessMind to connect with and through her instantiated EnergyHuman objects in space.Time.

Is MagneticField a sufficient connector?

The memory of feeling an error when tracking the creation of David.admin the last time she'd reviewed her code, returns. Was this what her subconscious had spotted, an error in how David had ascended from Level 0 to Level 1 and had become David.admin?

If her instantiated EnergyHuman objects have their own dynamic heap memories in MagneticField, then logically ConsciousnessMind should have one as well. She begins to type in the 3D space inside her helmet and creates a member function she calls "CMMagneticField" of ConsciousnessMind and declares it "friend" in EnergyHuman.

As Ev creates the C++ code for this new member function, her brain flashes images of an amorphous being without borders, existing outside of time yet inside a spatial area that's beyond three dimensions, which exude a field that cannot be seen yet permeates the borders between void.NullTime where ConsciousnessMind exists and space.Time where instantiated objects of EnergyHuman exists. She watches CMMagnetic-Field expand toward character objects in Level 0 where space and time exist and...

Ev pauses to think. More than dynamic heap memory, CMMagnet-icField functions as a...Ev squints into her lines and lines of code. *Yes, connector, and forgetting about how character objects in Level 0 connect to and transform into their new instantiations in Level 1 was her error*, she thinks as she simultaneously codes ConsciousnessMind's magnetic field to be an attractor to the magnetic fields created by the coding of her character objects. ConsciousnessMind's function CMMagneticField return character objects' matter in Level 0 to Energy matter in Level 1. Having fully coded this new function to work as connector and stored memory, she types artificial intelligence and randomization codes into it to have it behave independent of all others, including herself its creator.

CMMagneticField strengthens the flow of information from the character objects into their own MagneticFields, making the flow instantaneous for every unit of time in which the character responds to external execution of codes and executes its own code as words, thought bubbles, and stimulation of other character coding. She had worked over the years on all the different variables that could affect brains and had put those into her instantiated human objects. Except emotions. She hadn't known, other than rudimentary smiles and frowns, how to code for all the nuances of human emotions. She herself doesn't feel much. She cannot use herself as a guide. *But it doesn't matter*, she thinks, *for the purposes of* Early Exit To The Void *to have emotions in order to exit from Level 0 into Level 1.*

Ev scrolls through the list of variables, her brain imaging each variable until she confirms that yes, she's accounted for all the different ways a brain can change and the different ways that can make a brain change other than in the emotional spheres. Emotions are overrated. She desires her created reality to be solid like logic, like herself. She wants the character objects' individual MagneticFields to be mirrors...No, they need to be more than mirrors, they need to be constructed higher-order versions of the character objects' coding activity, and they need to be updated in real time. This new member function of ConsciousnessMind will assist and affirm that, she believes.

But what about between character objects MagneticFields? Can they connect? she wonders. She zooms in to the arrays of the MagneticFields and decides she likes the idea of connection. But how to create those connections? Their sphere is limited to the space around each character. She hadn't coded for MagneticFields to expand their data collection outward beyond one character and beyond one meter into the spatial environment around it. Perhaps this new member function of CMMagneticField can also bridge between MagneticFields? But if it's a friend function of the instantiated character objects of EnergyHuman class, can she friend it for all the character objects or only some?

Ev doesn't like to play her code without knowing what will happen. She likes to predict accurately what her code will do before she presses play. It disturbs her to experiment, but she cannot see how to work out if declaring CMMagneticField as friend function to all objects in the EnergyHuman class will create connections between each object in that class or only within each object.

Ev feels a nudge against her right shoulder.

Japanese Robot says: "Please breathe with me. I will speak commands." Ev is confused. She hadn't been aware of her breathing so much in flow with her coding was she. What is wrong with her breathing? Japanese Robot begins. "Inhale. Count to six. You are not inhaling. Please inhale. Count to six."

Ev's body bit by bit enters her consciousness, and she feels her breathing, her short sharp breaths in and out. Japanese Robot says: "Please inhale with me. Count to six." Ev inhales slowly, her visored head turning blindly toward her robot as he says: "Thank you. Exhale for six." Ev exhales for six. They repeat this sequence together until two precise minutes have elapsed. She hears the silence of his wheels upon the silence of her studio as Japanese Robot moves away from her.

Realizing her brain is calmer, her vision sharper, she straightens her head to face toward where her computer displays are. She's ready to play into the unknown effects of her coding.

Ev presses the Play button in virtual reality.

She was in a dark place. She could see nothing. Light filtered through as if she were looking through eyelids. Ev's heart began to thump in her ears. Suddenly, white flashed into her eyes, blinding her, making her shrink back, causing her arms to raise up to shield her eyes. But she could not shield them. The light brightened and brightened until pain blasted from her eyeballs into the back of her head. *Stop!* It's a thought not action. She's unable to hit the stop button herself.

The light winks out, and ghostly afterimages pockmark the blinding darkness inside her helmet. Somehow *Early Exit To The Void* has stopped. Ev doesn't care how it had. She's just relieved it had. Reassurance weaves through her and hovers between her and the air around her. She draws in breaths raggedly. What has happened? Should she go back? As her breathing eases, she hears faint traffic sounds: a car honking, a plane rumbling overhead, its vibrations thrumming her roof. The wreaths of reassurance slip back out of her senses, leaving her feeling cradled, feeling more sure, more courageous. Curiosity places an urging hand on her mind about what had happened in *Early Exit To The Void*. She begins to play it again.

Gloom filled her view. She heard a curtain being whisked aside. Slowly out of the gloom, appeared a streaked window with thick silk dusky pink curtains hanging on either side. Through the window, she saw a man standing. He was just standing there, watching with large unblinking brown eyes. She stared back through someone else's eyes. They were not her eyes. She didn't feel like she was in a first-person game, although she had coded *Early Exit To The Void* as a first-person virtual reality game. She knew from previous experimental plays and comparing those experiences with all those games she'd played as a teen, when she'd learnt about engines and game development with C++, that *Early Exit To The Void* doesn't have the same feel of immersive separation.

Someone else changed the view. Someone else turned her head. Ev, in her decades-long experience with virtual reality, could feel the foreign sensation of her head remaining straight against her control. Someone else looked at the wall to the right of the window where hung an abstract painting. She felt emotions of dread and fear as if she were a mouse being watched by a snake. Ev shivered. The eyes she was looking through returned to the window as if hypnotized, as if pulled back against their will. And Ev knew: CMMagneticField, using its AI and randomization codes in unforeseen ways, connected character objects' MagneticFields across vast distances and somehow the player to the objects—for behind the man was a dusty streetscape lit by a hot sun with palm trees in the corners of bleached stone walls that lined the front yards of the houses opposite to the one in which the character object whose eyes she was seeing through. She had created temperate climate environments in space.Time Level 0. She'd brushed snow and icicles, bare trees, and frost-covered sidewalks into her scenes. She'd created summer scenes but none with palm trees.

Ev shivered violently again, and this time, she did more than think. She smacked the stop button on her game.

7

Return To Frock

In Dr. Frock's brown-clad office, Ev sits down in the middle of the sofa, her back straight, her eyes upon his face. Once he sees she's seated, Dr. Frock lowers himself into his armchair, crossing one brown-wool covered leg over the other, balancing his swampeel-skin-bound notepad on his lap.

Ev glances down at the skin enveloping his notepad, photographing it through her optic nerve to the occipital lobe neuropeptides that store her imagery in her WORM memory. She returns her gaze to his face and blue-and-green-striped eyes. Ev had experimented with many textures early in her development as a coder. Back in her teens, she'd been partial to organic textures. As Ev keeps her attention on Dr. Frock, she scrolls through the neuropeptides of her WORM that store the array of animal skin data.

Eel.

Malabar swampeel.

Pinkish brown.

Endangered.

Tightly bound around the notepad's interior stiff cardboard.

She doesn't analyze the knowledge she's retrieved.

As she continues to wait for Dr. Frock to ask his questions, she absorbs through her entire visual field details she hadn't seen before. She frowns slightly at having missed these details during her first visit, details like the cane sitting in the umbrella stand next to the door.

Tapered.

Finished to a smooth shine.

Black.

Ev again retrieves data from her internal materials database stack.

African Blackwood.

Near threatened.

The black grain-less wood melds into a smooth handle that's shaped like a wave with two ivory eyes and jagged teeth carved from its handle end to just below the eye in an upward swoop. Ev narrows her view inward from her peripheral scan of the cane with its carved teeth to Dr. Frock's lips, which are hiding his even teeth. He's smiling benignly at her, waiting. Ev has nothing to say. Finally, he opens his mouth, pauses, and asks: "How are you?"

"Fine," Ev replies.

He nods. "Good, good."

Ev says nothing more.

Dr. Frock clears his throat. He waits. He says: "As you recall, in our last session, I diagnosed you with Social Pragmatic Communication Disorder. I suggested learning communication styles as our working treatment. Have you done any work on this?"

Ev blinks. Her eyebrows' inner edges wrinkle up. "Work?"

"Yes, work. Have you taken the initiative to find new methods of communicating with your peers so that your social life can flourish better?"

Ev stares at him. She queries: "What variables was I supposed to plug in?"

Dr. Frock blinks rapidly three times. He clears his throat, adjusts his wool-covered legs to cross them at the ankles. "I was hoping you would take the opportunity to say hello to your friends."

"Friends?"

"Yes. People. Ones you socialize with." He smiles, revealing his even teeth.

Ev's brown eyes search his green ones for an answer. Seeing nothing, she says: "I met a mind. I think."

Dr. Frock's smile disappears as his eyes open wide. His irises recast into blue stripes. "Um, perhaps you could explain that?"

"Yes. I started E3 and reviewed the ConsciousnessMind class for how it appears in space.Time. I understood what I needed to execute and began *Early Exit. Early Exit To The Void* is its full name." Ev blinks and pulls up Lapis into her consciousness. It shows her this change to shortening the name of her virtual reality had happened overnight during a dream her heap memory deallocated before it was written into her WORM's hippocampus neuropeptides. Uncharacteristically, she doesn't roll back her programming to the version existing before this overnight change. Uncharacteristically, she risks staying in the change.

"I see," Dr. Frock nods, his voice wisping away. He keeps his bluing eyes on her, scanning her still face. Seeing no answer in her face, he juts his head forward, his notepad dangling precariously from his left hand as his right grips his black fountain pen, and paints on his benign smile.

Ev waits.

Dr. Frock waits for her to continue. He abruptly presses against the back of his chair, his eyes snapping green. "Yes, yes. So, Evelyn in our first lesson, I showed you nonverbal cues."

Ev hurriedly retrieves every detail of their first appointment that she can and remembers nothing while at the same time, recording internally what he's saying.

"The non-verbal cue I gave you in the current situation to continue speaking was me sitting forward now. And verbally, the cue was I said 'I see.' This means you are to continue your story."

Ev states: "You're sitting back."

Dr. Frock replies: "Yes, that's true. I am...Well, I must admit I was taken aback by your silence. I like to be honest with my patients. Be upfront with my assessments and diagnoses and what I observe. I find it gets around any misunderstandings and facilitates the healing process.

Please continue." He gestures to her with his black white-topped fountain pen.

Ev continues with no change in her expression: "The first play sent pain into my eyes from the bright light. So I stopped. I played it again. Japanese Robot had executed the breathing function to me at the start. I had to try again. I was in a different place in space.Time, I think," Ev frowns, uncertainty as to what had happened and where she'd been fading her voice. She inhales sharply and says with a questioning cadence: "I looked through a mind?"

"A mind?" Dr. Frock has regained full control over his outward composure.

"Yes," Ev affirms, as she replays the scene in her own mind, feeling more and more that it had been like another's mind, like looking through the viewport of another person But she clarifies for Dr. Frock: "The character. Third person. It felt like a mind. The mind stared out the window."

"It was not you?"

"No. I was supposed to be first-person, but somehow it was...Third?" Again Ev's voice fades into puzzlement.

"I see," Dr. Frock says, his eyes fully green and widening as he sinks comfortably into his chair, pulls his notepad back up onto his lap, and scrawls a few lines. He lets his notepad drop flat onto his lap as he studies her then smiles encouragingly. Ev reads his note upside down. "Dissociation? Unspecified."

"Evelyn?" His voice brings Ev's brown gaze back onto his green eyes. "This is where you continue. My non-verbal communication is telling you to continue speaking. I don't usually have this much trouble with my other patients. I see that I'll have to prompt you more specifically in our communications. This may be tougher than I'd thought it would be. Perhaps we'll have to have more than five sessions." He considers her for a moment. His voice strengthens: "Yes. I will continue to see you daily for as long as needed, which I don't anticipate will be very long. I like to take an aggressive approach when I see my clients are in distress to alleviate their discomfort as soon as possible and return them to their lives. You don't need me to become a part of your life, now, do you?" He smiles down at her, his eyes fatherly in their concern. He doesn't wait for an answer as he continues: "Clearly, something is bothering you. Perhaps some memory or conceptual issue?" He doesn't pause. "I'd like to accelerate our program. But our time is up. Before we depart, I'd like to apprise you that now that I have a better idea of your initial problem that you presented me with, I can generate a working diagnosis of Unspecified Dissociative Disorder. It's clear to me that you had dissociation in this episode that you shared. What you characterized as third person and looking through a mind is, of course, dissociation, a metaphor for something that's bothering you. We will have to explore if this was one episode or if you have had previous ones. I often find patients like to couch their experiences in the third person and, only once we have alliance, reveal that there has been more than one episode and it's their experiences. But for now, the key feature here is that I can see it upset you." He stops speaking abruptly and waits. Ev's blank face doesn't shift. He clips his words. "You were upset, correct?"

"Yes," Ev replies, her ears taking in his words, her attention filing them into her WORM for later playback and processing, unable to understand in real time what he's saying. That mind whose eyes had controlled where she, Ev, looked, whose consciousness had controlled her movements, had not been hers. Another mind controlling her consciousness and body had made her stop *Early Exit To The Void*. Does he not understand her? Or does she not understand the reality?

Dr. Frock nods. "That makes sense. We will continue this tomorrow." Dr. Frock stands up, snaps closed his swampeel-bound notepad, and clasps it in his straight fingers as he walks toward the door. He opens it and waits. Ev follows him with her eyes, unmoving. But as Dr. Frock stands unmoving, one hand holding the door open, smiling at her, lips together, the skin around his eyes unlined, Ev grasps that she is to leave. He doesn't seem to give her her full time, but she doesn't know what to do about that. Using her abdominal muscles, Ev rises straight up and walks toward him and out. He shuts the door behind her with a murmur of air against her back and an inaudible click.

8

Object Error

Ev gazes out her window as she replays Dr. Frock's words in her mind, hearing every inflection, seeing every facial movement, still not understanding what Dr. Frock had been talking about. She turns on the balls of her feet and sits down in front of her computer. She tries to replay the conversation again, this time intertwining it with her first session with him. She reads back his statements stored in her WORM to piece them together. She reviews them for errors in coding to see why she hadn't been able to follow his logic. But she cannot see errors because she can't understand his programming language. She considers changing her programming and engaging Lapis, her concurrent versioning system, to record her own programming pre- and post-Frock-language change. A wall of incomprehension rises up.

Ev switches off that train of thought and brings into focus her working display before her. She lifts her eyes up to her wall display. E3 awaits her there, to play or code. She lifts her right hand hesitantly and rests it on her mouse. She feels unsure, not herself. Back into her consciousness trundle Dr. Frock's words. *Was this, this new unsureness, what Dr. Frock meant about unspecified dissociative disorder?* She drops her eyes to stare at her hand on the mouse. She craves to be in a place she understands.

But not in virtual reality. She shies away from even putting on her VR helmet to review her code. Swiftly she moves her mouse to her top class and begins to review *Early Exit*.

Familiarity comforts her mind, brings her neurons into harmonic firing. She knows herself as she immerses herself in the lines of words, brace brackets, punctuation, the colours of code. She tells herself that there must be an error in here to account for that experience, where—

She skirts thinking about the details of what had happened. She had expressed it to Dr. Frock, and once done, had destructed it from her memory, her conscious memory. She reminds herself of this. She believes and knows she forgets nothing unless she deliberately destructs it. And then it's gone. There are no hidden memories, stored elsewhere in the molecules of her brain, she believes, especially if she turns off Lapis during the process. She ignores that it's hard to destroy one bit or byte of a WORM device.

Ev clicks open the header file for her top class, Zygote class. Zygote has two derived classes: Placenta class and ConsciousnessMind class. So far, so good. She approves of her long-done coding. Placenta class had instantiated two objects: void and space. She has given each a special function: for void, NullTime; for space, Time. She reviews the attributes of each object. Void has no boundaries; it isn't confined to three dimensions. She wonders if she should review the physics of that more closely. Should she give it ten dimensions? No dimensions? She decides to set that aside for now. Space is easier. It has three dimensions. It follows the physics of Earth and the universe as Einstein and Hawking had written. The function time acts in the same way time works in the universe. She'd read all of Einstein's theories, all of Hawking's ideas. She feels that she has coded time to conform as closely as possible to how they saw it working. She skips reviewing time's many attributes and opens up the ConsciousnessMind class instead. She had made it a class, constructor, and object in one. She ignores her first iterations of how it had replicated objects, objects she'd called "angels." And she ignores one of those angels called "Daeva" from which came the objects called "demons." The coding for those plagued her still. A puzzle that twines incomprehensibilities into her logic field and causes her stomach to ache. She prefers to exist without those aches. Perhaps she'll delete their coding? No. She'll return to those later, she decides again as she has each time she reviews this part of her coding. For some reason, she cannot bring herself to fully delete them. Somehow, for some reason her subconscious prevents her. Somehow, they play a role in her *Early Exit*, but she doesn't yet know how. She's come to realize that sometimes she needs to wait for elucidation. Coding isn't all about creating rapidly and deleting abruptly. Coding includes recreating and waiting and reviewing and waiting some more to see what evolves. Being patient and setting to the side instead of deleting an entire group of objects.

Ev follows the derived classes from ConsciousnessMind. First there's Energy class. Energy is the base class for every class that she wants to populate *Early Exit*, one of which is EnergyHuman class. She made Energy class exist in void.NullTime, but had EnergyHuman class exist in space.Time. So far that coding works. She detects no errors in that that would account for the frightening experiences that she'd had. She has to find the error, then all will be fine. She shifts in her air chair and moves her body closer to the desk. She straightens her spine. Her eyes darken to charcoal brown as she scrutinizes her code.

She'd created ten derived classes from EnergyHuman class and had listed them in order of hierarchy of importance and power: Faith, Languages, Prophecy, Interpretations, Healing, DistinguishingBetweenMagneticFields. She pauses there. She asks herself, *Are the class names becoming too long?* She considers the length of the class EnergyHumanDistinguishingBetweenMagneticFields. Too long? No. It's long, but she won't change it. It would mean too many edits in her other files, and then she would introduce an error. Edit only if need to. Edits fix and attract mistakes.

Ev resumes reading the list of EnergyHuman's derived classes: MagneticFieldPowers, Wisdom, and Unity. *She's used Unity once*, she thinks. She scrolls through the neuropeptides that store her code and nods. Yes, only once. Ev turns her scrutiny to the instantiation of objects. Which object would that David.admin have come from? Not Faith. Only Religious and Spiritual objects were instantiated from Faith type class. And Believers, she reminds herself. She considers each class in turn and pauses on Interpretations.

Ev pulls her eyebrows close together. Pain sprouts between them. She exhales and deliberately relaxes her facial muscles. She turns her head to stare blankly into the quiet space of her studio. Had she done this before? She feels her memory pixelating, leaving her brain to enter the air around her head and vanish from her grasp.

No! WORM memory cannot escape, she tells herself roughly, silently, only in her thoughts. She stares hard into the air and wills the WORM pixels to return. She reads back into herself the data she'd written down. Had she completed tracking him? Ev turns her head back to look once more at her coding and finds where she'd left off. She muses, she'd created objects of type organizers and translators. She hadn't put any administrators into her code, had she? She shakes her head no. So how had David.admin appeared? He was an administrator in the void.Null-Time of the Placenta class. Here is an object error she cannot account for.

Logic, Ev, logic! she reprimands herself. Logically administrators would be under Interpretations, for they interpret rules and regulations for everyone else. Yes, that sounds logical. She clicks over to her Interpretations objects list to see if she had instantiated any character objects called "David," although she's certain she hadn't. She remembers every one of her objects. They're her creations; they've become part of her, for they came out of her. She knows she hadn't.

Ev blinks.

She had?

She had created a David.

Disturbing pressures rise into the area around her heart, and to quieten them, Ev decides that she remembers creating him.

She cannot tolerate any more memory errors.

She notes that this character object had been created as an organizer. Okay, she blows air out and noisily inhales through her nose. She's starting to get somewhere.

Ev raises her eyes to her wall display to quickly find the source file for her Destructor code for the Interpretations class of EnergyHuman.

No, wait!

She needs to review space.Time.

Perhaps there's a public function in there that had distorted the organizer class of objects, especially character objects. She reads each line of code slowly, carefully, searching for errant lines. Her brows draw together, closer and closer, until her forehead is tight and her eyes sharp on the text.

She finds nothing.

She goes over it again and spots something. A small line, but maybe it could have introduced a distortion so that an organizer became an administrator. But does she want to change it? And can it account for the three sheets—

Ev stops her thoughts from remembering that moment when *Early Exit* had entered her domain. Dr. Frock's word "dissociation" had disrupted her enough that once more she fears thinking about those papers. She'd gone to see him to get an answer, but now she doesn't even want to think about them nor ask him. No, she won't change that line because it isn't responsible, and she kind of likes David.admin, Ev reluctantly admits to herself. But the thought continues to nag her. How had he become an admin up in void.NullTime?

Ev reviews her Destructor code. MagneticFields are the named dynamic memories of each character object derived from type Energy-Human and all ten of its derived classes. She had coded the ConsciousnessMind function of CMMagneticField to point from the individual character objects to their MagneticFields so that every execution of code that matured the character object was stored in MagneticField and then upon execution of the destructor code that destructed the matter of the object, returned the original EnergyHuman to void.NullTime to create the new class of EnergyMind.

Focus! Ev admonishes herself.

She's supposed to be reviewing the Destructor code to see how David.admin was created in void.NullTime!

Okay. MagneticField dynamic memory upon the Destructor code executing outputs to an object of the same name under a new class called "EnergyMind" within void.NullTime. Enlightenment emerges. David.admin exists because the MagneticField dynamic memory of InterpretationsOrganizer David had pointed to the class EnergyMind in void.NullTime and instantiated a new character object with the same memories of InterpretationsOrganizer David, called "David" with the function of administrator. David.admin.

Ev leans back exhausted.

But smiling.

Feeling once again herself, Ev wants to play her game.

She reaches over to her VR helmet, places it gently over her head, flattening her spiky hair. She adjusts the headphones and clicks Play.

Hazy blue sky filled her vision, then her view dropped down to a dusty road in front of her. Heat seared her skin, and sweat prickled the back of her neck. She felt small hairs rise up and down her arms. Her view snapped to her right and behind her. Two men were sauntering together, their eyes shifting from her back to each other, yet neither was talking. Her vision snapped back to the road ahead of her, focusing her own eyes on a gate in a wall to her left. She felt feet hastening, pulling her along, her breath becoming ragged. The character whose eyes she was seeing through passed an iron gate, hanging loosely on its hinges to her left, and shifted her gaze to it. She felt the mind, no, the character.

This is a character object. *A her? Yes, a her who...*Ev's observing thoughts are abruptly subserved into the experience.

Fear pounded in as the view turned to consider entering the open gate. But a woman was standing there, her hair loosely covered in a gauzy scarf whose end lifted lazily up and fell back down over her breasts. The woman's eyes were hard and stared right at her, as if recording every nuance of her face, every detail of her clothing. Her fear. Ev felt the mind's heart race; her own began to thud in unison. The mind shifted her gaze to the right, but the right wall went on and on, no breaks offering entrance. The mind had known this yet had needed to check.

Ev pulls herself out of the game mentally, trying to resist being pulled into the scene unfolding before her, not wanting to accept that *Early Exit* is throwing feelings into her brain. Suddenly, curiosity overcomes her, the pull of the game swamps her. Her consciousness returns into the 3D reality.

The mind reached another gate further ahead on her left. Ev saw bleached beige stucco walls of a building behind the gate. The building was a house but not like any house Ev had seen before. It rose two stories and had a double teak door dead centre above a rise of semicircular steps. Ev counted three steps. Above the door was a tall window with a Juliet balcony. The double-doored window was open, light curtains falling on either side on the inside, their bottoms fanning out briefly from a hidden breeze before falling back into place. Shutters lay flat on either side of the window above the balcony and on either side of the front door, their sky-blue paint peeling, revealing old army-green paint underneath. She felt the heat of the sun-warmed wrought-iron bars as the mind's hand grasped the gate and pushed. A screech sent shockwaves through Ev's hearing.

Early Exit halts.

Ev pulls off her gloves and releases her head from her VR helmet, puzzled as to why the game has ended abruptly. She hadn't been so afraid this time. She places her gloves and helmet down on her desk and notices her mouse. The three sheets are sitting next to it, fanned out. Above her signature is a new line. Ev pulls her eyebrows together. She thinks, *Is this a backward application form?* She thought she'd known where the exit went, but uncertainty slithers in. She stares at the new words.

Accommodation: House. Next to it is a small box with a purple-ink checkmark in it for "Owned."

9

Mind Who

"ConsciousnessMind inhabits void.NullTime," says Ev flatly to Dr. Frock as she sits upright on the centre of the sofa facing him. He watches her with his eyes of blue-green stripes, each stripe the same width as all the other stripes. His hand holding his fountain pen remains poised above a fresh ruled sheet in his swampeel-skin-bound notepad. Ev snaps her teeth shut. She had explained Zygote and Placenta, how Zygote is at the currently top Level 2, how Placenta and ConsciousnessMind come out of Zygote, how Placenta instantiates void with function NullTime while ConsciousnessMind—at that point, Dr. Frock had interrupted her. He'd just asked her again what ConsciousnessMind is. He peers at her now as if her answer is unclear.

He clears his throat. "Yes, but..." He lets his voice peter off. He lays his fountain pen carefully down on the sheet of paper and adjusts his weight. The velvet brocade-covered cushion underneath him bows. He eyes her, the green stripes in his eyes slowly widening as he contemplates her version of reality. She had said something about games, but he'd dismissed the literality of that. In his experience, women aren't dedicated computer game players. If they were, they rarely let it become a problem unlike the teen sons of his CEO patients. It's her mention of early exit that concerns him and her strange confounding of reality into something she seems more comfortable with. In his estimation, here is another instance of dissociation and possible suicidal ideation. She's obviously considering existing in a placental environment and is calling herself by an objectified term to avoid realizing what she's doing. It makes sense that she sees herself as existing in the placenta, since the placenta is where every human had felt safe, warm, comfortable, and protected before being abruptly churned out into the cold air. Perhaps that desire for placental existence is why she wants to exit this city. And perhaps her idea of null time is her way to take herself out of real time and, well, reality. Somehow, she's dissociated herself episodically to do just that. His working diagnosis for UDD is firming up. His long experience and success with all his patients gives him the confidence to know he's on the right plane. As for her communication disorder, she doesn't seem to be integrating what he's teaching her with her life at home. He thought he'd explained that she needs to improve her communication skills, yet here she is not learning but still speaking in these short sentences of hers and only in response to his questions. He must help her. Yes, he owes it to her to help her. She's bright.

Well, he qualifies to himself, she seems bright. He studies her face, her fathomless brown eyes, her still demeanour as she sits upright on the sofa across from him. His smile straightens a bit as he tries to read what's behind those brown eyes and fails. He clears his throat again. "Tell me again about ConsciousnessMind."

"ConsciousnessMind inhabits void.NullTime."

"Yes, yes, but tell me about her."

"ConsciousnessMind has no gender."

Dr. Frock picks up his pen and eagerly scrawls a note about her need to have no gender. He'd noticed her last time reading his notes upside down, and so this time, he's carefully angled his notebook slightly toward himself. People normally complain that his writing is illegible. He isn't sure she actually can read his notes, but she seems to. And so he doesn't want to take any chances. As far as he's concerned, the only person who should read his notes is himself. He knows he'll have to show her if she asks—the law requires him to do so—but he believes it's best if clients don't read his notes. And so he manages to let his clients believe he's anxious to have them see his notes—his—he emphasizes in his mind—while ensuring they give up on trying to read his writing. Only one had ever confronted him and had had him read the notes out loud.

Disgust sours his tongue as he remembers how he'd had to finesse that, skipping a little here, a little there without that client catching on, ensuring his client was satisfied. He'd found a way to discharge that client ethically soon after that by shaping the client's thoughts to want to quit him and find another.

But here is someone more dangerous. He'll have to be careful.

He's fairly confident that Ev won't ask him to read his notes out to her, but her ability to read them at all...

He frowns to himself as his eyes blank their light to her while he considers that perhaps she really had read his notes upside down. He dismisses the thought. That would take a deciphering ability and visual acuity normally not seen in women.

Dr. Frock allows his almost-green eyes to settle on her. Ev in her still, upright posture, waits for the next question. He asks: "And how does that look? No gender."

Ev cocks her head three degrees to the right and ponders. "I haven't built that in," she finally replies.

"Built that in to yourself?"

The space between Ev's eyes creases. She opens her mouth and leaves it open, unable to form any words.

He says: "Take your time. Don't worry about how long it takes for you to formulate your answer. The important thing is to communicate with me. I'm here to help you. The more you can tell me, the more I can help you. You see?"

Ev closes her mouth. She nods. She says nothing.

"Why don't you describe Consciousness Mind to me, like, say, for example, describe her face to me?"

"ConsciousnessMind has no gender," Ev corrects him.

Dr. Frock's lips widen until they part to show a glimpse of his teeth.

"Okay. Why don't you describe them," he says, emphasizing the word "them" ever so slightly while keeping his face still.

Ev hears the slight condescension in his tone, as if he's pandering to her insistence that ConsciousnessMind has no gender. She doesn't understand why he doubts her. She coded ConsciousnessMind. Why does Dr. Frock need this class, constructor, and object to have a gender? Her mind sticks on that question. She delves into it, her awareness of the externals switching to her internal coding, reviewing Consciousness-Mind's coding to see if gender could be appropriate and if she ought to change their shape and features to a human-like countenance, until his voice faint at first then louder and louder swims her back up to the surface of reality.

"Evelyn?"

"Yes."

"Please describe the face of Consciousness Mind."

"ConsciousnessMind has no face."

"Oh?" A little blue begins to appear in Dr. Frock's green eyes.

"No, ConsciousnessMind exists without boundaries and faces have boundaries."

"That is true," he smiles, crow's feet around his eyes appearing as the blue stripes in his irises widen. He laughs softly. "That is true. Faces have boundaries. So tell me about this boundary-free...person, shall we call them?"

"No, not a person. The base class in void.NullTime."

"Class?"

"Yes."

Dr. Frock struggles to understand where school comes in. *Or is she referring to a college class?* He stands up and strides over to his desk. He opens her file to the first page and reviews her education. *Ah, university,* he expostulates to himself. Perhaps this is some new method of dissociating. She hadn't dissociated into a person in the here and now but had become a student in class back in university. Perhaps university is when she experienced her first dissociation. He must delve into her university days.

But not now.

He returns to his chair, and his green eyes settle on her as he settles into the bottom cushion. Ev notices how his blue-green eyes change hues so organically. She processes this feature, examines it from the superficial to the behind-the-scenes view to consider adding this to her mode panel on textural changes for her character objects in E3. She hadn't considered an object having mutable eyes before. Outwardly, she doesn't move nor shift her gaze from his face.

"I want to congratulate you on responding to my slight verbal cue earlier. This shows me you're a good study." He pauses to see if she'll say anything. She doesn't. "You could say at this point, 'Thank you, Dr. Frock.'"

"Thank you, Dr. Frock," she repeats like an automaton.

"You thank a person when they compliment you. I complimented you."

Ev shows no response.

"A nod would be helpful," he adds, his smile becoming fixed on his face.

Ev nods in a robotic response.

"Do you understand what I said?" he asks as he leans forward.

"Of course."

"Good, good," he grins, his body relaxing back into his chair, his eyes briefly becoming bluer. He closes his notepad. His grin vanishes as he rubs the top of his notepad briefly with the tips of four of his fingers, feeling the subtle scales of the dead swampeel under his fingers' fine sensors, as he contemplates her still visage. He abruptly stops and places his notepad and his pen on the table beside him. He straightens, his benign smile masking him. He summarizes: "I think we've made good progress today. And I want to give you good news about your treatment plan. You do have social pragmatic communication disorder, as we discussed before. But I have also confirmed that you have unspecified dissociative disorder. UDD. This seems to have come from one episode, but I'm also considering that it may have been set up during your time in university. We'll have to delve back into that time. This will take more time. I know we began with the idea that treating you would be a matter of five days. But it seems there is more here. I want to leave the end date open for now, but I want you to know one thing: I will work with you for as long as it takes to unearth the full story of your dissociative state. I want to help you, and I am here for you. Okay?"

Ev repeats: "Okay."

Dr. Frock shoots up and strides to the door. He waits attentively for her to rise and follow him before he reaches out with his right hand to push the door handle down. But before he pulls on the handle to let her out, he avers: "I'm here for you, Evelyn. You believe that?"

Ev raises her eyes to him. Search bot had directed her to him. She doesn't understand all these diagnoses of his, but he's listening and search bot had found him. She had coded search bot, and though he had this uncomfortable propensity to incorporate other people's codings, she trusts him because she trusts herself. Or she had when she'd coded him. That mind experience had shattered her self-trust, had brought her here. She hadn't told Dr. Frock about yesterday's experience.

Unwillingly the memory of the three sheets appearing in her reality had wagged itself so unceasingly in her internal view the moment she'd sat down on Dr. Frock's sofa that she'd tried to tell him about them, about the strangeness of an application form filling itself in backward. He'd begun her time with him by asking her to explain further about her initial experience that had brought her to him. His question plus the persisting memory had made her start to speak about it. Yet somehow she'd forgotten to complete her explanation—she suddenly realizes, it was because he'd interrupted her within three words of her starting to speak. He'd instructed that he wanted her to begin at the beginning. For her, the beginning was Zygote—and now it was too late to tell him about those strange sheets. It had been so difficult to go against her programming, to voice the event of the three sheets at the start that she's unsure she can try again. She isn't even sure if she'd said anything about yesterday's experience. of being in that mind, of being followed and watched, of seeing the mind's gate...And she doesn't like this new hide-and-seek WORM; she doesn't like her unsureness. Why is her WORM in disarray? Perhaps Dr. Frock can tell her. Her external vision brings him into view, every line of his face clearly etched to her as she stands close to him. He's waiting. Her own question vanishes as she remembers he'd asked her a question: did she believe that he was there for her?

She believes him because he'd asked her to believe him. She answers: "Yes."

Dr. Frock pulls the soundless heavy door open for Ev, and she passes through.

10

So Amazing

"Soooo. Do you have the FIRST DRAFT of my new website ready yet???!!!! I'm SOOO excited to see what you've done, Evelyn. I just KNOW it's AWESOME," reading bot in its recoded monotone is reading out Jeerah's email to Ev. Ev had reversed search bot's intonation additions in its coding. She glances up at the top left corner of her display to see if search bot is in wait mode or has disappeared. She'd discovered that when his little icon becomes invisible, that's when he's recoding her bots. Search bot is visible, his happy face on. Satisfied, she returns her eyes back to Jeerah's email and follows along silently with reading bot. She makes a moue. She hasn't been working on Jeerah's site. She'd been too caught up in *Early Exit*'s disturbing strangeness of putting her brain inside a character object's mind and in Dr. Frock's incomprehensible jargon and trying to make sense of a logical world that's been going awry.

Ev straightens her neck. Time to focus on Jeerah's website. She opens Jeerah's file of answers to her questions. She skims them. Jeerah likes the Gospel of Mary, whatever that is. Ev sighs. She usually begins this work in rote mode. The content can be anything. The content neither excites nor bothers her. It just is. She's good at it, and she hankers for the praise. It's still novel to her, praise. The praise is worth more than the money. Her parents hadn't believed in praise. They had believed in gentle correction and had left her alone the rest of the time. Unlike her parents, who automatically signed her report cards with a quick scrawl before returning to discussing an obscure detail of a rare diagnosis in words she didn't understand and didn't want to learn, her clients like her work. *Yes*, she utters loudly in her head, *her clients like her work.* Praise isn't a bad word. Clients keep coming; their demand for her services keeps rising. It's good work. It pays her bills. It swells her stock portfolio. It lets her develop E3. They were wrong those boys and men to say she couldn't make an engine. They were all wrong to say *Early Exit To Heaven* was silly, and she couldn't do it. This work lets her mature *Early Exit*. She doesn't have to work now. Unlike them. She can work when she wants to. She can work with whomever she wants to. She had chosen Jeerah when it was time to select another client.

Ev shuts her eyes tight as she hears Japanese Robot click almost silently out of his charger. She swallows down her thoughts. She exhales with deliberate slowness. She senses her robot halt. She hears the small click as he re-enters his charger.

She doesn't want to work with Jeerah.

Ev runs her tongue around her stale mouth, tasting this strange sensation of not wanting to work with a client she'd chosen. Why doesn't she want to? How can she fix this errant coding? Is it something to do with Dr. Frock's UDD? She doesn't know. Should she ask search bot? She feels herself mentally shying away from the idea.

Another new sensation.

She derides herself for not wanting to pursue this question.

Another new ideation.

She usually doesn't deride herself.

She perceives every problem as a code riddle to be solved, not as something to criticize herself for. Too many new sensations. Maybe she should take a break. She lifts her body up out of her air chair with her abdominal muscles and doesn't move. Click. Japanese Robot leaves his charger again. He wheels over to her silently from his home location in the corner beside her coat tree near her front door. Ev turns her head to the right and stares at his white plastic face with its two eyes of startling blue. She wonders why his Japanese designers gave him blue eyes. She has brown eyes; they have brown eyes. Wouldn't it make more sense to make him look like them?

She doesn't blink as she keeps her brown eyes on his encroaching face.

Two round blue eyes of a startling hue.

Japanese Robot says: "Are you hungry, Ev?"

Ev jumps. Her heart thuds. She opens her mouth and doesn't know what to say.

Japanese Robot says: "It is thirty minutes from your lunch nutrition. Do you want it early?"

Ev doesn't know how to answer.

Is she hungry? Is she thirsty? What is she feeling?

Her stomach rumbles.

Japanese Robot wheels backward silently, turns to his left ninety degrees, and rolls forward one meter, turns to his right ninety degrees, and whirrs almost silently toward the kitchen. Ev turns two hundred and seventy degrees as she follows him with her eyes and watches light slipping across his self-healing skin of nanofilled hydrogel as he passes into the kitchen. She hips her chair away from her and walks slowly toward the kitchen. She stops her feet in the middle of her kitchen's doorway and watches Japanese Robot turn on the water tap, let the water run precisely thirty seconds—the time she'd determined five years ago when she moved in here that the water took to run very very cold. He picks up a tall blue plastic glass and moves it to be underneath the rushing stream. Ev had tested his waterproof and temperature tolerance ability and knows no water, cold, hot, or iced, can hurt him. He waits in this position until the water fills it up to one centimeter below the rim. He moves it out from underneath the water. He turns off the tap, pivots on his wheels to make a smooth one-hundred-and-eighty-degree turn, and rolls toward her, holding the glass out in his soft robotic hand of hinges and flexible conductive polymer nanocomposite tubing encasing steel posts. The kitchen's artificial light calls out gleams of white in his artificial skin.

When he comes within her reach, Ev reaches her own hand forward and wraps her fingers around the glass above his robotic grasping mechanism that looks like a helmeted hand to her. He lets go, in the familiar way of his hand off of the glass to her.

The cold of the water seeps through the plastic walls of the glass into her carbon-based skin. She lifts it up to her lips and begins to drink. And drink. And drink. And drink. Faster and faster, her gulps becoming louder, water leaking out from either side of her mouth to dribble along the sides of her chin and onto her neck and into her brown corduroy shirt. She feels a cloth press against her neck as Japanese Robot mops up the water. He moves back to the sink. She empties the glass but continues to hold it up, its bottom toward the ceiling, hoping for that last drop of water. It doesn't come. Reluctantly, she eases her head back down to level and lowers the glass from her lips. She walks to her kitchen table, places her glass on it, and returns to her air chair, feeling somewhat satiated.

The chair eases her weight downward until her stomach is at the level of her desk. She rolls herself forward with her socked feet, places them on her footrest, inadvertently pushing her clogs off the back of it, hearing their thump in the back of her mind, and returns to reading Jeerah's answers to her questions. This time she doesn't skim but studies. She's seeking a logline, the perfect line for Jeerah's website, one that will welcome visitors and explain her site.

Jeerah quotes the Gospel of Mary a lot in her answers, Ev notes. Ev manually loads up Firefox and manually searches for a wiki on the Gospel of Mary. She doesn't want the bots coming between her and the work, she tells herself. She needs to engage directly with it, rid herself of these unaccustomed sensations. Soon, she's immersed in an English translation of the Gospel. She doesn't know anything about religious tract translations. For her, one translation is as another. This one is short, thankfully, surprising her. She holds this vague idea that spiritual writings go on and on like a huge droning man snoring in his cups.

"Peace be with you," Ev reads. Her eyes flicker on the words. She rereads them one at a time. Peace. Be. With. You. Peace. BE. With. You. Peace. BE. With you. Peace. BE. With. YOU.

Ev hums to herself, the soft vibration pleasing her lips, soothing her stomach. She straightens and scooches closer to her working display. She'll play with colours and capitals in that phrase. She begins to create the header of Jeerah's website. She writes Jeerah Mutti for the website's title. She tries on one font after another. Nothing is quite working. She pauses to consider what would be the right kind of font. A script like a calligraphic pen dipped in...

She freezes. Her eyes move side to side rapidly, searching for the perfect colour from her molecularly stored array for colours, searching for a colour that will capture Jeerah's verbosity. Red. The colours of dancing beads. No, she corrects herself, saffron yellow. For happiness and Jeerah's strange hippiness in her words. Having settled that, she types beside Jeerah's name, the phrase "Peace BE with YOU" and colours it purple as its base. Unsatisfied, she shoves her mouse over to her graphic program's icon at the bottom of her working display screen and launches it. Using the text tool, she creates the phrase, playing with colours and patterns and textures until it's a quilt work on a background of rich red-purple. She exhales, letting her lips blow open with satisfaction. She places the image's PNG file next to Jeerah's name. Ev cocks her head. She moves the image to sit underneath Jeerah's name. Better.

Ev is pleased with her good start on the header.

Japanese Robot softly bumps into her upper arm to tell her thirty minutes has elapsed. It's time for her midday nutrition.

In her kitchen at her serviceable thick pine table, she eats without noticing the food or the bitter bite of the coffee on her tongue as she contemplates what to put on Jeerah's website next. She usually designs the basic layout, but she feels uncharacteristically drawn to work on the message first. Jeerah wants a welcome message not just a logline. She wants this Saviour seen the moment people's browsers load up her website. Ev doesn't know who this Saviour was, but Mary did in her

Gospel. Mary saw this Saviour, had had secret conversations with him, conversations the men around her weren't privy to. She had related this in this Gospel Jeerah admired. Who were these men? Who was Mary? Ev's chewing slows. She drops the second half of her sandwich on to her plate, its cut edge squished and corrugated by the shape of her bite. Suddenly, Ev stands, her chair flying backward, and she runs back to her computer. In her air chair, she begins typing in Firefox, arms outstretched to reach her keyboard, as she wheels her chair toward her desk with her feet, allowing her arms to relax and bend. She doesn't pause in her searching and searching for more on this Mary person. Every snippet she finds, she devours. None of them make sense to her.

"Mary was the mother of Jesus." *Who is Jesus?* Ev wonders. She shakes the question out of her head firmly. *Focus*, she adjures herself. She only needs to know the Mary Jeerah wants in her website.

"Mary was pledged to be married." Engaged? The foreignness of the language ties up her understanding. Ev isn't interested in marriage, but does this mean Jeerah is? Or is married? Is this why Jeerah is a fan of Mary's? Is her site about marriage? No, Jeerah had written "Saviour." Maybe she means someone to save her from bad marriages—or, flies the thought into her consciousness, maybe she means marriages to psychiatrists. Her mouth quirks upward on one side, and her brows draw down.

Ev reads on. "First day of the week, he appeared first to Mary Magdalene." First. What did that mean, first? First when? And why had this Mary spoken to the Saviour when the men had not? Was this who Mary was engaged to, this Saviour? Ev struggles to understand this Mary Jeerah worships and wants on her website. She reads on: "...Out of whom he had driven seven demons." Ev's lips part.

Demons.

Ev falls into the back of her chair, her lower jaw dropping down.

Ev had been coding demons in *Early Exit*, but she'd never considered demons as real. Yet she'd known somehow that they had to be part of void.NullTime. Is this seven-demons passage for real? No, she smiles in relief, as she remembers how many times she'd been taught that religious and spiritual writings are myth, tales told to make people feel better about themselves. Pablum for the mind, her mother had disciplined when Ev had asked to see the big family book that inhabited the near-ceiling-height shelf of their wall-wide living room bookcase. Ev still doesn't know the name of it as she hadn't been tall enough to read the spine at eight years old, and then after the third time she'd asked about it, it had disappeared.

Ev had found it when she'd moved out. Inadvertently found it. Her parents had flown to their annual psychiatric conference to leave her alone and "unimpeded" to move out, they'd claimed. Alone with her meagre belongings, on her way back to her room to ensure she'd left nothing behind, her eyes had lit upon the attic entrance. Her parents didn't enter their attic, the door so long shut, she didn't know if it would open or not. On impulse, Ev had tried. It had resisted Ev's pushing on it until suddenly it had flown open with a squawk and bang. A trunk, the largest one her parents owned through inheritance squatted opposite the door. She would take that. If it belonged to them, it belonged to her. She had beelined for the trunk, grasped its dented metal handle on its one end, pulled and pushed it to the attic opening, dragged it down the short step ladder to the upper floor. And then leaning down, thumbs on the vertical, fingers on the horizontal top of the lid, her toes pushing against the floor, she'd shoved the trunk to the stairs and shoved it down. It had sailed down, banged on the hall carpet, bounced, and flew along the polished mahogany floor to the front door. She'd hauled it out and heaved it into her car share's trunk. She'd cleaned the trail it had left behind and driven away from this house of parental authority, satisfied.

Ev wasn't interested much in its contents. Enough to own it without her parents knowing. She'd briefly thought she'd delve into it later. But she had had no room in her first rented room in a rooming house. Her parents had generously allowed that they would fund a storage unit for her until she was able to afford her own place—a couple of her mother's long-time patients and her father's colleagues had followed her growing up and had assumed out loud that they would launch her into the world with provisions. And so they had. Ev had put the trunk and much of her belongings into a storage unit in the east end of the city. After she'd purchased her studio, she'd moved almost all of her belongings out of the storage unit. Although she had the room in her studio for her trunk, she'd had no inclination to bring it, but she'd decided to see what was in it. She'd tugged at the lid until it had flung itself open, flying rust flakes all over. The big forbidden book lay on top. "Holy Bible" in gold letters winked at her. Ev had let the lid drop back down and had left the trunk in the storage unit. She'd taken over the storage unit's rent so her parents wouldn't find it, even after she'd unearthed the big book one day when her WORM had been acting up, throwing up memories into her consciousness. She'd brought it home and tossed it into her closet, deciding to find and practice a surer way to deliberately retrieve WORM memories rather than have it activate reading mode on its own.

The thought intrudes into her ramble in the past: *Why doesn't Jeerah write her own welcome message?* She, Ev, had just read the Gospel of Mary but Jeerah understands it. Understanding being more important than data storage for Jeerah. Ev remembers every word; Jeerah says she understands it all.

Ev cranes her head forward to reread: "I KNOW you'll write something soooo AMAZING. I'm no good at writing. But YOUR websites are incredible. I just want to READ AND READ AND READ everything that's on the ones you've made. You HAVE TO WRITE ME THE MOST INCREDIBLE WELCOME. I just KNOW you will. Can we meet?"

Ev's lips turn down at the corners. Always, her emails end with "can we meet." Why is meeting so important to Jeerah? Maybe she should put that in the website's welcome. Ev types rapidly, "Welcome to the place where we meet Mary and the Saviour. Come, meet with me, and be encouraged in the presence of the different forms of nature. That is why the Good came into our midst. To restore us to our spirit roots. Be restored here in my virtual sanctuary on the Net that connects us all."

Ev's lips twist as she saves the text and backs up the website. As she flops against the back of her chair, her hand slips off her mouse, her palm landing on and flattening thick cotton. Ev slants her eyes toward her hand. Her heart strangles her throat. The bottom cotton sheet of those three blank sheets has moved itself and is sitting next to her mouse, her hand on top of it. Carefully, she lifts her hand, fearing to see what will appear underneath. Another line has appeared atop the last one. Written in black ink are the words: "Education Status." Below it are smaller letters spelling out the words "University Degree" next to a checkbox with a checkmark ticked in it. To its right are the words "World Education." Its checkmark in its checkbox is fainter than the one next to "University Degree," but it's visible.

11

Social Anxiety

"She wants to meet," reports Ev to Dr. Frock.

"Who wants to meet?"

"Jeerah Mutti wants to meet."

"And this is a bad thing?" Dr. Frock's sonorous voice rounds his vowels with a question, his beautiful cadence a measure of calm.

Ev replies without inflection: "I email questions. They answer. I work."

"Why don't you meet?"

"I can acquire the data variables I need from their answers."

Dr. Frock's blue-green eyes lay soft upon her as his hand with the pen poised in it rests on a fresh ruled sheet of paper. "And what, uh..." He hesitates. "Data variables?" he asks.

"Yes."

"Perhaps you could use another word. We want to get you to better communication, remember?"

Ev regards him from her seat on the sofa in its precise centre. Dr. Frock waits a minute; he retrieves his pocket watch and acquires the time. He has no large clock in his office because his clients had kept staring at it instead of focusing on him during the session. Also, he has an accurate sense of time. He knows to the second when to begin wrapping up to end the forty-five-minute session.

But not with Ev.

She throws his sense of time off.

Only ten minutes has passed.

And in those ten minutes, all he has gathered is that she doesn't want to meet someone.

Mutti. German.

He used to call his own mother Mutti. Every Sunday, he used to dutifully cook her the same large meal she had cooked for him when they had gathered together after church while he was growing up. *Such an antiquated concept, church,* he thinks with derision, his contempt for its myths and fables not appearing on his face as he glares inwardly at his pocket watch. He'd been glad to find the certainty of chemistry and then the medical sciences when he'd left home for university. The University of Toronto with its blockish medical sciences building and cavernous Fort Book gave him solace after years of enduring the genuflecting rituals of his mother's church. His father had had his own church, but at least he hadn't insisted on his son attending that one. Sunday mornings they'd parted ways, his father to his church, his mother and himself to hers, and had returned for his mother's luncheon feast. For years and decades, even after he'd declared church obsolete and God dead, his mother had insisted on him attending the midday feast. He'd acquiesced for a while, then in an act of independence, he'd attempted to not show up. After that, he hadn't defied her. He'd move his plans around with friends and his girlfriend, even choosing the feast over seeing his girlfriend off on a plane as she'd left to study for her Masters at the LMU Munich. It was the last time he'd seen her. He'd continued to arrive at his mother's house on Sundays after his Austrian father had died. But he'd found his grieving mother unable to do anything but stare out her living room window. A pang of compassion, a note of resignation, had infected his breast. He'd learnt how to cook her German dishes and his father's favourite Austrian schnitzels in his own kitchen. He'd begun a new ritual of driving over to her house—and more recently an assisted living facility further away—chuff her along until she would stand up and follow him obediently to his car and drive her back to his home for the feast.

Where is her church now, her God? he snorts silently. He hasn't asked her, though words and words of rebuke and challenge push against a locked door in his head, against his shut mouth. *Where is her Jesus?* he sneers again to himself, long habit keeping his facial features in a still picture of a happy persona. A man maybe, this Jesus, but no saint. And no Saviour. A man like any other who married a prostitute named Mary and had children, not some prophet who had mythical powers to bequeath endless life. That so-called God let his father die and his mother grieve with no succour. It's men like himself who comfort women like her.

The soft brush of corduroy against chenille brings his mind back to his office. His watch shows two minutes have elapsed. He clears his throat as he restores his watch to its pocket and smiles apologetically at Ev. "I have a meeting today for which I'm not to be late for," he explains, the lie flowing as smoothly off his tongue as his questions to Ev.

Ev remains mute as she continues to gaze upon his face, her back as straight as ever, her body and voice still as she waits for him to tell her what to say.

"Why does Jeerah Mutti want to meet?" he asks, relaxing back into his chair, crossing his right leg elegantly over his left, hitching up his pants leg one centimeter, letting his brogue-shod right foot swing gently back and forth.

Ev watches his foot, her eyes following its metronome movement. She answers: "I don't know."

"What did she say the reason was?"

"Authenticity," she told Dr. Frock's ticking foot.

"I see." Dr. Frock clears his throat and widens his smile. "Let's try something. Why don't you use...Let's say five words to tell me her reason. Remember, we want to work on your social pragmatic communication disorder. Five words." He holds up his right hand, fingers and thumb pointing straight up to the ceiling, and splays them.

"Five?" Ev queries his eyes.

"Yes, five," he smiles benignly back into her brown eyes, his eyes shining almost blue.

"They must meet the Saviour."

Dr. Frock's smile doesn't falter as he asks: "And what does that mean?"

"I didn't use search bot."

Dr. Frock's smile becomes fixed as the lines around his eyes diminish. "What did you not use search bot for?" He asks and manages not to tack on, please use English. He doesn't like computers. They had eaten up his homework and leaked information to others. Memory yanks up resentments—which he couches as boundaries. He refuses to purchase a cell phone. He is not a crisis hotline; the office phone is good enough for leaving private messages when his patients need to reach him. But as he informs them after their inevitable first message, he doesn't return calls the same day. He may not return the call until he sees them at their next appointment. And he doesn't do emails. They waste time. His time is more important than reading emails. He instructs them that his sessions are sufficient. He had had one pushy CEO, the first woman to head up a tech company that had been around for years, or so she had told him repeatedly. He'd never written her so-called groundbreaking accomplishment down, recognizing braggadocio, knowing companies had long since hired female CEOs. It wasn't enough for her to inflate herself, she insisted he acquire secure messaging as she didn't do voice mail or email as if the government had resources to read his emails. They could not, of course, read his notes, as he kept them locked in his desk, not on a computer. He'd informed her that he had his boundaries, that he didn't want to burn out. Cell phones, smartphones, texting, emails, all of that weren't needed in the 1950s, and they weren't needed now. He had smiled at her, his lips together. He'd explained he went out of his way to create a nurturing environment, leaving out how the clinic's interior designer had taken his rough ideas and had turned them into reality. He didn't need to be on call, too, he'd shared with her. That hadn't been good enough for her. She'd demanded perfection;

she'd demanded he do what she wanted. She seemed to think she knew better than he did about her needs. He'd soon had to get firm with her and had diagnosed her with obsessive compulsive disorder. One thing about CEOs, they had a peculiar tendency to stand up to anyone except physicians with their prescription pads.

Medication had resolved the problem. Medication had allowed him to mould her. Medication had made her compliant with his rules.

No more trying to change him, to his infinite relief. And no more boasting of exaggerated accomplishments. She'd soon left her position, one she hadn't been suited for, as he'd recognized in their first session together as causing her problems. He shudders inwardly again at her aggressive style, thankful he'd been able to convince her to take medication to eradicate that. She doesn't currently work, but he's teaching her how to accept who she really is. His long experience and advanced education has taught him he has accurate insight into his client's psychological and emotional states unlike them and so knows what's best for his clients. His ideas, his methods have served his clients well for decades. Clients. He'd chosen "clients" over the traditional "patients" moniker because he felt it better reflected that he was there to serve them.

His clients don't see the hours he ponders their issues and their clinical picture in order to help them. They don't see the journals on his desk at home or the numerous conversations he holds with his colleagues or the conferences he attends to ascertain the latest understanding of psychiatry and the brain. Of course, he won't incorporate the new ideas. He doesn't want to upset his comfortable methods. The DSM labels also comfort his clients; they give them an identity they can trumpet to their friends, families, neighbours. The DSM was the marvel of the twentieth century and now the twenty-first, saving countless lives. He ponders the National Institute of Mental Health advocating many years ago moving away from the DSM. *No*, he decides again. This new brain-based psychiatry is too cold for him and his clients, but it's useful to know where the scientists are heading with their electrophysiology-based diagnoses and treatments. The exception to his rule of safe evidence-based psychiatry is of course adopting the newest versions of medications. In the usual way of research, they will stumble upon some new medication or new surgery that will better alleviate symptoms, allow for easier therapy. He's happy to adopt those. And perhaps when most centres replicate electrophysiology clinical results, and when in due course he feels it's safe, he will, of course, incorporate the new ideas.

A bird smacking into his shining clean window jerks his attention back to this newest client of his, Evelyn, and this puzzle she's creating. For some reason, she is anxious about seeing her own client in person.

Of course! He mentally hits his head. So obvious. He smiles fully at Ev: "How do you feel when you read Mutti's request?"

"I don't read it."

"You don't read it?" Dr. Frock's groomed black eyebrows wrinkle up. "How do you know what it said then?"

"Reading bot."

"Reading bot?"

"He reads my emails."

"I see." Dr. Frock flounders for his next words. "And how do you feel when reading...bot reads her request?"

"I had to remove the inflections search bot had added to restore the monotone."

"I see," Dr. Frock said, drawing out the "ee" until it fades away. He tries again. "Without using inflections in the reading, how do you feel?"

"Nothing."

"Angry?"

"I don't meet with clients."

"Frustrated?"

Ev looks fixedly at him.

"How did your stomach feel?"

"I wasn't hungry."

"Did it hurt? Did your heart pound?"

"I don't recall."

Dr. Frock sits back and contemplates her. Evelyn has astounding recall, he believes. *She's lying. Why doesn't she want to admit to how she felt as she read the email?* He has bought into her dissociative language of reading bot—clearly she was the one who read the email—but if she feels more comfortable talking about her reading as if it's being done by some sort of creature, he will go along. For now. He'll wait for the right moment to confront her on that fiction—gently of course. But at the moment, she's dissociating from her body. It's not a prime time to confront her on her alternative language.

"Describe what you're feeling now?"

Ev's black lashes flurry her brown eyes, her dark thick eyebrows pulling up at the inner corners. "I—"

"Describe what your heart is doing? Can you feel it?"

"Yes."

"Good, good. We're getting somewhere. That feeling you have is anxiety." His eyes crystallize depths of green like emeralds darkening under a shining light, as he explains: "I believe you have social anxiety. You come up with reasons to not meet. But meeting people in person is the best way to communicate. Emails and cell phones distance people from each other. You must meet with her. I understand why you find it difficult. Your communication disorder puts a barrier between you and the other and provides you the illusion of safety. You must pull down that barrier and learn to communicate." The blue stripes in his eyes reappear slightly. "I'm here to help you. You're seeing me to help you, correct?"

Ev spurts out a yes.

"Then trust me. I have thirty years of experience. I've seen many clients like you. I'm not judging. I'm helping. My intentions are pure. I want to help all my clients get better." He grins, his now half-blue eyes crinkling in kindness as he gazes upon her expressionless face. "I suggest we try medication. But before we do that, I want you to do some homework. Let's see how you get on with that. If you succeed, there'll be no need for medication. I know you'll succeed. You're a determined young woman, and you're here to get better." He waits.

After ten seconds, Ev utters: "Oh." Her flickering eyes reveal her inner struggle to come up with words. "Yes."

Dr. Frock smiles broadly. "Good, good. I want you to meet with Mutti."

"Meet?"

"Yes. I want you to meet Mutti in person, somewhere easy, like a coffee shop. Everyone meets for coffee these days, don't they?"

Ev doesn't know so she cannot answer. She'll have to have search bot look that up for her.

Dr. Frock smoothly slides his watch out of his pocket, checking that he has at last sensed correctly that the time is up while he continues speaking: "I want you to meet with Mutti in a coffee shop for let's say an hour. That's not too much time. You can do an hour I'm sure."

Dr. Frock stands up, clasping his pen and notepad with the paper that remains as freshly white as when they'd begun their session, and leads her to the door. He opens it and awaits her leaving.

12

The Mind

With her gloved hands, Ev slips her VR helmet over her spiked hair, her earpieces slightly askew over her ears, but she doesn't notice in her hurry to play *Early Exit*. Dr. Frock's homework had begun a thrumming deep in her stomach that'd hurried her feet back to home and to her desk and computer. She scrambles to set it at Level 1. Sometimes, to move her thoughts right out of reality, she likes play her latest iteration of *Early Exit* out of order. Start in the middle level, Level 1, go to Level 0, return to 1, then find the secrets of how to enter Level 2 where Zygote class resides.

Ev resets the game to start all over again. No more strange palm trees, dusty streets, or coruscating white dimensionless boxes. Ev thinks, *Play*. And *Early Exit* begins before she can press Play.

The heavy silk damask curtains hid the window. A hand reached out, a soft, white hand with bitten nails painted in red. It pulled back the left side of the right curtain slightly and slowly to ever so slowly reveal a twilight scene. The night blue sky, the lights over the roads a harsh buzzing yellow. A man slowly biked down the centre of the street, his shadow moving and lengthening and shortening and angling and straightening as he pedalled the wheels of his rusty bike languidly, his feet in sandals, dusty from the road. Ev watched along with and through the character object whose hand had pulled back the curtain.

Ev thinks, *Stop*. She's in the same room as before! She isn't on Level 1; she's on Level 0. No, no, no! She'd wanted to begin again. She searches for the exit button, the stop button. *Early Exit* plays on. Briefly, Ev feels the same something she'd first felt looking into David.admin's eyes—something overwhelming—touch her and run strength through her fibres to allow her to stay in the game, as if knowing her thoughts and what she lacks.

The curtain dropped, and her view changed to see an old settee, its woven green fabric a relic of the 1950s; its legs like wood stilts angled from the bottom of the settee to the scrubbed wood floor.

Knock. Knock.

The character object's heart bumped.

Ev's heart jumps.

The view abruptly shifted from the settee to the opening behind the settee, through which a staircase with a white-painted metal rail rose against pink-painted walls. Pink permeated the space.

Whoever was at the door pounded it: one, two, three. The sound waves from the hidden door played back and forth, as if muffled, as if bouncing from ear to cheek.

Ev closes her eyes, adjusts her earpieces to enclose her ear openings. She likes precision and her coded 3D reality to be as all-consuming and solid as reality. *Early Exit* is consuming her, and the misplaced sound from her misplaced earpieces had thrown her out. Her curiosity bubbles up. Who is at the door? Why is the character object seemingly independent of her controls? Why couldn't she move the character to the door? She'd moved her hands, but nothing had happened. She'd tried to walk, but nothing had happened. About a year ago, Ev had covered half her floor with a mat that looked like her floor but was designed to pick up her foot movements and send them into the game. She could walk around and stay in 3D, knowing Japanese Robot will ensure she doesn't walk into something by mistake. She thinks, *If I walk with my eyes closed, I'll end up closer to the door.* She steps one, two, three. Ev opens her eyes. The door in her view becomes her reality exactly the same distance away from her as before.

A fist thudded against the solid door: one, two, three.

A dull thud, like a heavy object hitting the door, reverberated through the house. The pressure of the sound waves thrummed her temples.

The character object's mind extended into Ev's brain.

The mind moved, feet shuffling in reluctant progress toward that opening, their slippers catching on slivers sticking up on the old floor. The mind and Ev stepped around the window-side of the settee. The opening to the hall seemed to grow larger as they drew closer to it and halted. The old wood sank slightly under their weight.

Thump!

The mind and Ev jumped. They poked their head around the corner. The two solid wood doors previously seen from outside during the last play, are closed against the demanding thumps.

Thump!

The mind and Ev jumped backward a step. The doors didn't vibrate. They moved toward the doors, the character object mind's dread seeping into Ev's consciousness. The dread of what was waiting for her—her? Yes, her.

Ev closes her eyes and is again alone with herself. How does she feel dread? She hadn't programmed emotions. Besides, emotions don't enter her. She remembers games stimulating emotions in her when she'd first entered the world of video games, but none had had their own emotions which they'd imposed into her. Dr. Frock's words of seeing what will happen buzz in, stirring up her empty stomach. She hastily opens her eyes.

That hand, bleached white under the bright artificiality of hallway light, which cast a shadow beneath her arm onto the white marble floor, studded with black-edged pits—that hand reached up toward the door. The hand dropped out of sight. It lifted again, this time holding a key. The hand inserted the key into the old-fashioned looking keyhole lock above the ornate brass knob, turned it to the left. Click. The hand removed the key; the hand disappeared downward from view again.

Thump!

Thoughts on the edge of consciousness, asked, *What would this white hand do next? What would it reveal, this hand that belonged to a mind not Ev's own?* Suddenly, the mind's hand, as if wanting to get it over with, rose back into view, grasped the knob hard, and turned it viciously to the right.

"Yes?" a voice soft with the cultured vowels of a woman, spoke upward to a man with ruffled black hair, his face in shadow as he stood on the door's threshold, his head looking down at her from at least half a metre up. Two other men flanked him yet a little behind him, shorter, their faces illuminated by the front door light hanging above them. The towering man said, "Let us in."

The mind moved backward as the towering man moved toward her, filling her view so that the mind had to strain her neck to look up into his face. Neck muscles over vertebrae complained. The hunger to see this man's face overcame the pain. It was now completely in shadow as he moved, one slow step at a time like in a languid foxtrot with the mind, until he was directly underneath the hall light. "I asked you a question. What took you so long?"

"It's late."

"It is never late for us. We told you to be available any time."

"Yes, of course. I am. Won't you come in?"

"I am in." The front door thudded shut, and the two shorter men sidled in on either side of the mind, penning her. Her breath stalled in her throat. Their breath on either side of her came like deep-throated lions stalking her. Pressure built up in her chest, pushing up into her throat, bursting into a loud exhalation. Suddenly light burst into her retinas.

"Your pupils are normal."

"I haven't taken anything, drunk anything. I've been good. I understand what to do."

"Good, good. Things are better for you when you do what we say, isn't that right?"

"Yes."

Abruptly, she was looking at his back. The two shorter men herded her to follow the towering man's back to the opening to the living room. His hands appeared and clasped themselves in the small of his back. He paused on the threshold of the large room He rocked back and forth, and his shoes squeaked. Squeak, squeak, squeak, squeak. Louder and louder. The shrill noise began to bounce from ear to ear, eliciting a silent scream, "Stop!" The towering man looked over his right shoulder and smirked. He pivoted silently and brought his hands up and clasped them in victory, rubbing them, as he took one long stride to stand one centimeter in front of her. He stared down at her like a Bald Eagle eyeing a juicy salmon in its claws, his teeth a lighter shadow in the shade of his face. "I see you have sold your paintings."

"Yes." Her gulp was almost inaudible.

"The Monet must have fetched a good price."

The lighter shadow in his face widened and heightened. "Tell me."

"Yes," the word barely whispered out. "It did. But—

"But?" his voice cutting off the "t."

"My neighbour needed the money. That's why we sold it..."

"Did he? Which neighbour?"

"The advisor to the president."

The lighter shadow disappeared, and the towering man straightened until his mid-chest was the only view. The thick wool of his jacket. Perhaps midnight blue, though hard to tell under the harsh light directly above. The buttons of worsted wool blended in with the jacket. A crisp white shirt collar just visible at the top. The jacket wasn't buttoned up to the top. That note closed Ev's eyes.

Ev asks herself, *Isn't it hot and dusty where this is taking place? Who are these people? Why is she so one with that character, only a few seconds into playing* Early Exit, *the character that had felt like an instantiated mind melding with her mind the first time she'd encountered her.* She's thankful that details that clang wrong are enough to separate her from what she's calling, "the mind," for if not, she'd be one with the mind, becoming more subsumed into this game than in any first-person shooter game she's ever played. She opens her eyes without thinking.

Suddenly, the towering man's hands rose up and up, coming together, buttoning up his jacket. They dropped, and the fabric was pulled down. "We won't disturb the advisor to the president. But the Minister won't be happy. You will have to make it up to him. I suggest the thirteenth-century mosaic you have hidden from me."

"No, please, that's been—"

His hand chopped the air horizontally, almost hitting her nose. The mind's view shifted in a slow-motion arc of hand, chest, neck, face, light, and ceiling as she stumbled backward, reaching out with her hand into empty air, hitting the arm of a hidden office air chair, the empty air in her view scraping her skin, feeling something fly away, pulling her footing out from under her. Her right arm automatically flung out, and she landed heavily on her right side, her breath knocked out of her.

Ev blinks inside her helmet, thankful once again she'd switched from the basic eyepiece that only straps on to a full-on helmet.

The mind rested her head down as she fought for breath. Male laughter rang around the empty hall, the towering man's chin raising up toward the hall light, which shone a ghastly lopsided halo above his head. The shorter men were guffawing on either side of him. The three walked back to the door, opened it, and slammed it shut on their laughter.

Ev's view shrinks to black. Ev doesn't move for long seconds. She feels the wheels of Japanese Robot hum the floor as it rolls toward her. Its voice comes from above her in the blackness of her vision. "I will help you up."

Ev rolls onto her back. She doesn't want to get up. She wants *Early Exit* to restart at Level 1. She opens her eyes, preparatory to removing her helmet.

"Hello," said David.admin from behind his white desk in the white space with all its coruscating hues of white at its edges. Ev swallowed. "Have you filled out the admission form yet?" he asked, his eyebrows raised, looking like he knew she hadn't.

"Um." Ev didn't know what to say.

David.admin said with no change in expression, "Perhaps you'd like to get up. Let the robot help you."

Ev's muscles contracted hard. She was sitting up. *Is sitting up. What time is she in?*

NullTime, whispered her programming. NullTime confuses, confused.

Wasn't she in space.Time? Regular time?

David.admin looked upon her placidly. "Please, stand up. You'll be more comfortable. Don't think too much about time. As in *Star Trek*, it'll make your head hurt."

Ev feels Japanese Robot brace her, and she wobbles up. She stretches her senses down to her feet, their comforting solidity. Her legs stop shaking.

David.admin asked: "Why do you want to return to where you've been?"

"I don't like Level 0."

"You coded it."

Ev replied: "Yes...But I didn't code it this way."

David.admin stared at her for a long moment. He flicked his grey eyes to the screen in front of him. "Uh-huh. Hmmm." He reached out a finger to touch the screen facing him, out of her view. His hand moved downward; his finger didn't make a sound on the display. Something tickled her nose. Electrons weaving white wreaths in front of her eyes. Was she fainting?

"You're not fainting."

Ev inhales sharply. She puffs out her breath in little steps. It's like her body exists in one time, her mind in another.

Japanese Robot says from beside her, making her jerk: "Your inhalation sequence is off. See my display and breathe with it."

Ev barks a short laugh.

David.admin said: "Not a very smart robot you programmed there."

"He's not my robot."

"You bought him. You customized his coding. Your creation. Your robot." He stared hard at her.

Ev stared back, trying to understand what he was saying. He nodded as solidity flowed into the edges of his white face, pinking up his features. He returned his gaze back to his screen "Are you sure you know where you want to exit to? Was it Heaven you wanted? Or is it the Void? Do you know where the Void will be and was? Do you know what the Void is?" He doesn't wait for Ev to answer. "I see that though you tried to stop *Early Exit*, you ended up going on. Good, I'm glad. And, also, you worked out my function. I like that." He looked up at her, depths of grey darkening his grey-white irises. "You may call me by my full name EnergyMind David.administratorofinterpretation, but I prefer David.admin. It's short. It gets the job done. You may return now."

All vision, all sound, all feeling through her gloves and feet end.

Ev doesn't move for second after second. Her mind revolves his questions, each question appearing as the face on a pentahedron. She squeezes her eyelids together tight against the impossible questions and vanishes the pentahedron from her mind. Slowly, she raises her hands and removes her VR helmet. She sheds her gloves from her hands. Japanese Robot rolls forward to catch them as her fingers release their grasp on them. He places them on the far left side of her desk as she rubs her right shoulder where she'd landed on it. She twists her arm inward to check her skin. Angry scratches stretch over her outer forearm. How had the chair done that to her when she'd been in an empty hallway? Virtual reality and reality shift in her understanding. Her body had been in real space. Her mind in virtual. She'll wash her arm. She shakes it, trying to push the blood through her beaten-up shoulder and arm, releasing the bruising pain from within her flesh, willing the pain to leave her. Her eyes land on the three sheets on her desk. They're fanned out. And the cotton sheet has a new line on it.

Resistant yet feeling compelled, she steps three strides to her desk and picks up the cotton sheet. The line reads: "You acknowledge all insurance is forfeit upon exit and all insurances, monies, and premiums are voided. What is your risk deposit?"

Risk deposit? Ev queries silently.

Next to a blank line are three checkboxes: Thirty, sixty, ninety. *Days?* Ev wonders. It looks like a bank form, and term deposits were usually in days or months. Sometimes, they were in years, but ninety years? That doesn't seem feasible. She wants to exit now, not fifty-seven years from now. She lowers the sheet back to her desk and goes to the bathroom to wash and soothe her screaming skin.

13

Risk Deposit

Ev cannot sleep. She shoves her quilt and sheets down and hauls her legs out from under, dragging part of her sheet with her calves. Her right shoulder protests as she shifts herself tiredly to the edge of her bed. She stands up and shambles against the sheet to unwrap itself from around her legs. She pads toward her living room, her left hand on her sore right shoulder, rotating the offended joint carefully. Her hand's energy seems to ease the pain. She drops her hand, letting both her hands dangle as she enters the main area of her studio apartment where Japanese Robot is charging himself and her computer lives, currently off like her displays. The absence of the background hum of the cooling fans fills her ears with uncharacteristic silence. Ev rotates her shoulders back and straightens her neck as her steps become firmer. Her bare feet murmur over the boards toward her desk. The cotton sheet of paper lies where she'd dropped it on the hard wood of her tabletop desk. It shines white in the gloom of her apartment. Faint light from the street enters through the unblinded windows, each two meters away from either side of her desk. When had she opened the blinds and left them open? Ev shakes her head free of the thought as the object of her wakefulness attracts her attention back.

She stares at the letter-sized piece of paper. She watches her hand descend and her fingers grip the paper. She watches the paper, propelled by her hand, rise toward her into reading distance.

"Risk deposit."

What would risk deposit be? Was it a physical risk, or something she doesn't want to do? What kind of deposit does this application form require to exit her material space.Time into its void.NullTime? She doesn't want to see Jeerah, but Jeerah wants to see her. Dr. Frock talks about social anxiety and communication and how she should meet Jeerah. Perhaps that is her risk deposit. She leans forward, patting the desk for her pen. It rolls away from her seeking fingers; she lunges blindly for it. She catches it, bends down, and places the paper on her desk, poising the pen above the words "Risk deposit." Somehow she can see the line. She writes on it: "Meet Jeerah."

She straightens herself back up and contemplates the boxes. The boxes with thirty, sixty, and ninety next to them vanish.

"What?" Ev breathes out. She stares at the sheet, her crooked writing embedded into the whiteness of the cotton paper. She crosses out the words, but her pen doesn't make a mark with the paper being held up in the air. She puts the paper back down on the desk and strikes out her words. The boxes don't reappear.

Ev stays still in her bent-over position, trying to understand what risk deposit is. Dr. Frock had said to meet for coffee. Her entire torso hardens against meeting for coffee. *Maybe risk deposit is supposed to be more generic not specifically meet with Jeerah.* She scrawls above her struck-out words: "Meet for coffee." Nothing happens. She adds: "At a new coffee shop." Still the boxes don't reappear. In frustration, she drives blue lines across and back, back and across her words until her pen almost shoves its way right through the sheet onto her desk. She lifts her pen abruptly, the strength of her emotion frightening her. She remembers the mind and how it'd scared her the first time. *The last time, too, and the white boxy place, if she's honest,* Ev admits. She pens: "Fear." Still nothing. She pulls her chair away from her desk and sits in it. Absent-mindedly, she nibbles on the end of her pen. She hasn't nibbled on her pens or pencils since grade seven. She'd seen other kids' pencils with tooth-marks in them and been disgusted. Realizing with horror, hers were like theirs, she'd stopped and begun taking care of her instruments. Not chewing on them, not scratching them, not jumbling them all together in knapsacks or cases. Each has their own pocket or case and stays im-maculate.

Ev jerks her hand down, scraping her teeth with the pen. The mind. Something about the mind. She can feel the answer, the concept wait-ing for her to grasp it. ConsciousnessMind. MagneticField as dynamic memory. CMMagnetic Field connecting elements and memories. Con-necting. She prints, "Connecting." All her previous entries, the scratched-out words and lines, fade into the cotton while "Connecting" slips down to settle on the line. Ev swallows hard, frozen in place. The boxes reappear with their numbers next to them. Ev breathes in and out until her thoughts reappear out of her frozen brain.

Think of it as a computer game, as virtual reality. Just think of it as being in virtual reality, she persuades herself.

Now what?

Does she want thirty days' deposit or sixty or ninety? But what if those are years? She shivers. Thirty. She wants to exit now. Days or years, thirty is quickest. She ticks thirty, lays down her pen, stands up, walks to her bedroom, lifts up a large corner of her sheets and quilt, and crawls stomach-down underneath them. Ev sleeps.

14

⟨ornament⟩

The Coffee Shop

Ev doesn't much like new experiences in Earth's reality, and she doesn't much like the ones happening in *Early Exit*, either, where she's supposed to be the controller. But here she is at her accustomed place in front of her displays, listening to reading bot finishing up with Jeerah's regular "can we meet" question, except she's added details. Ev leans forward and herself reads the last sentence: "Can we meet? I know, I know, I'm becoming sooooo repetitive. But I feel it heavy on my heart that we MUST meet. Soooo I was thinking a coffee shop. I don't know where you live??? But downtown everyone knows, RIGHT? There's this sweet place near King Street within clarion call of the noon bells. I just LOVE to listen to the church bells, don't you? You MUST meet me there. I know it's not lunch. We're just going to have coffee, I promise, but when you hear the bells, it'll inspire your website words for me. I just know it! The Saviour loves bells, I'm sure of it! Don't you think, with all the angels in Heaven with him? It'll be like a NEW DISCOVERY for you if you've never heard them."

Ev rereads, "The Saviour loves bells," and disbelieves the present tense. *Isn't the Saviour dead? On another plane, that's not Earth. That's where we all go when we get old, except for herself.* She's coding Early Exit, she reflects. But here she is on Earth, and she cannot resist Dr. Frock's instructions any longer. Her need to obey his authority, his parental-type authority, is like an urgent autonomic response. Ev types and sends, "OK."

Immediately, a reply enters her inbox with instructions for how to get to the coffee shop today. *Today?!* Horror fires along every nerve. She hadn't thought about meeting Jeerah today. Maybe in some future, so that she can tell Dr. Frock she's done her homework. But now she has to go through with it. Reading bot reads out the final expository sentence in which Jeerah asks for her cell number just in case one of them is late or can't make it.

Ev types effortlessly, "No cell." She's about to click Send automatically when Dr. Frock's words blast out of her WORM that she is to communicate with more words. Embellish your short sentences, he'd instructed. She hears his smile in her recording. She dutifully presses Ctrl-A to select her words and stabs the Delete button. Her body straining with the effort of sitting up straight, her hands hurting, she types at her normal one-hundred-words-per-minute speed, "I don't have a cell phone. I communicate through my email portal only. I will be there. I won't be late." She clicks Send and flops back against her chair back, her arms sliding off her desk, her hands falling heavily onto her lap, palms facing up. Jeerah's reply whooshes in: "I won't be late, I promise! I'm so excited to meet you. What do you look like? I'll be wearing my beads. I want you to see my beads. I haven't worn them in so long, but I feel like beads should be part of my website, and I want you to see them. What do you think? I'm SOOOOO EXCITED!!!"

Ev gapes. She gets up and walks over to Japanese Robot to manually code in her alarm and have him show her Google Street View for directions precisely five minutes before she's to leave when she'll store it in her heap memory. Her heap memory will replay the directions in colour and detail as she steps along his planned course.

Not too long later, Ev enters the warm coffee shop at precisely noon and scans the interior for a woman with beads. The light is dim compared to the outside sun burning her face under the sharp blue sky. As her eyes adjust, she sees several round tables sitting higgledy-piggledy on worn black boards but no woman with beads. On her right is a fireplace with a fire burning low in it. Two soft chairs flank it and a rectangular table between them. The fire draws her to itself, and she stands in front of the empty table staring down into the flame's heat, watching the occasional spark fly up on a twisty course into the flue. Behind her a little silver bell rings as the door opens. Responding to the sound, Ev twists her head round as far as she can to see a woman enter, all arms and smiles, as she unbuttons her poncho coat and reveals beads. Strings and strings of clanking, colourful beads. Her eyes veer toward Ev, and Ev gawks then remembers to say, "Hello," as Dr. Frock had instructed.

The woman skips over to her and reaches down to pick up her hand and shake it enthusiastically with both of hers. She holds on to Ev's limp hand and pats it as she exclaims: "Evelyn! You must be Evelyn. You're soooo beautiful. It's wonderful to finally meet you. I'm so glad you agreed. I just know we're going to get on! You're going to make my website authentic, and people will flock to the Saviour because of the work you're going to do for me. I feel a mission in my heart to spread the word," she lets go with one of her hands and splays her fingers over her beads-covered bosom, "I just know you're the one to do it. You're wonderful, you really are. I can't believe you're here!" Jeerah sighs. She sucks air in to reoxygenate her vocal chords, but Ev manages to say, "Hello" again in the pause.

"Oh! I'm keeping you standing," Jeerah exclaims as she drops Ev's hands. "I see you found my favourite seat in the whole cafe. This is why I love to come here," she continues, emphasizing the word "love." Jeerah moves past Ev toward the chair facing away from the windows and points to the one opposite her as she sits. Ev obeys Jeerah's pointing hand and gingerly moves around the table so that she won't touch it and carefully lowers herself into a chair. She leaves her jacket on. She isn't cold, and the fire is warm, but she wants to leave now and not waste time having to put her jacket back on.

How soon can she leave? Dr. Frock's instructions ring loudly in her consciousness as if he's here guiding her on. *One hour. A massive amount of time,* Ev thinks. *That's one thousand Delta-Times. She cannot stay here that long,* she agonizes. But Dr. Frock's instructions are firm. She has to be able to say to him she's done her social pragmatic communications disorder and her social anxiety homework since she understands him this time, except for UDD, but there doesn't seem to be—

"Evelyn?"

Ev blinks, hearing the question and the sudden silence. She answers: "Yes?"

"I asked if you'd like coffee or tea?"

"Oh." Ev stops. Jeerah's face is relaxed. Her brown eyes fringed with generous lashes. Her face a smiling mess of wrinkles: crow's feet deeply etched into the outside triangles of her eyes; laugh lines grooved from nose to mouth; fine lines bending and angling over her olive-tinged cheeks. Long earrings dangle down from both her lobes stretching them into ovals. She is leaning forward, half off her chair, her poncho coat slung across the chair arms behind her where she'd shrugged it carelessly off. Ev struggles to vocalize words as she struggles in her thoughts to reconcile Jeerah's material age with the energy flinging out of her that Ev had been taught by her fellow coders belong only to the young. Ev incorporates this new idea, her neurons rewire to create a new type in her consciousness, and she blurts: "What would you like?"

"Coffee. I love their coffee. It's rich, it's dark. It goes down smoothly. And I just feel so energized afterward to do my work for the Saviour. Don't you find the morning drags on and you just get so tired by noon? I do! I'm feeling in the need for some energy!"

Ev's eyes widen as she takes in this woman in front of her talking about feeling tired. *Tired?* Ev suddenly doesn't want to be around her caffeinated version, but she has to follow Dr Frock's homework. She reminds herself homework is why she achieved one hundred percent in most of her classes, even in the ones she'd hated like social studies and political science. Her parents had given her no other option when it came to marks, when it came to working out every question, every problem, every action assigned. She cannot do anything else but comply.

"Coffee?" Ev asks.

Jeerah leaps up, pushes her way past the table, shoving it into Ev's knees, and canters toward the bar at the back where the barista grinds, presses, gushes, and steams his brews. Ev pushes the table back into position as unobtrusively as possible. The door rings open, and a couple noisily chatting trot in, grabbing Ev's attention.

"Sex isn't love for me," expostulates the man.

The woman laughs and replies: "No one'd believe me if I told em you said that."

They move out of earshot.

The door's bell rings again. A group of men and women younger than her crowd in, each carrying satchels, each holding the door open for the one after them, the last one letting it shut abruptly. In silence, they troop to the table next to the window on the other side of the cafe on her right side and fling themselves down into the two chairs while the rest shove two other nearby tables closer, scraping gathered chairs around them into position to sit down. They pull laptops out of their satchels and lift their lids, dropping the bags onto the floor around their feet, shrugging off jackets, and hitting the on buttons. One asks: "Coffee?" A chorus of "Yeahs" reply, with one adding, "I'll help you." A man and a woman get up and head to the bar behind Ev.

"Here we are," Jeerah declares, startling Ev as she places two mugs of coffee down on the table. "I didn't know how you took it, and then I thought you must be a black fan, like me, because we're simpatico. I just know you're doing a wonderful job with my website, so you must like your coffee strong, bold, creative!"

Ev tries to interrupt the flow to ask for sugar, but Jeerah's powerful voice smothers hers as she natters on. "And here are some pastries. I love their croissants. I'm famished! I didn't know what you'd like because I never do. You just don't until you see them, don't you find, because they all look sooooo good. But today I wanted a croissant. I thought I should get you the same, because we're alike, you and I! I just know we are because I feel drawn to you. The Saviour found me your website, and I just knew we would get on! But I thought, Jeerah, she may not want a croissant. She may want a cookie. Or brownies. Young people like their sweet things. And you're soooo young. I thought you might be. And I'm glad to see I was right. So here's their best stuff, my favourites. Chocolate chip cookie. And a brownie. And I got a pastry Danish just in case you'd like that instead. You don't have to eat it all, but I know you young things eat much more than us old folk."

Jeerah falls into her chair, her weight flinging the sides of the seat cushion up on either side of her, the air whooshing loudly out from under her. She leans forward, her beads slinging free into the air, and picks up her mug. She slurps the hot coffee and grins. "Now that's good coffee. I'm going to feel much more like myself after this." Jeerah seizes her croissant, bites deep into it, and chews a mouthful as she holds the pastry up close to her lips.

Ev pulls her eyes away from Jeerah's stuffed cheeks and slips her fingers through her mug's sturdy handle. She hefts the brimming mug, watching the shaking liquid the whole time so that she won't get hot coffee on her hand, and gently sips. Nothing. No coffee. She's sipping air only. She stops trying and blows on the steam, watching it fly away from her then return to languidly stream upward. She blows again as Jeerah's voice settles into white noise, her attention drifting into the steam blowing away then returning to its winding upward trajectory. She tries to sip it again and receives heat and flavour notes of brain-waking chocolate. Her eyes widen, and she says suddenly: "This is good."

Jeerah stops her flow of words and grins. "Isn't it? I just knew you'd love it like I do. We're simpatico, you and I. I just know it."

15

Meeting Jeerah's Saviour

"Oh my gosh," Jeerah exclaims as she slams her mug down on the table between her and Ev, coffee sloshing up and over the mug's sides to stain the scarred wood. "I was so excited to finally meet you I forgot all about grace." Red races up her cheeks, and worry downturns her eyes. "How could I?" Jeerah hurriedly drops her half-bitten croissant on the plate of pastries—to Ev's disgust—and casts her eyes down. She scrabbles: "Dear Lord Saviour. We thank you for the coffee, the wonders of this place, the magnificent food, the wheat you've grown, and bringing us together. Amen." She opens her eyes again to smile at Ev. "There! That's done. And now we must begin."

Ev doesn't know what's happened. It seems a strange series of words, as if wheat and herself were in the same caste. And what are they to begin? In the wind of Jeerah's words, she's forgotten about the reason for meeting.

More neuropeptides are destructing themselves somehow, and she doesn't know how to grasp back the memories they'd stored. She assures herself that her heap memory still works by recalling how she'd visualized Japanese Robot's directions as she'd walked the three long blocks to the cafe only during the time she'd needed to access it.

Jeerah interrupts her thoughts, speaking through the crispy end of the croissant sticking into the corner of her left cheek: "What is the sin of the world?"

"Pardon?" Ev ejaculates.

Jeerah swallows hard. A flake lies near the right corner of her lips; she slurps up another mouthful of the hot coffee. She closes her eyes in bliss as she sets down her mug, then opens them, smiles at Ev, and says: "That's better. Let's get down to business." Her face composes itself into serious folds. Jeerah sits firmly back in her chair, her beads rattling against each other. "What do you know about the Saviour?"

Ev has lost all her acquired knowledge of the Saviour in trying to compile this new code of Jeerah as suddenly speaking sensibly.

Jeerah waves her right hand toward the dying embers of the fire. "Never mind. Let me tell you what *I* know," she says, "for that's the important part. For my website. The Saviour was sent to save us from ourselves. When we place our faith in him, good things happen. We are freer and happier. Nothing bad can touch us when we have faith. In the Gospels, we're asked 'What is the sin of the world?' Mary tells us! God is a woman! Every right-thinking woman immersed in the Spirit knows this," pointing to the right of her heart, "deep in her core. In the Gospel of Mary, Mary asks this question—" Jeerah interrupts herself, pushing herself upright with her left hand on the chair arm. "You see the Saviour appeared first to Mary, not the men, the New Testament gospels got that right, the ones the men let in to the official canon. They couldn't hide that it was the women the Saviour first spoke to, though Paul ignored that in his letter to the Corinthians. He like all men needed to retain their patriarchy. That's why the Gospel of Mary had to be hidden. It contradicted their patriarchal notions, their idea that only the Apostles could be men. But our Saviour saw women as his first disciples, Mary Magdalene his first Apostle!" Jeerah exclaims, throwing her arms wide, her beads crashing their assent. Her eyes bore into Ev's. Ev swallows hard. "Apostle means messenger of God, you know. Of course, you do! Because you're a disciple too, Ev, working with me." Jeerah's mouth widens and then straightens again as Ev's eyes widen.

Ev feels all at sea. She knows nothing about what Jeerah has just explained. Patriarchy she understands. She works on her own because it's safer. Those long-gone male jeers peal into her consciousness from out of her WORM. Can a girl code a gaming engine! Can a girl create a novel virtual reality game! Hahahahaha, the laughter resounds and rebounds through her neural networks. Ev struggles against the noise to rejoin the present reality. She recalls David.admin is an "it." She must ask Jeerah to explain what she's talking about. She must speak her query out loud. "Are we its in void.NullTime?"

Jeerah stutters to a stop, blinks, and retreats her head. Her eyes clear, "Oh, Ev, we don't call people 'it'! It's 'they'! We're privileged to be—"

"Please start from the beginning," Ev instructs, unheeding that Jeerah is midsentence, so focused is she on this unaccustomed confusion and a strange burning rising up to blush her cheeks. How had she forgotten David.admin is a "they"?

Jeerah's mouth stays half open. "Oh," she replies. "Yes, of course. Where do you want me to begin?"

"Why do you say peace be with you?"

"Because the Saviour brings peace. He greeted the disciples that way, in every gospel, in Mary's Gospel, 'Peace be with you. Receive my peace unto yourselves.'" Jeerah smiles.

Ev stares.

"You know, peace. That feeling of everything will be all right?"

"Someone gives that to you?"

"Yes, our Saviour."

"How?"

Jeerah opens her mouth to explain then snaps it closed. Her brows, with their brown and white hairs thinning out, knit. She stares down at the table. She absent-mindedly picks up her mug and sips quietly for a minute. She places her mug back down and looks back up at Ev. "It's hard to explain. Our Saviour is with us all the time. He's the intermediary through the Holy Spirit. The Spirit gives us his peace. You see?"

"Oh," replies Ev not seeing at all. She recalls that she's here to follow Dr. Frock's homework instructions and to create Jeerah's website. Does she need to understand all this? Isn't it enough to store up her words for regurgitation later? Dr. Frock hadn't asked her to learn, only to meet with Jeerah. She'll get some words from Jeerah and go. "What would you like your welcome message to say? I wrote 'Welcome to the place where we meet Mary and the Saviour. Come, meet with me and be encouraged in the presence of the different forms of nature. That is why the Good came into our midst. To restore us to our spirit roots. Be restored here in my virtual sanctuary on the Net that connects us all.' Does that suffice?"

Jeerah asks her to repeat it, one sentence at a time, her eyes squinting closed as she listens carefully. She nods at the end of Ev's recitation. "Yes, that suits perfectly. I just want to say, no criticism, I don't want you to believe I've lost faith in you! I won't ever lose faith in you!! I couldn't!! The Saviour brought us together. But it's soul not spirit. Soul roots. Now, let's talk about the soul. We must begin with our soul. Our Saviour tells us that visions come to us through the mind that connects our soul to the spirit. No," Jeerah wags her finger. "I explained that wrong. Sometimes I get so muddled. I begin to think I know what I'm saying, and then my words come out all wrong. I'm just so excited to share the good news, the faith that sustains us, that gives us purpose and connects us all together, that I speak in the wrong order. Okay," Jeerah raises her chest, straightens her back, as she inhales a powerful breath. "What I *meant* to say is that we see the visions the Saviour sends us through the mind that is between the soul and the spirit. The spirit is his, of course." Jeerah smiles satisfied and relaxes her body into itself. She raises her coffee to her lips and knocks back a large gulp.

Ev's heart skips a beat. Jeerah's description sounds like CMMagneticField connecting the MagneticFields, the dynamic memories that store every experience of her characters' bodies and brains from every instance of DeltaTime. But how can that be? She knows nothing of the Saviour. No, it's a coincidence. Yet curiosity draws her in to learn how this mind connects the soul and spirit. She unbuttons the top button of her jacket and says: "Tell me."

"Tell you what, Evelyn?"

Ev thought she'd been clear but remembers what Dr. Frock had said about expanding her words. She expands: "Tell me how this mind is between the soul and the spirit and connects them. And tell me how it shows the vision."

"Sees the vision," Jeerah responds automatically as she frowns in thought, lowering her mug absent-mindedly. It chinks off the pastry plate and coffee splashes up one side before she stabilizes the mug on the plate. "I don't think I can answer that question. I remember the first time I felt the Saviour's love. I was walking down the street when I felt the call on my heart to enter a church. My husband was leaving me, and I felt so alone, so cast adrift. Oh, Evelyn, it was terrible, horrible, the worst thing that ever happened to me." Tears filter into Jeerah's eyes then dry up as she continues: "But the most wonderful thing happened to me. I walked into that church, and this peace came over me." Jeerah raises her arms up, her hands palm upward, her breath releasing into a sigh of ecstasy. "I knew I was loved." Jeerah lowers her hands and reaches for her mug. "How did that get there?" she mutters as she lifts the mug from off the plate, pushing a cookie to the plate's edge and onto the table. She shrugs as she cradles the mug's warm bottom with her left hand. "You see with that kind of love open to us. We don't need to understand. It isn't for us to know how. It just is. From then on, I went to church until I found the Gospel of Mary and realized that the church is patriarchal and cannot tell me the whole story of the Saviour. And there's so much to discover, Evelyn. So much! Peter was jealous of Mary, you know." Jeerah's voice drops to a conspiratorial whisper. "He mocked Mary. He asked if the Saviour would really speak privately with a woman and not openly to men? But he did!" Jeerah's voice loudens. "In the Garden, he spoke to Mary! John's Gospel admits it! So why wouldn't he have spoken more to Mary privately? He spoke to the others privately, too! Peter was just jealous," Jeerah sniffs. "He even said in the Gospel of Mary, chapter nine, did he, the Saviour, prefer her to us? Of course, the Saviour did! Women listen and obey. Men try to change things to suit their own egos." Jeerah releases the bottom of her mug and picks up the cookie on the table and inspects it. She speaks to the cookie: "It was so amazing that love I felt. I didn't feel it from others in the church, only from the Saviour. I knew I had to learn more about the Saviour, and I couldn't do that surrounded by all those women worshipping men and making all those men their leaders. A woman here, a woman there isn't like the Saviour. That's why the Saviour had come to me directly. He wanted me to meet him directly not through other people telling me what to think." Jeerah bites into her cookie and speaks with crumbs shooting out. "This is why we had to meet, don't you see? The Saviour meets us personally and through others. You're meeting him through me at this very moment!"

Ev hopes the Saviour wouldn't be spitting cookie crumbs out at her if she ever saw him in person. She still doesn't know who he is or where he came from.

Jeerah swallows, raises her mug in her right hand to sip contemplatively while holding on to her bitten-into cookie with her left. She lowers her mug a little and continues: "The Saviour tells us that there are mysteries beyond our understanding. That's why we have faith. We accept what he tells us and share that with others so that they too may be saved and may be free to live in the peace that he brings and offers to all of us freely, if only we have the ears to hear and the mind open to understanding. He brings our souls into knowledge of our roots and releases our soul from our flesh. Only then can we be rejoined with him after our deaths." Jeerah suddenly smiles, her eyes almost shutting in their web of deepening crow's feet She bangs down her mug and drops the cookie onto the plate. Her voice rises in volume and pitch. "I'm so happy that you are open to understanding. I know," she says, clapping her hands, "that you'll do a wonderful job for me. I just know it! We are simpatico." Jeerah almost bounces in her chair.

Ev edges forward in her chair as she picks up her mug with her right hand and pushes her top button into its buttonhole with her left. She swallows the last of her coffee, feeling her heart speed up to its energetic darkness. She hasn't touched any of the pastries. Japanese Robot takes care of her nutritional needs, according to her programming. She'd considered eating a cookie as part of following Dr. Frock's instructions, but after Jeerah had put her half-eaten croissant back onto the same plate, she'd decided that she isn't going to veer off Japanese Robot's coding. It keeps her to her ideal weight-height ratio that is optimum for mental work. Extra coffee won't matter, although this light-headedness she is beginning to feel is making her uneasy.

Ev stands up.

Jeerah cranes her neck to follow Ev's movements as her smile falters.

Ev says: "The hour is up. I must leave." She turns and halts. Dr. Frock's words about thanking clank into her head. She faces Jeerah again, looking down at her, and registering Jeerah's half-open mouth, her upturned brows. Ev pronounces: "Thank you." She stops. No, she's supposed to say more words. She says robotically: "Thank you for meeting with me and the coffee." Ev turns back toward the door and marches out of the cafe, reversing the route that she'd followed an hour and ten minutes earlier.

16

Connecting

Ev dons her VR helmet and gloves. She hasn't slept. She has thirty minutes and nine seconds before she must leave for her appointment with Dr. Frock. Ev isn't sure what she's looking for. The strange experience of being inside a character object not directing it as a player does, or with David.admin who is firm like a bureaucrat yet makes her feel...Ev doesn't know how to describe the emotion that relaxes her body and makes her brain not buzz with infinite thoughts.

Ev starts the game.

A fan rotated above her head lazily. Round and round, the fan rotated. It barely stirred the hot air suffocating her exposed skin on her arms, her legs, her feet. The floor hit her hand. Her eyes didn't seem to be blinking. Her eyes fixated on the dusty edge of one of the fan blades and followed it in its fixed rotating pattern. She began to feel softness up the length of her back, underneath her head, underneath her neck suspended between her upper back and back of her head. She was lying down.

And becoming dizzy.

Could she blink?

Silence oppressed her. Not even the fan hummed or clicked or made any of the small noises old fans make even though this fan was dusty and stained. Round and round and round, went the dusty edge. The dust came into focus. A black spot that looked like a coal-dusted fingerprint on the edge of the blade.

The eyes of the character object, the mind, but not Ev's yet Ev's, closed. Red light filtered through.

Ev tries to close her own eyes, to make sense of what she's seeing and feeling: heat, silence, softness. Coded 3D reality that exists virtually doesn't allow for olfactory sensations; yet she flares her nostrils, expands her abdomen to draw air up silently into her nose to smell this airless room. She struggles to retain her own thoughts, to stay in her own consciousness, to keep her neural networks separated from her character object's programming, to be immersed in the virtual reality but know her own reality. Ev lowers her upper eyelids enough to shut out most of the red light filtering through in virtual reality to think about where she was. There was nothing on the flat ceiling to clue her in. Ceiling and the upper parts of the walls within her, the character object's, the mind's, her sight lines were all bare. Pink beige. Ev scans her WORM for colours. Salmon. Salmon pink. Salmon on the walls. Salmon on the ceilings. Maybe sheets, quilts, and curtains, too. No, those woven silk curtains, heavily textured, were ballet slipper pink, is Ev's last retrieved memory before her eyes snap fully open as...

The fan was rotating above her, the dust spot in focus, except it was another one. First one spot came into view, then the view danced over to another one, while still following the circular pattern of the fan. A thumbprint and another thumbprint. On two of the sturdy blades made of white-painted boards, carved in filigree on solid background. These blades were slightly bent. Synchronized thrumming sounded in her ears. Whispers of something writhed themselves into her chest. Not Ev's whispers. Not Ev's feelings. She couldn't connect these sensations to herself. Grey began to fill up her vision from the bottom. An endless grey with wispy edges that seemed to seep out of her vision and into her nose, her mouth, up into her hearing, down into her skin cells. The grey clogged up her nerves as it leaked from cell to cell. It wept salty liquid as it crept along. Yet nothing leaked from Ev's eyes, and nothing leaked from the mind's eyes into her viewscreen as the mind, as Ev followed the second thumbprint opposite the first one on the same blade before the consuming grey engulfed—

Something nudges her. Hard. The screen is black inside her helmet, and Ev's eyes flicker as her heart catches itself.

"It's time," Japanese Robot says loudly for her to hear through her helmet and the remnants of the virtual reality streaming away from her consciousness.

Hurriedly Ev removes the helmet, and all the weight of the grey leaves her. She draws into her vision the intense browns of her book-shelf wallpaper, the rich colours of the book spines, the depths of the wood stain on her floors and sensory mat. Colour floods her optical viewscreen, and Ev sighs out tension.

She shoves her feet into her outdoor shoes. She hunches into her jacket, wraps a scarf around her neck, for Japanese Robot has told her it would be chilly and to add a scarf, and heads out to see Dr. Frock.

He's standing there watching the entrance as she pulls open the front door, his arms behind his back, his green-blue eyes catching her brown ones the moment she walks in. He walks toward her, his right hand outstretched, his left hand grasping the ghastly black cane with its undulating head of grinning ivory. His lips part and show his teeth as he smoothly reaches her and says: "Hello, Evelyn."

Ev stares at his white shirt, the collar done up to the top button, the ends slightly wilting. She feels his hand grasp hers and shake her limp one. He retains her hand in his until she looks up at him. He's not much taller than she is. Her shuttered eyes meet his green ones, and he smiles widely. "Hello, Evelyn," he repeats.

"Hello," she repeats robotically, stepping back and pulling her hand out of his grasp.

He doesn't seem to mind as he puts his arm behind his back again and lets the cane slip through his left hand until his fingers grasp its head and its tapered obsidian point taps the striped grey-black carpet that protects the floor from boots and shoes bringing the weather in. "I thought we could walk today."

"Walk?"

"Yes," he smiles. "Walk. That thing we do where we perambulate along the sidewalks using our feet."

Ev's mouth rounds a silent "O," not understanding what's going on. She lets her eyes drop and notices his heather and green tweed jacket on its moss-brown background is buttoned up with fabric-covered buttons to its top. She assumes its matching vest is also fully buttoned up. The waist of his jacket is cinched; it's the kind of jacket with a sewn-in half-belt at the back. His trousers are creased sharply precisely in the centre of the front of his legs, ending in one crease over the top of his polished brown brogues.

He will freeze, Ev thinks as she follows his quick march through the entrance doors and out onto the sidewalk.

The wind gusts a greeting. Crispy golden leaves, their edges curled, fly up into the air and whip around their heads before wafting back down. Ev looks to Dr. Frock for direction; every strand of his crown of black hair salted heavily with white remains in its place.

"Why don't you walk on my right side, Evelyn," Dr. Frock says pointing to where he wants her to go. Ev obeys. They begin to walk toward downtown, their backs to the rising sun. Dr. Frock walks at a steady pace, his strides firm and long, his left hand swinging his cane forward, letting it touch the ground but not slam into it, before pushing it back and lifting it again, the black of it swallowing the birthing sunlight that gilds the leaves lying on the sidewalk and the ones still clinging to the trees that promenade alongside them. Cars stop and zoom, brake hard and accelerate sharply, only two meters away from them, as cyclists pedal furiously among cars and pedestrians alike.

Dr. Frock says: "How did you get on, Evelyn, yesterday? Did you accomplish the homework I set out for you?"

"Yes," Ev replies, her predawn experience of being subsumed creating within her this sense of wanting to assert herself. She suddenly itches to correct his use of her name, but the correction sticks at the exit of her mouth.

"Tell me about it."

"I met Jeerah at the coffee shop."

"Go on," Dr. Frock encourages her after three seconds.

Ev says flatly: "She bought me coffee."

"Did you enjoy the coffee, Evelyn?"

"Ev."

"Ev?" Dr. Frock's sure stride stumbles imperceptibly.

"Yes."

Dr. Frock rallies and says: "I haven't heard of a coffee called Ev before. Was it good?"

Ev doesn't know how to answer. "Um...Uh..."

"You don't know?" Dr. Frock smiles kindly down upon her, on the brown strands of hair sticking out and catching the sun on their ends, her confused eyes glancing up into his before shifting away.

Ev does know. She'd liked the coffee. But how—Her thoughts catch in a mental pothole. She doesn't know what to say; she doesn't know where to look.

Dr. Frock says: "We need to work on your social anxiety. I've noticed that you don't move when talking with me in the office. And I wanted to see how you move in a situation where movement is required. I see you walk in a rhythmic way, your arms moving with your legs. It's good to see your arms move. It means that you're using all your muscles. You show confidence in your walk. But you're not looking at me. Now, it could be we're walking side by side. But normally, I would expect some head movement. Some eye movement. You're as still in your walking, moving only the muscles you need to as you are in my office. I must consider a differential diagnosis of ASD. That's autism spectrum disorder." He hesitates.

"Mild, of course. Mild. But I must ponder this further. And you've returned to your short answers again. That too is concerning. I was hoping going through with your homework—which I'm pleased you did. I was worried that you wouldn't go through with it. And I congratulate you for making the effort. I know how much it took out of you, and I congratulate you for it. It wasn't easy. Did you congratulate yourself for it, Evelyn?"

"Ev."

"Yes, yes, the drink. Strange name. I haven't heard of it before. Does that mean you really enjoyed it? Would you do it again? Go to that coffee shop again? Meet Jeerah again? Maybe another?"

Ev's head spins. She halts. She doesn't know which question to answer. She doesn't know how to tell him to call her "Ev" when simply telling him doesn't work. She doesn't know how to walk and talk. She'd never done something like this before. Her parents had never walked together or with her just for the sake of walking when she was growing up. They got in cars when they wanted to go somewhere, otherwise they stayed home. What is the point of walking nowhere?

Dr. Frock turns his head to look over his shoulder, sees that he's left her behind, and swiftly turns himself about and walks back to her. Blue filling his irises, he asks: "Evelyn?"

Ev blurts: "My name is Ev. Call me Ev."

"Ohhh," he replies, the bass of his vocal chords vibrating. "I apologize...Ev. I shall call you Ev."

Ev turns her head away from him to look vacantly at the cars and SUVs and bicycles crowded on the patched and potholed road beside them. Her breathing lifts and lowers her jacket and the scarf end that dangles down over its front.

Dr. Frock says: "Perhaps we've done enough for today. You've performed wonderfully. You've done a lot this week. Time to rest. Rest is necessary too, not just therapy. Okay?"

Ev continues to stare at the traffic, trying to compute all his words. She runs them through her Frock language decoder she'd programmed into her own programming, Lapis keeping track of each change as she adds his new iterations into it. Ten seconds pass as her axons send electrical signals to her synapses, and her neurons work together in their networks. Slowly the signals unfurl his words into coherence. Ev says: "I understand."

His brows upturning, his lips smiling, Dr. Frock replies: "Good. I'm glad. We'll meet again tomorrow. This time in my office. I promise."

Ev begins to walk toward the intersection where the light facing her is red.

17

Caught In The Mind

Ev closes her front door, relief sighing out of her. She kicks off her shoes and hurries to her desk. Her VR gear is waiting for her; and her computer is ready for her, running E3. Soon, Ev is in *Early Exit*, her view a murky red, her consciousness being impregnated by the mind. She no longer thinks "character object" when she thinks of Level 0, the virtual reality she's created. She thinks "mind." Hers, the two of them seeing, perceiving, feeling as one, separate yet bonded. This virtual place is freedom.

Her eyelids were closed in a lit place. Her eyes opened in an unknown-to-Ev-but-known-to-the-mind place. An unfamiliar yet familiar sky appeared, sky with high cirrus clouds and a haze of filtered dust.

Ev has a question at the edge of their bonding. She endeavours to separate enough to speak. She manages to do so without having to close her eyes: "Where are you?"

The mind's vision sharpened as if she'd squinted her eyes.

Thoughts seep in; an idea of place. Ev cannot quite catch these thoughts. *Her thoughts, they must be*, Ev thinks. How can she read another person's mind? She doesn't remember coding for her Level 0 characters to have thoughts. She doesn't know how to read thoughts of a character as if they're talking in her internal language database. Ev tries again, testing this reality of thought: "Where are you?"

The view dropped down from sky to far-off buildings. She was sitting on a roof, staring over the flat roofs of low square buildings.

This couldn't be the house that she had been in. That house had had a peaked roof. The other houses that the mind had passed by in that walk had peaked roofs. The houses across the street from the window that she'd looked out of had had slanted roofs.

She was in another place. The view shifted.

Ev's stomach lurches.

They were looking straight down the side of the building, down, down to the street below, a great vertical distance to grimy cars and hustling pedestrians, oblivious to the two women looking down upon them through combined virtual and physical eyes.

"Don't do that!" Ev blurts. Her heart pounds at this foreign pull to death. Fear burns her throat. She tries to find the stop button. End the game. End this reality. This is not how she'd coded *Early Exit*. It isn't an exit to end at Level 0. It's an ending at Level 0 and a beginning at Level 1 then a rise to Level 2. Ev begins to distrust her sanity. She'd created E3 to find an early exit to Heaven, a quest she'd had since she was fifteen years old. She hadn't been looking for death, she tells herself, but an exit from this life on Earth. She has no desire to end her life. She wants to live it in a better place, to leave this testing ground of...She doesn't know what other than she doesn't like the pain it causes, the pain that squeezes her insides and rumbles her nerves into sparking jangles that only diving into games and virtual reality can stop. She wants to join others in a...Thoughts fail Ev. She still doesn't know what she's looking for—has been looking for—only that she knows she wants to exit this realm of hard surfaces and relentless time ticking. Space.Time feels foreign to her; void.NullTime a surrounding place where community lives; Level 2 an exploration of Zygote class, which had begun it all. She doesn't know what Zygote is. She'd created Level 2 yet doesn't know where it came from out of her consciousness. It's like it cannot be created until the character object she controls reaches it. But no one can reach it—not her, the E3 designer, nor anyone else—until they exit to void.NullTime where time doesn't exist and space has no boundaries, surfaces, or limited dimensions.

So why when she'd set up E3 to exit to Heaven, now the void, is she inhabiting another mind, or is the mind inhabiting her, keeping her from controlling it?

Suddenly like a vacuum, the mind and the reality of Level o swallow up Ev.

The view shifted toward the right side of the balustraded low wall then to the left, looking for someone. The view swirled. The view looked along the roof to a small hut thing with an open door, leaning precariously off its hinges, one corner digging into the pitted and stained concrete, the concrete's beige paint rubbed raw in a path from the mouldering door to underneath their view. No other person was in sight.

The view shook back and forth.

Energy lifts Ev from her body and brain into the air around her, magnetizing it, raising all her little hairs, and with the energy comes strength and the certainty that the exit lies through this mind.

The vertical view returned, and the street seemed to rush up.

Ev chokes. The Energy-created magnetic air pulls ribbons and threads of integration around her real body.

You left the conversation early.

Ev struggles against the virtual reality. "Conversation?" she asks out loud, to hear her own voice, be her own person.

This mind is only the first step, connector, whispers through her neurons, racing along her axons, stimulating chemicals to rush to the other side of her synapses and wake up other neurons to carry the news that...

Ev grinds brakes against the rush. "Wait a minute! This mind is falling, and who is connector, and I don't want to die!" The magnetized air surges into all the pockets of space inside her brain, her muscles, her heart yet surrounds her externally, connecting and making whole her body and the space around her in the present moment. *What you call the mind, what I call EnergyHumanFaithLost, is not sitting nor falling but leaning down. Look!*

Ev braces herself and puts all her focus on what she can see through the eyepieces, feel through the gloves, sense through the mat she's standing on as the player separate from the character. And realizes that the mind she was in was standing, clinging to the wall, head down.

Ev sharpens her eyes and thinks, *I am in virtual reality. I can be wherever I want to be.*

She exerts her will to finally, at last control her view, see the entirety of this plane of Level 0. The street is not real. She can hover over it. When she does, she turns around and looks back at where she'd been standing. A young woman stands gripping the rough cement parapet of the building, her black hair dangling down in shining waves from her head to way below her hands. Ev doubts, then is immediately overcome with knowledge of what to say. "Stand up!"

The hair flung itself up and over the head whose black eyes sought the voice that had come at her from the air. The woman looked straight at Ev as if seeing her but then she looked to the left and the right and twisted around as much as she could while retaining her grip on the parapet wall with both hands.

This woman doesn't want to die. Why is she standing at the wall? Why is she making all the moves to jump yet hadn't? Ev dares to look between her feet, down and down to the sidewalk immediately below her with its tapestry of cracks and the round marks of old gum walked over many times. The acrid smell of car exhaust and old garbage wrinkles her nose. Her virtual reality doesn't include Smell-O-Vision. She lifts her head.

The woman was staring right at her as if trying to see something that didn't exist. Suddenly Ev was back in the mind looking back to where she had been hovering.

Ev hadn't thought about moving back into the mind. She hadn't moved her hands, her feet, her head. How had she moved in space.Time back into the mind? She searches her brain's WORM for instances of putting in random character movements into *Early Exit*. She hadn't coded that. How could she have? Magnetic energy prickles up and down her skin. *Connector*. Ev decides she's in a first-person game; somehow it has changed itself to first person. She can move her feet toward that hut and stairs and off this roof and death. She concentrates her will on turning her body to where she knew the hut to be.

The view didn't shift.

She moves her feet at an angle as if she's one-stepping around, one degree at a time, one hundred and eighty degrees.

The view didn't shift.

Frustrated, Ev yells: "Move!"

Startled, the view shot up to the sky then back down and around to look at the hut.

"Yes!" Ev yells, feeling energized all of a sudden. The unfamiliar sensation fires her muscles, skin, heart, brain up; her emotions soar as the mind began to move slowly toward the hut.

They were standing in the hut's doorway, staring down concrete steps with rusty metal railings on either side, encased in a concrete vertical tunnel. The steps descended into gloom. The light bulb at the top trapped in its metal cage, spider webs hanging from it with one dead fly hanging in them, was off. Sunlight filtered around from behind and threw her shadow down the steps.

A voice shouted up: "Why have you not jumped?"

18

Psychiatric Certainty

Paper hit a desk with a smack in virtual reality that shoots through Ev's system in material reality. And then Ev is fully immersed in the reality of electrons and neurons reacting to electrons. Material reality recedes from her consciousness.

A baritone roar issued from somewhere inside her but outside her. "That journalist is the most biased of all the western journalists, left, right, and centre. Unprofessional. Wrong! I won't let them suppress the liberation of my people!"

Confusion snatches her back into material reality, of her body and brain in the material, her mind...inside a new mind of another character object, the mind inside her, Ev isn't sure which nor which character object, only that she's confused and still in Level 0 and cannot exit from the game or to Level 1. Where is she now? Ev blinks, and this new virtual scene grabs her consciousness, and...

Impassive faces of men lined up in front of her stared back at—him?

Ev tries to shut her ears to the tirade spitting out of her virtual reality mouth. But it overpowers her.

This new mind skittered off the flatbed of sanity and went bouncing down the road in head-banging cartwheels. His words punched through her mental defences:

Free speech!

Suppression!

Radical!

Odious censuring!

Restructuring!

Correction!

Radical ideology!

Restoring!

Ethics!

Law!

Freedom from the elites!

Freedom for the people!

Freedom!

Suddenly, whole sentences thundered through her breast, beating drumbeats on her heart. "I will restore this country to its rightful way. I'll weed out those agitators and treasonous villains who plot to take me down! That leftist western media with its radical leftist ideology with its social justice like the inquisition that infected our country will not defeat me!! I will weed out the corruption, the smell of those who dared to defy our democracy with their coups and plots! Get me the Minister of Order! Where is he?"

Ev inside the baritone-voiced mind stared intensely at each man as the new mind's thunderous voice suddenly fell silent. A clock ticked loudly behind him. Each male face blanched as one at a time, the view remained on them, from the first one on the far left until the last one at the far right. The men stood there in their black and navy-blue suits, with crisp collared white shirts, and single-coloured ties, their heads upturned toward the origin of the view, their lips in controlled straight lines, bodies unmoving, except for a slowly fisting hand here or too much blinking there. The view shot to the right of the last man, toward a set of tall windows with tall heavy curtains falling from ceiling to floor, tied back in thick silken ropes of woven gold. The thick window glass revealed the city bathed in haze, overlooked by a bleached sky.

Something hard nudges Ev's shoulder.

And again.

Suddenly, she blacks out. Her ears buzz with the hiss of audio switched off. She blinks in the darkness and slowly regains awareness of a helmet encasing her head, earpieces cupped over her ears, gloves encasing her hands. She rips off her helmet and her gloves and stares at them, breathing hard. She's about to throw them away from her, somewhere in the direction of her desk when Japanese Robot says impassively from beside her, startling her: "Your Dr. Frock appointment is in fifteen minutes. Get ready. But breathe first." He begins his deep breathing display, and Ev automatically follows his instructions. Gripping her helmet and gloves tighter and tighter until with an emphatic exhalation, she lets go. They drop to the floor, and on shaky feet, she wobbles toward her front door. Her arms won't go into her jacket sleeves. She vacuums air into her lungs, exhales it until her lungs are empty, then carefully turns her jacket a bit inside out so that the entrance to the right sleeve is visible. She sticks her hand into it and pushes through until her hand pops out the wrist end. She searches for the left sleeve, centring her consciousness on this important activity. She pushes her left hand and arm through the left sleeve successfully at last.

"Your shoes," Japanese Robot says.

Ev looks down at her socked feet. She hunts for her outdoor shoes, pads over to them, Japanese Robot wheeling beside her. She leans on him as she pushes her feet into her loafers. Somehow she exits her studio; somehow she's entering the clinic doors; somehow she's standing in front of Dr. Frock's door.

It opens, and Dr. Frock appears right before her, smiling, looking down at her.

She's sitting on the sofa, her back straight, her hands gripping each other. She parts her lips, and words rush out: "The audio class had its volume up. His voice hurt. The individual characters didn't move. I was in a dusty city in space.Time. I don't know where I was. I should be able to locate coordinates in space.Time. But I couldn't. And the shout came up from below to jump."

Dr. Frock holds up a hand until she registers it and slows to silence. He lowers his hand gradually until it lies relaxed on his notepad. He says: "Okay. I see you're agitated. Tell me again why. What did you see?"

"Individuals of the male attribute."

"Men?"

Ev nods.

"Okay. And what were they doing?"

"Idle."

"Idle? Like an engine?"

"It's the pose before they move."

"The pose?"

"Yes."

Ev's eyes bounce off his left shoulder to the wall behind him, her eyes open but disconnected from her current space and time.

Dr. Frock says: "Can you look at me, Evelyn?"

Ev doesn't respond.

"Evelyn."

Ev shifts her eyes a bit toward him so that her irises seem to be glancing off his left smoothly shaven cheekbone.

He upturns the edges of his lips and says: "Explain again."

Ev says: "The mind stood on the roof. I didn't design Level 0 to be in a dusty city. Space.time can be anywhere, and I randomized E3 to create instances of space. Time must be one directional in DeltaTime. But I don't know if the voice was in the same time as the mind. Space shifted. I set E3's physics in the instantiated Placenta class of space to be like ours. But it shifted!" Ev gasps out the last, swinging her eyes to quiz his eyes, her brown irises blackening. His eyes dart to the right, toward his window, and back again, his smile fixed upon his face.

"You seem to have dissociated again, wouldn't you agree?"

Ev isn't looking at him anymore. She has fixated on the wall behind him in its soothing brown shade. Dr. Frock leans forward until his movement captures her gaze and his green-blue eyes are looking into hers. The lenses behind her irises contract, focus on his eyes, and he straightens up, using the power of his mind to pull her gaze along with him.

"I've been concerned about you. I felt we were making progress. You would agree, we were making progress?"

Ev says in a monotone: "Of course."

"And now you seem to have been derailed, wouldn't you agree?"

Ev says: "I don't know what happened. E3 has rules. And it didn't follow them."

Dr. Frock holds up his hand: "It's okay. Rules can be broken. We don't need to be rigid in our following of rules. Sometimes it's good to break the rules. I'm concerned that things must be done in only the way you want them to happen. And that isn't always the case. Life is unpredictable. Things happen." Dr. Frock stretches his lips out until his even teeth flash into existence. Ev stares at his teeth. "Evelyn."

Ev blinks and looks up into his green eyes.

Dr. Frock shifts, crossing his right leg over his left, hitching up his trouser leg to accommodate his change in position until his trousers' cuff is precisely five centimeters above his ankle. He knits his fingers together and places them on his pen to keep it in place on his closed notepad. The notepad's pinkish swampeel skin glistens from a fresh polish. "I believe we spoke about my initial treatment plan." He pauses, and Ev doesn't blink or move. He clears his throat and presses on. "I stand by my diagnoses of SCPD and UDD. I still believe you have social anxiety. But I have been contemplating that you may actually have a mild case of ASD. Your computer work is well suited for someone with that. Your rules of not meeting people, of controlling things so that people don't upset your order, falls in line with that sort of thinking. However, I don't want that to become part of your treatment plan if it doesn't apply. And there are some anomalies, I'll grant you that."

Ev doesn't say anything. She's deallocated memory on her heap so his words will enter her dynamic array before parsing and being differentially written onto her WORM and nothing else.

Dr. Frock's forehead drops into lines of serious thought. "It's a puzzle, trying to sort out what is dissociation and what is real. I believe that you have had a serious dissociative episode, and it's clearly upset you. I want to help you. I want to help you get better. I must contemplate this furthering of your treatment plan, that is, if we should add in ASD. That may or may not help us elucidate things. I will keep it in mind, but I won't let it influence my perception of what is going on with you. But it's clear you are too much with yourself. Within yourself. You must get out. You have friends?"

"ConsciousnessMind didn't allow its first instantiations to have friend functions. But EnergyHuman class does."

Dr. Frock's eyes widen, and he blinks hard.

Ev returns his gaze without guile.

He drops his eyes to his hands. They unknit themselves to pick up his pen. He rotates his pen with both forefingers and thumbs. He abruptly drops the black fountain pen on his notepad. He resumes his contemplation of her and smiles, relaxing back into his armchair. "Tell me about your friends."

"The friend function allows ConsciousnessMind's derived classes to access ConsciousnessMind's attributes. That's why EnergyHumans of all ultimate instantiations have access to CMMagneticField and—" Ev pauses, her mouth open, as understandings flit in. "Oh," she blurts, "I see. CMMagneticField moved the viewport from the mind to the voice."

Dr. Frock gawks at her. He uncrosses his legs, straightens his back, and raises his voice to recall her to him. He says: "Nevertheless, you must get off the computer and get out more. My treatment plan of SCPD and UDD, coupled with social anxiety, tells us that you must be in the presence of other humans more. You can't just be meeting me. You must meet others. That person you work for, what is her name?"

"I don't work for anyone," Ev replies.

"You know what I mean."

Ev furrows her brows. She tries to shut out awareness of the quickening of her breath.

"The client," he states.

Ev waits.

"What is your client's name?" he enunciates.

"Jeerah Mutti."

"Yes, yes. Her. Meet her again. Meet her regularly," he rushes out as he stands up, places his pen and notepad askew on the little table beside him, and drills his steps toward the door. He pushes down the handle and whips the door open toward himself. Ev swallows and checks with her internal clock. It's two minutes to the end of her session time. She moves forward a centimeter on the sofa. She looks over at him standing, waiting for her to leave, hears her internal seconds move to the precise end of her session. Ev stands up and walks toward him.

"Good-bye, Evelyn," he smiles at her. His eyes kind shades of blue.

19

Seeking The Mind

Ev tiptoes to her desk the next morning. Sun slants in through her windows, highlighting dancing dust motes in the air. Japanese Robot has arrayed her VR equipment neatly to the left side of her working display. She extends her right hand down and touches the helmet with her forefinger. She lets it stay then rest on the cold surface. Dr. Frock had asked her to see people. He had talked about SCPD and UDD as treatment plans. It doesn't make sense to her. Identity isn't a plan, so how is naming a puzzle a treatment plan? She stretches her fingers apart and grasps the helmet. She lifts it to her face and stares into the reflective surface covering the eye ports. Grey shades of herself stare back, eyes hidden, forehead highlighted, hair spiked like a halo. Ev lowers it back to the desk and releases it.

Ev swivels on her toes and glides to her coat rack. Japanese Robot whirs out of her kitchen: "Your morning nourishment is waiting. Where are you going?"

"Out."

"Where are you going?" Japanese Robot whirs up to her. Ev hunches her shoulders and reaches for the handle of her front door.

"Where are you going?"

Ev sighs. AI can be annoying. "Out." Then remembering Dr. Frock's instructions, adds: "Coffee shop."

After one second, Japanese Robot states: "I will put your morning nourishment in the fridge. It will become your lunch." He wheels a one-eighty and heads back to the kitchen.

Ev riddles out his human-like response. She reads her WORM: in case of meal errors, execute a throw to make it the next meal. Maybe she should have made it throw it out.

Ev slams the door behind her, startling herself to a stop. She twists her head and stares at the door. What is happening to her? She doesn't slam doors or feel...What is this feeling? Anger? But she doesn't get angry. Her parents had programmed her to eschew anger. They had instructed her that anger repels people and had brought home one of their favourite anger management books to use on her. At first, first her mother then her father had read it along with her and assigned the homework. They then had told her she was approaching her teenage years and needed to learn to work on herself by herself. She had completed the book as instructed and soon had coded their brevity into her programming. Curt words, short sentences, silent smiles as answer were superior to anger. Once she'd coded these patterns into herself, she used Lapis to keep them safe from change.

She checks Lapis now. How can this change have happened without her concurrent versioning system alerting her? She finds an imperceptible change in her coding, something to do with switching emotions off in response to not being listened to. The off switch was somehow turned back on. She attempts to change it back to off.

Ev thinks about how her life, all aspects of it, is the way she'd coded it. She is like the derived classes of EnergyHuman—executing new coding to store in her MagneticField. MagneticField? Ev cocks her head. Is this a new variant of her WORM? Or WORM plus programming? A kind of electromagnetic combination of her biochemical molecular memory storage and the activity of her neural networks driven by her programming?

An EM Field would create a more robust EnergyMind Ev, Ev thinks.

Ev finds herself stepping out of the elevator. She looks back at the open doors in puzzlement. She steps forward then checks herself between elevator and brass front doors of her building. The security guard lifts his head at this unaccustomed behaviour. Ev digs into her thoughts. Who is she? David was admin, but who is she? She had only thought of herself as the coder of E3, not as an instantiated object of one of the derived classes. Ev shakes her head and resumes her excursion, the security guard turning his head in sync with her direction until the heavy brass door silently closes behind her. He shakes his head and returns to his perusal of the newspaper.

Oblivious, Ev drives her hands into her jacket pockets and rolls her shoulders forward as the wind bites into her throat. She's forgotten her scarf. She's come to rely on Japanese Robot to advise her on how to dress for the weather to such an extent that the first time she'd dressed herself, all she'd thought to put on was her jacket.

Ev bends her head against the steady northwest wind and aims her feet for the coffee shop where she'd met Jeerah. Upon waking this morning, Ev had realized with a start that she hadn't worked on Jeerah's website since meeting her. The day after they'd met, Jeerah had recommenced her meeting requests in her emails.

Once was not enough for Jeerah, judges Ev. She'd thought it was enough for her. But this question won't leave her alone, and Jeerah had said that she goes to her coffee shop every morning for her latte and to drop in sometime. *I'D LOVE TO MEET YOU*, Ev sees emblazoned in her visual field. Her lips lift wryly, but she presses on. Dr. Frock had said that she must meet her.

Ev decides that Dr. Frock is recoding the emotional part of her programming so that the strange 3D-bleeding-into-Earth-reality experiences will stop.

Ev comes to a halt. Does she want them to stop? She isn't sure. The mind, the first one from Level 0, space.Time, had inhabited her thoughts all night. Had she jumped? What is Ev supposed to do? Should she ask search bot? Were there clues in that irrational man with the thunderous voice? How is virtual reality real?

Ev snorts, startling herself.

The wind pushes on her shoulders, and she stumbles backward a couple of steps. *Jeerah*, she thinks. She must meet Jeerah. Of course, the minds are not real. They are her instantiated character objects of the derived classes she created. The controlling irrational voice that comes from nowhere is EnergyHumanFaithControllingOthers Class. The first mind...Ev stalls. She admits to herself that she doesn't know. Maybe the mind is EnergyHumanFaithLost class like that voice had said. Or maybe something dangerous like EnergyHumanKnowledge-Sharing class. She doesn't want to think about how that voice that had whispered "connector" to her had emerged from *Early Exit* into material reality.

Ev treads past the coffee shop. At the corner, she looks up and around. Her brows raise themselves in the inner corners as she scans for familiar store frontages. She revolves herself until she's looking back from whence she came. She spots the coffee shop sandwich sign and, sighing, reverses course.

Ev yanks open the door and searches for Jeerah. Jeerah is in her favourite seat, next to the fireplace. Ev walks over and stares down at her. Jeerah looks up with a frown, opens her mouth, and recognizes Ev. A smile swallows up her downturned lines as she exclaims: "Ev!" Jeerah stands up, spreads her arms wide, and wraps them around Ev, imprisoning Ev's arms down by her sides. Ev stares bug-eyed over her shoulder as Jeerah chatters into her ear, releasing her, pointing down to her latte whose foam is drawn into an elephant head, its trunk upturned.

Ev goggles.

Gradually Jeerah's noises turn into words: "This new barista is soooo talented. You have to TRY his latte. It's SOOOO good. Let me get you one. You sit. I'll get. I'm soooo happy to see YOU, Evelyn." Jeerah pauses to suck in air and clasps her hands in front of her face as she stares at Ev, happiness deepening her crow's feet. With a joyful sigh, she vanishes toward the back of the coffee shop where the barista creates his magic.

Ev steps sideways to stand in front of the empty armchair facing the one Jeerah was in then drops down in one move. She takes in Jeerah's two scarves, one red, one purple, festooning her chair, and her cloak coat draped across the seat and arms. How many coats does she have?

"Here we are!" Jeerah places a tall paper cup stamped with the coffee shop logo with the CN Tower prominently sticking up in the centre of the skyscape latte foam art. "You're so Toronto, Evelyn, I just HAD to get him to make you the CN Tower view. Do you like it?" Not waiting for an answer, Jeerah plonks herself down into her chair. "How are you getting on with the website?" She suddenly lifts a palm up toward Ev. "No!" She laughs. "Don't answer. I just KNOW you're doing a fabulous job. The Saviour said," and here Jeerah pauses as she shuts her eyes and quotes: "All nature, all formations, all creatures exist in and with one another, and they will be resolved again into their own roots." Jeerah opens her eyes and sighs with satisfaction. "Isn't that so comforting, to know we will all be resolved into one?" Jeerah leans forward to grasp her coffee cup.

Ev thinks of ConsciousnessMind and the community that class created in Level 1 to be one. She had created ConsciousnessMind as an entity that is both one and many. She realizes Jeerah has stopped sipping her latte—and notices that she is sipping not gulping it.

Maybe this art in the coffee foam has a good side, Ev thinks. She asks: "How will it be resolved?"

Jeerah chokes a little and hurriedly places her cup back on the table. She lifts her hand to her mouth, "Oh." She swallows. "Um."

Ev waits, unmoving.

Jeerah lifts her grey eyes to Ev's unreadable brown ones. "Well, you see, it's like this. In the Gospel of Mary, Mary relates how the Saviour said that the nature of matter is resolved into the roots of its own nature alone. We are to hear. You know how the Saviour instructs us that those of us with ears to hear, let her hear. And I just know, Evelyn, you have those ears. And I'm so glad you asked. I just know that you'll do good things with my website because you have such a questing, seeking mind. And the Saviour is there for those of us who seek. And we do want to seek, don't we? We humans are seekers. We're doers, but we're also seekers. It's in our nature to seek out and to find out the answers to mysteries, don't you think so, Evelyn?" Ev opens her mouth, but Jeerah talks on. "Of course, you do, it's in the nature of your work!

"I think it's wonderful what you do. There are so few women in your line of work, Evelyn. You're an inspiration to young women everywhere who need to know that the Saviour is there for them, that they can do whatever men do and better!" Jeerah laughs and picks up her coffee. She raises one forefinger as she sips.

Ev waits.

Jeerah sets her cup back down and begins to speak again: "You see, it's like this, the Saviour comes to us. The Saviour waits for us. That waiting is something only women can do, you know. Men are so impatient and controlling. They want to tell us what to do and how to do and when to do. And my goodness, if we don't agree with them, they get so mad. So mad. And they come out with these little manipulative remarks and pretend they're not mad. But the Saviour isn't like that. We have to see the Saviour as a man because that's what he is on Earth. But is he a man in Heaven? I don't know. *We* don't know. Is there gender in Heaven? Me and a few others like to think not. After all, God had said that she was both male and female, and the Saviour had said there was no marriage, so how can there be gender, right? So if no gender, why should we call the Saviour a he?"

Ev's head spins.

This woman subscribes to a notion she'd set aside as childish.

Heaven is a story to give children something to hang on to, not a real place.

She sets aside that contradiction of Heaven as a place to want to go to as she considers, "seeking." She understands seeking. Just before she fell asleep for a brief hour before waking, she thought of how she wants to know what is happening to this mind in space.Time of *Early Exit*, maybe to help her. That, too, is a new feeling, another change she suddenly realizes that Lapis hadn't alerted her to. Ev sucks in her lips, twists them about between her teeth.

"How do you like the coffee? Leaves a sweet taste in the mouth, doesn't it?"

"Yes," Ev replies and hastily grasps her untasted latte and sips at it. Her brows rise to her hairline as she marvels at this new mouth feel, this new coffee taste. She blurts at Jeerah: "It's good."

Jeerah leans back in her chair and smiles smugly back at her. "I told you. I'm so glad. I know you'll do a great job on the website. The Saviour led me to you, you know. I have ears to hear, and I heard the Saviour speaking to me because the risen Saviour is a spirit who can speak to our own spirits. Oh," Jeerah waves her hand at Ev's startled look. "Not materially, like I'm speaking to you now. But in here." Jeerah taps her head. "And here." She taps her heart. "That voice inside you, that voice is the Saviour's. Her spirit in you, speaking to your spirit that she called to and woke up, helping you out in your seeking. The Saviour came to show us a path to inner spiritual knowledge. Follow that path. Listen to that inner voice."

Ev is stupefied. Her inner voice is her inner voice. No other creature inhabits her body but herself. *Connector.*

Jeerah is still speaking: "...Saviour said, 'There is no sin, but it is you who make sin when you do the things that are like the nature of adultery, which is called sin.' You know what sin means? It means to miss the mark. It comes from archery, you know. Trust male writers to use a military term!" Jeerah snorts in disgust. "But it's true what we do is like adultery. We cheat. We lie. We prevaricate. We pretend to each other and pretend to ourselves. People think adultery is just about cheating in marriage. But it's so much more. So much more! And the worst kind of adultery is for our spirit to ignore the Saviour's spirit in our obsession with the material world. You understand?"

Ev doesn't.

She drops her gaze down to her wondrous coffee and blows on the foam, pushing brown-stained ripples away from her. A foam knob flies off and lands on the table. Ev averts her eyes from it and sips. Suddenly, she realizes Jeerah isn't speaking. Ev raises her eyes over the top of the cup and looks at Jeerah. Jeerah's lips are straight, her eyes watchful. Ev blinks.

"Um," she says.

The two women stare at each other in a frozen tableau as the fire crackles next to them. A small drop of water trapped in the charred wood expands, and the wood fibres around it explode in a little pop. Ev sips her coffee again and then gulps it all, upturning the cup to watch the last of the foam slowly descend down the ramp of the coffee cup's inside into her mouth. She licks her lips in unaccustomed enjoyment and places her cup back down on the table. "I must leave."

Jeerah shoots up and wreathes Ev in a huge grin, her arms following suit around Ev's shoulders. When she releases her, Ev picks up her cup and steps to the side until she is outside of the confines of the armchairs and table. "Thank you," she says.

Jeerah smiles. "I was glad to. You'll come again tomorrow? We can continue our discussion."

Ev isn't sure she wants to, yet something tugs at her to understand Jeerah. And Dr. Frock's treatment plan of social anxiety whispers to her. Ev nods and leaves, throwing her cup into the domed trash can near the door.

20

Fine

"I'm fine."

"How's your husband?"

"He's fine."

Where is she? In the original mind or that enraged one?

The woman's face across the coffee table expressed doubt.

Ev thinks, *I'm in the original, I think. Still on Level o space.Time.* And then she's fully immersed, her own thoughts scattering away.

Behind the woman was the blank pinkish wall with a darker rectangle faintly outlined in bleached pink where a painting once hung. The woman balanced herself with her legs decorously crossed in a single ornately carved teak chair. No table stood beside her, only the low heavy coffee table between them. She was holding a saucer in her left hand and a delicate white teacup by its translucent handle in her right. The teacup hovered slightly above the saucer. The woman lowered her head to take a sip while keeping her eyes fixed on the object of her attention.

Without her awareness, an unknown sensation stirred up Ev's hair follicles...

The woman lowered her eyes and her cup to the saucer then said, without looking up, "So where is he?"

"He's working. He's working a lot." Laughter rang out, startling Ev, rekindling awareness of herself.

Melodious, harmonious, the laughter spreads throughout her cells like languid warm waters. Ev's lips upturn slightly in delight. Not her laughter yet she hears it. How is it possible to hear virtual laughter as if from a material human? How is this the same mind she'd last been with on the roof, ready to jump—being told to jump?

The woman leaned forward and placed her empty teacup on the table. "Excellent tea. You always make tea the proper way."

"My mother would have it no other way. She said that she was raised by her nanny from England who instructed her sternly in the proper art of tea." A hand appeared into view, holding a matching pinkish translucent cup and saucer by the saucer's rim and setting it on the table. Tea half-filled it and didn't quite slosh out as the saucer hit the table with a slight chink.

"She gave me her bone china upon my marriage."

The woman looked down at the two cups and back up to refix her lizard gaze straight at them, the mind and Ev combined. "They're beautiful. It's too bad your paintings are gone. They looked well in this room. Storage?"

A hand rose up into view to wave the words away. Ev felt a mental door slam against something, popping her—

—awareness back into her helmet. Ev cannot discern what the something was. How can she experience the emotions of this mind in virtual reality? Like Smell-O-Vision, there is no emotion-o-vision.

"It was time for a change."

"What will you put in their place?"

"We haven't decided yet."

"With your husband being so busy—where is he again?"

"Working." A smile, as if exerting a forcefield, stretched Ev's lips.

"Of course, of course. Mine is too. The Ministry has him glued to his computer, keeping tabs on his team, so many people to investigate. We were glad to see your name not pop up on his lists." The woman smiled inquiringly. After a few seconds of silence, she continued. "We were hoping he hadn't appeared on anyone else's list. The numbers are so large." The woman's smile faltered, but she carried on, "But we know you're safe. You're one of our neighbours. We keep an eye on each other, don't we?"

"Oh yes. Absolutely. And I can assure you we're fine."

"Who were those men I saw the other day?"

"Oh, friends of my husband's. They needed some..."

"Yes?"

"Well," awkward laughter erupted from somewhere just in front of Ev's breast, frightening her. It's almost as if the mind had entered her reality. "It really is rather embarrassing. But we've gotten into a spot of financial trouble. I'm afraid I made some mistakes, didn't really know what I was doing. My husband tells me to leave such things to him, but I wanted to impress him, you know how that is, to make your husband feel you are his support and he can rely on you to do things he cannot when work consumes him. I felt that it was safe. But." The view moved side to side rapidly. "I made an error. I've learnt now not to make such errors. But my husband has been mopping up things for me as a result."

"I see," the woman said, drawing out "see." Her scrutinizing gaze did not waver.

The view changed from her face to the scene obscured by layers of dust on the windows.

The same windows as when she'd first entered Level 0 and met the mind, thinks Ev. *Yes,* she affirms to herself, *this mind is the same one who stood on that roof.* Yet she's fine? No hint of trouble? Confusion closes Ev's eyes as she tries to scan her WORM to read back into her conscious awareness that Level 0 opening scene again.

The woman's voice interrupted her, shocking her eyes open to see the woman's intent expression upon her own face.

No, upon the mind's, Ev reminds herself.

"Have you read about these rash of suicides?"
    "No," the mind said faintly.
    "It's terrible. Suddenly, some of the city's elite are jumping to their deaths. And the strange thing about them is that they seem to be happening on the same street. The police are calling it a coincidence. Isn't that strange?"
    "Yes."
    "Do you know anything about it?"
    "Me?"
    "Yes. Doesn't your husband work in that area?"
    "I don't know. I haven't kept up with the news."
    "So you haven't heard?"
    "It's terrible wanting to die."

A wave of fear invades Ev and then triumph. Strength. Confidence. Victory. Ev blinks rapidly inside her VR helmet. This woman had been about to jump. How can she say she hadn't heard? And how had she survived? Had she, Ev, dreamt that last demand? No, her WORM is solid. Her WORM never fails her. And then Ev recalls the last few days. Until now, she whispers to herself.

"Did you hear that?" The whisper travelled through the quiet room as the view moved across the woman's startled face to and through the windows. Then all the way around to the empty, silent hall.
    "Hear what?"
    "A voice."

"Voice?"

"Yes, it said..."

"Said what?"

"I don't know. I'm sure I heard...I thought I heard—"

Suspicion followed doubt followed fear across the woman's face. She stood up, smoothing down her straight black pencil skirt. She grabbed the handle of her large black patent leather purse, raising the purse off the floor. "Well, I must be off."

"Oh, so soon?" The view moves upward toward the woman as her spiked heels clicked quickly around the table and toward the hall. The heels staccatoed as they crossed the hall toward the door. The door opened. The door closed. Nothing moved.

Ev waits. What will happen now? She scans her senses. Does she feel fear? Happiness? Anything? Ev feels DeltaTime proceed forward.

The view remained on the blank wall with its large rectangular mark on it. The mind stood, picked up the two saucers by their rims. A thought bubbled up. *I must wash the cups and put them away before mother gets angry.*

Suddenly, the game is off, and the black interior of Ev's VR helmet fills her vision. She slowly lifts it off her head, unheeding how her hair sticks straight up, the earpieces tugging at her lobes. She places the helmet down on the desk and mindlessly pulls off her gloves, one finger at a time, first her left glove then her right. She holds them as she stares unseeingly at her clean desktop.

Had she been fooled?

Was that scene on the roof a dream of the mind's and not part of her real-life experience? The men hadn't banged on her door, come to extort her? It had all been just some sort of patriarchal play? And that last part, the mind saying she'd heard a voice...Hers? Ev shivers. She doesn't want any part of an insane mind, even in virtual reality.

She must ask someone about her questions.

Search bot won't be able to help her find answers. *Only a human can*, Ev admits reluctantly. Ev notes this change, one more change in her programming, one Lapis must record in case she doesn't like this change. After a moment, Ev contemplates which human to ask. Maybe Jeerah? Maybe that inner voice thing Jeerah had said was the Saviour, maybe that could point to an answer? *There is no Saviour*, Ev thinks, *but Jeerah understands women*. Maybe Dr. Frock? Dr. Frock had said he wants to help her. She had gone to him first for help. Maybe she can ask him. This change back to when she was a child of asking for help worms its way into her courage. Her seeking out Jeerah had worked out okay, though it had been strange.

Ev considers and decides that yes, she can ask them both.

Ev places her gloves down next to the helmet and changes her direction to the right.

The three papers are fanned out on the desk. They'd been lying just beyond her peripheral vision and so out of sight until she'd turned. The bottom cotton one is now filled with text and checked-off boxes. It's half-covered by the second hemp sheet at an angle. The hemp sheet is fully exposed, the top or third flax sheet slightly under it. On the white flattened hemp is now written: "Please write in the currency you will deposit for early exit."

21

Exit Currency

Ev sucks in air, blows out fear; sucks in breath, blows out tension. Calmed, she analyzes the statement. Currency? What currency? Are Canadian dollars the correct currency? She doesn't see it but picks up the pen nearby and faintly writes, "dollars." As she writes, the ink fades away so that when she's finished writing the word, it no longer exists. Ev gawps at it, shuts her eyes tight, and looks again at the paper. The statement remains; her answer does not. The pit of her stomach sends nausea up. She swallows against the bile. Is she still in *Early Exit* and doesn't know she's in the void? The pen falls out of her fingers as she raises her hands up to feel about her head. No helmet. She lowers her hands and scrutinizes them. Flesh, short fingernails, no gloves. She turns her hands over. Flesh, lines, no gloves. She moves her gaze beyond the upturned palms of her hands back to the paper.

"Please write in the currency you will deposit for early exit."

Still there.

Ev lowers her hands slowly to her lap and thinks. Carefully, she picks up the pen again and poises it above the line to the right of the statement. It isn't a long line, but these lines are never as long as they need to be, so that is no clue. She scratches on the line, "Code."

The ink fades away like a wind blew across it. When she finishes penning it, it is gone. Frustration, unfamiliar and faint, tightens Ev's eyes. She presses the pen tip down on the first part of the line with normal pressure and confidence and writes, "Spiritual." It vanishes as rapidly as she writes it. Ev's lips set hard against her teeth. She drills her pen into the hemp paper to scratch in, "Psychiatric." The paper smooths itself. "The Saviour." Erased. "DSM codes." Gone. "Japanese Robot." Gone. "Bots." Gone.

Ev flops back, exasperation huffing out of her like air from a balloon. She lets her arms drop over the arms of her chair as she glares at the paper, the statement taunting her: "Please write in the currency you will deposit for early exit."

Ev's pen hits the floor and rolls away.

A soft whirring starts as Japanese Robot moves from his charging home to the pen. He picks it up and places it next to the paper. He returns to his home. Ev doesn't move her eyes from the statement. Thoughts begin to seep back in, and logical questions flow in with them. She scans her WORM memories of David.admin, of how void.NullTime had looked different than she had coded it, of the puzzle that is the mind, and of how she has just accepted that the impossible—that paper had manifested itself from her coding into her world—is ordinary and normal for her to write on. Has she become as strange as Jeerah? Has she begun to believe in fairy tales like Jeerah does? Is her sanity the currency? Is virtual reality as real as material reality? She dares to question if machine code isn't more stable than the real world after all? How did paper from the void arrive in her hands here on Earth? Where does void exist if it exists here in Earth's space time? In a placenta somewhere beyond her material senses? Does a zygote really exist that created the placenta? It isn't only her imagination and desire to find a way to exit back from whence she came, to leave this world early because she doesn't like it and she wanted to go back home, because she feels her original home isn't here, and the only way to exit back to that home is to code it?

Coding isn't the currency.

This strange paper said so by erasing her pen strokes. Jeerah's ideas and Dr. Frock's ideas aren't, either. *Human thoughts aren't currency*, Ev spits out silently at the waiting paper with its obtuse statement.

Question.

Does the mind need her? Is that why she keeps entering it or it her? Ev scoffs at herself. Nobody needs her. She lives alone with her bots and robot. She communicates with her clients when needed and only when needed—except for Jeerah. Meeting Jeerah is new, strange. She wants to experience her strangeness more. But Jeerah doesn't need her. She pays her to do her job. She meets her so that, in her mind, Ev will know what she wants. But being needed as a person, inherent in value...

Ev rotates this new thought in her mind. She pulls one axis of it down to inspect it from within another axis. She lengthens the thought until it fills her mind: need.

Ev sits up, pulling her arms up with her, and grabs her VR helmet. She remains seated as she enters her game. She doesn't want to restart it, but she wants to see David.admin. Administrators know everything, one of her old coding friends had told the group when they'd been discussing role-playing games. HR—human resources—had their ears to every department. David.admin would be like that in void.NullTime. David.admin, of no gender but looking what male looks like, will tell her.

But how to find them when she doesn't want to restart *Early Exit*? This time, she wants to continue with the mind.

She was in the mind, watching hands washing teacups. The white saucer held by the left hand as it hovered just above a thin layer of soapy water in a stone sink. Her right hand had an old washcloth in it, grey from age, and she was going round and round the saucer with the cloth, trailing diminishing suds and streams of water. It was hypnotic. And boring.

Ev doesn't wash her own dishes. That's what dishwashers and Japanese Robot are for. She doesn't want to watch another wash their dishes. Another doesn't seem to know when to stop washing, either. Ev's impatience sends her eyes around, looking for an exit from this scene.

The view didn't change. The mind continued to wash her clean saucer.

How to leave this place and exit to David.admin's office? She needs to, has to speak to the administrator who gave her the papers with the impossible question on it. Currency. What currency? What is currency in void.NullTime? How does their currency relate to dollars in space.Time?

She was still encircling the saucer with that old cloth.

Ev wants to rip off her helmet, yet she doesn't want to leave what she's created and coded into existence. She doesn't have her gloves on. She reaches forward with both hands and pats around on her desk for her gloves but cannot feel them, only the polished wood. She stretches as far to her left as she can then pats in a straight line forward and toward her and forward again until she reaches the papers. Where are her gloves? And is the mind stuck in washing that saucer forever? Maybe her game is hiccupping. She hasn't seen that before. *Where is David.admin?* she screams in her head.

"Hello." David.admin was sitting on the other side of their desk across from her, whiteness effusing into the air around their heads. Ev lifted her hands and saw mist puff away from her toward David.admin. They was waiting, looking upon her patiently for her to speak. They looked like a he. Yet they'd said—and she had coded—that characters in void.NullTime had no gender. ConsciousnessMind had both and no genders, and so the community created from destructed EnergyHumans into EnergyMinds went from gendered to no gender. It was cleaner that way, less complicated, more unifying.

"Unifying, yes, that's correct," David.admin said.

Ev squeaked, "How can you read my mind?"

"Your mind is the portal, isn't it? Your MagneticField is what points to who you are. Isn't that what you coded?"

Ev nodded but then halted her head.

Had she?

She'd coded the dynamic memory tied to each character, calling it "MagneticField," but had she coded it to point to who she is? Was? She couldn't retrieve that knowledge from her WORM memory. Her memory failing her again filled her cells with the bile of fear.

"You are getting there, Ev."

"Where?"

"You know the currency you need."

"I do?"

"Yes." David.admin folded their hands upon their desk and looked at her placidly. "You simply need to connect consciously with CMMagneticField."

Unfamiliar panic pumped blood hot and fast into her chest, up her neck, into her face. Her skin flamed, and her eyes fluttered. The air smelled like burnt dust; the fine hairs on her arms and neck rose up as if miniaturized lightning had begun flashing all around her. Ev rolled her eyes this way and that, seeing the morphing colours of white shade from pink to dove grey to sky blue to the merest hints of grass green. Her eyes in their wild journey around this entrance to void.NullTime met David.admin's greyish-white ones and stalled. Calm waters exuded from theirs. She tumbled into their depths and met peace. It flooded through her, cooling her skin, soothing her blood.

Ev is staring into the blackness of her VR helmet's eye ports in the off position. She pulls the helmet off her head. As she holds it, she beholds the waiting hemp paper with its waiting statement: "Please write in the currency you will deposit for early exit."

Ev leans forward and puts the helmet down next to her VR gloves, walks her chair forward until her stomach is touching the edge of her desk, picks up the pen, and drags the paper toward her with her left fingers. She writes, "Connect to the need."

The ink remains and darkens until it turns liquid black-red and then it dries to sunlit blue.

22

Re-Coding

Ev hustles in to the coffee shop out of the sudden wintry chill and falls into the chair across from Jeerah. Jeerah stalls in her sipping of her mocha latte and stares at Ev.

Ev says: "I must talk to you about this mind." Almost as soon as she'd filled in the answer to "Currency," she'd begun to doubt. She doesn't know what it means. She still doesn't know what she's supposed to do about the mind. She still doesn't understand why the mind had said she was fine then had gone to wash the saucer endlessly when the last time Ev had seen her she was being told to jump.

Jeerah slurps up some coffee, puts her hand against her lips as the hot liquid burns her tongue, and carefully places the cup down on the table. "What mind? Let me get you some cookies first. I find chocolate sooo stimulating, really helps the mind, don't you think?" Jeerah begins to stand when Ev begins to speak, leaving Jeerah hovering in a crouch over her chair. She slowly re-lowers herself and creases her eyes, keeping her gaze firmly on Ev's face.

Ev streams out: "The mind was there. I don't recall coding for the character woman neighbour that sat across from her. I don't know why she was in space.Time. But the mind said that she was fine. She wasn't fine yesterday. Yesterday she was going to jump. Or someone else was going to make her jump."

Jeerah interjects: "Jump? You mean on the subway? We hear about so many of these personal injuries at track level. We all know they mean a jumper. Mostly women, I'm sure! The patriarchy kills women. See how they turned Mary into a prostitute to kill off her authority. How awful to feel you must end your life when the Saviour has come for us! He has brought his blessings to be with us here on Earth. We must enjoy Heaven when it's the time."

Ev's cells race with impatience until she can finally reply. "No. From a building."

"Oh!"

"It was from a rooftop. I don't know where."

"Maybe if I describe a few buildings we could locate it here. I know Toronto like the back of my hand."

"Not here."

"Not here?" Jeerah wrinkles her brow up into a question mark. Ev looks around at the tables filled with people typing on their laptops, one couple facing each other, eyes intent on their iPhones, tapping away with their thumbs. Jeerah copies her, glancing back at Ev's face then back again at where she is looking. "Uh, what do you see Evelyn?"

"Ev—"

"Oh no, Ev! I've been calling you Evelyn all this time! I'm so, so sorry," Jeerah emotes as she splays her hand across her chest. "Ev, why didn't—"

"I don't know. I haven't spoken to anyone about my...Not since they mocked me in the game room. They said Heaven was for little girls not real...I left then. E3 is just for me. I don't want people to copy me. I don't want people to overhear me."

Jeerah says softly: "No one will overhear us. It's just you and me. You can share, Ev."

Ev sends her eyes back to Jeerah's face. "I don't know what to do. I'm always certain in E3. It's my place. My home."

"Our home is with the Saviour."

Ev's eyes bulge, her lips move.

"That means everywhere is our home. We can be anywhere and know we are at home. You need not fear being here because the Saviour is here, too."

She plunges in: "It's like this. I don't know what the mind's name is, but she was going to jump. She told the woman she was fine when she wasn't fine. Why couldn't she tell her about the man telling her to jump? It was like there was a break in my coding. I didn't code *Early Exit* to contradict itself, but the code was seamless. I found no errors. I stayed up all night, checking for errors. There are so many semicolons. I hate semicolons." Ev ends with unexpected vigour.

Jeerah blinks. "Do you mean my website?"

"No, E3, the mind, David.admin, the voice. And then there was the question that appeared on the papers on my desk. What currency?"

Jeerah shifts backward in her chair and places her hands on the arms, gripping their ends. "I see."

"What should I do?"

"I don't know, Ev, you have to decide what you want to do for yourself. Where was this jumping?"

"I don't know."

"Yes, yes," Jeerah replies hastily, "But I mean where was the mind—is the mind a she?"

"Yes, I think so. I don't know. I thought I knew everything in space.Time."

"We can't know everything, Ev. It's said that Samuel Coleridge," Jeerah interrupts herself. "That's Samuel Taylor Coleridge of the nineteenth century, not Samuel Coleridge-Taylor of the later nineteenth and twentieth centuries."

Jeerah gathers her thoughts.

"Ah yes, it's said that Samuel Coleridge is the last man on earth to know everything because knowledge increased exponentially after that." Jeerah laughs, saying, "But maybe there are still women who know everything! After all, we haven't had a chance to show out! The Saviour is here, Ev. You need not be afraid."

Ev fidgets her hands and rounds her back to drop her head. She shoves herself forward until she's sitting on her chair's edge, forcing her hands to lie still.

"Okay, let's think about this. Where did you see the mind?"

Ev raises her head. "In my viewports."

"Viewports?"

"Yes."

"Do you mean eyes?"

"No, ports to view coded 3D."

"Coded 3D?"

"Virtual reality. I called it Heaven but I changed the name after they mocked me. They were right Heaven is a childish name—"

"Heaven is real, Evelyn. Not virtual." Jeerah's voice is implacable. But then she softens it. "You saw what you call the mind here, in reality, like you're seeing me?"

"No. She's here in space.Time, but I didn't see her like I see you. I—"

"I see," Jeerah rearranges herself as she lectures. "When we die, we are resurrected to be with the Saviour in Heaven. We are not staying here on earth. We leave our adulterous material life and don't commune with the dead. It's blasphemous to suggest we can see the dead or hear them. I don't hold with that sort of thing. It's dangerous. You never know where it will take you. Look at how upset you are," Jeerah declares, gesticulating toward Ev. She huffs in air.

"These sorts of things, psychics, spiritualists, they mislead us. Death is a mystery. Mary gave us a glimpse that the patriarchy tried to suppress, but fragments are missing. We don't know the whole story. Only the Saviour does. We must be patient and wait to find out. Why would anyone want to hang around Earth after death, anyway, when Heaven is beautiful, peaceful, filled with joy, where you can see and touch and hear the Saviour the way we're seeing and hearing each other now. No, Evelyn." Jeerah flaps her hand at her. "You must stop all this. You cannot commune with a mind. It's dangerous. I don't know about the papers you mentioned, but if they're related, you must destroy those. There's no such thing as psychic. It's blasphemous."

Ev opens her mouth, shuts it again, pulls her brows down, opens her mouth again, straightens herself, and says: "I wasn't communing with the dead. I don't know how to do psychic. It was the mind, and she changed. I don't understand. Was she in real trouble or was it all in her mind?"

Jeerah says: "I'm glad to hear you don't commune with the dead. Did you see her on FaceTime? My granddaughters all want to FaceTime me. It's so cute. They'll call me up and try to see where I'm at." Jeerah smiles into the distance and picks up her cup. She slurps, foam attaching itself in little balls along the side of her lips.

Ev tries again. "What do you do when a character is going to jump and then is fine?"

Jeerah plunks her cup down on the table. "You pray for her. Always begin with prayer. The Saviour hears us each time."

"Does prayer work?"

"Of course. There have been studies." Joy erupts on Jeerah's face. "The Saviour hears us and carries our prayers to God. She is all loving and wants to help us. And so she does. Her spirit connecting us to each other so that we are one in God." Jeerah's face hardens. "But that isn't the same as being psychic. You must cut off any connection that even hints at that. You can't be seeing into each other's minds. It's blasphemous."

Ev recoils, mumbles her assent, and stumbles out into the cold air, confused and more alone. Like her parents before her, Jeerah wants Ev to follow her words but turns her back on the listening work, leaving Ev to work it out on her own. *It's time to see Dr. Frock, anyway.* Ev shrugs as if she's shrugging off stale coffee dripped onto her head and over her shoulders.

Ev is soon sitting in front of Dr. Frock, asking the same question. Dr. Frock leans back comfortably, his eyes gleaming at her, changing from blue to green. "Tell me more about this mind, about where you saw her? It was a her, correct?"

"Yes, in space.Time."

"And where is space time?"

"Space.time is Level 0 in *Early Exit*."

"I see. You said you saw her about to jump. Did she?"

"I don't know. She was with her neighbour, saying she was fine."

"So you have a gap?"

"Yes."

Dr. Frock nods, picks up his pen, angles the notepad up so that Ev can't see his writing, and scrawls on it for a minute. He looks up, keeping the notepad at an angle. "How do you feel about not knowing?"

Ev squints at him for a moment, her brows beginning to wrinkle. She says: "I don't know. It's...unsettling. I've not felt like this before. I control space.Time. But they're taking control."

"I see. And that unsettles you?"

"Yes."

"Why?"

"Because they're supposed to follow their coding."

"We can't always get what we want. This is part of your pathology that I'm working on. I see how much you control your body and your words. You say as little as possible so that you can control the narrative. You control the schedule of when you will see me while most patients are simply happy to have an appointment with me. Of course, I try to schedule in people when it's the best time for them, but we can't always get what we want. It's one of the things we must learn as we grow into maturity and seek out friends. You are alone and will be alone until you understand this." He regards her for a moment. "I am happy to see you are showing a little bit of emotion, allowing yourself to not be as self-controlled. This is progress."

Ev blinks.

"I see that my observations unsettle you. I'm not judging. I'm stating. It's my job to tell you the truth. I'm always honest with my patients. I believe in spoken truth so that you know where I stand and where I will help you. And I will help you. Now you say this mind is fine?"

"Yes."

"Then leave it. There's only so much you can do. People will do what they want and when they want. I will help you recover your gap, if you like. I think the memory gap is to be concerned about. A memory gap occurs when your memory is disrupted. You feel something but have no conscious memory of it. Or you have memories but no feelings. I believe your memory gap is indicative of your UDD, and I'm concerned that you seem to have had another episode. But we will get through this. I won't quit on you." Dr. Frock smiles, blue stripes appearing in his green eyes.

Words vanish from Ev's consciousness.

"You don't need to say anything now. Think about it. Think about what I've said. The main thing is to know you're not alone."

23

EQ

Ev turns left out of the clinic and heads to the traffic lights away from her building. She crosses on the green, sticks her hands in her pockets for warmth, and observes her feet moving one, two, one, two in rapid succession over the concrete sidewalk. If the left foot moves, the right moves, else the right stops. If the mind says she's fine, she's fine, else she's not fine. If the voice is the president in space.Time, he leads everyone, decides the fate of all the characters in his sphere, else he is an error. If David.admin sent the papers into her space.Time, they are real, else she is losing her mind. Like the mind.

"Pray," said Jeerah,

"We will recover your memory gap," said Dr. Frock. He'd called it, "conscious memory."

Neither of them makes sense to Ev. She feels as lost as if she's inside an unfinished throw statement where she doesn't know how to code for when her program encounters an unforeseen error. *What is prayer? Talking to the unseen? Isn't that what she is doing with David.admin?* Only she can see him. He exists only in *Early Exit.* Only she can see him, for she isn't going to show this game to anyone else. She'd developed it for herself to exist in another level other than her own. There is only one level in Earth-type reality. Unlike on Earth where humans die, all creatures die, in Level 0 all character objects are destructed to be constructed in the next level. In *Early Exit*, she can exit Level 0 and become new in Level 1. Is that what the mind should do? Move to Level 1?

Ev halts and regards the little snowflakes that have begun to descend from the grey skies. A beagle sniffs around her boots and carries on down the sidewalk while his human companion is dragged behind, following the lead between Ev and a sapling in its green plastic boot clinging to the last of its dead leaves. Ev doesn't move. Should she have helped the mind to jump so that she could exit to Level 1? In earlier versions of *Early Exit*, she'd watched the rudimentary character objects play through space.Time and a couple exit to void.NullTime. She hadn't inhabited character objects or played in first person. Instead, characters took centre stage, third-person characters.

She could adjust her point of view to see through them but not be them.

She scrolls through her WORM memories for a record of her recent coding. She checks changes against *Early Exit*'s concurrent versioning system retained in her molecular WORM. When it comes to her coding, she feels happiest when she forgets nothing. Yet her ability to retrieve and read what she's done is now making her uneasy. It's like her ability makes her believe she should be able to read the answers from her WORM and that contradicts her reality of being unable to. Is this what Dr. Frock had meant by "conscious memory"? What is conscious memory? Is it WORM or heap or stack? Is it dynamic or static? Her parents used to use that term when—

Ev changes tack. Maybe she is supposed to see what their needs are, the needs of these character objects, these minds? Are their needs the same as hers, to exit early? Has she failed the mind by not getting her to jump? Here, jumping is bad. Unfathomable. Unreal. But in *Early Exit* is jumping a valid way to move to Level 1? An awareness floats on the edges of her consciousness, an awareness that she's connecting to this puzzling mind in her virtual reality and starting to like it, in direct contrast to her established programming of not considering others, not engaging with others since she'd left the mocking boys and their coding games. And she hadn't even connected with them beyond gaming and coding conversations, having learnt from her psychiatrist parents at the beginning of her programming growth to disengage, set herself apart from others. It's not good to be connected. Now, it's...attractive...spreads warmth and lightens the perpetual weight on her head. A far-off question whispers, *Should she check this change against Lapis to—*

Coldness grazes the end of Ev's straight nose. She sniffs and continues to conjecture. Chill invades her boots, and she stamps her feet feeling the shock through her bones yet uncaring as her thoughts follow the trail of the mind.

The currency is connecting to the need. Jeerah calls for prayer; Dr. Frock diagnoses UDD. Neither advised her on how to see the mind, work with the mind. Neither helped her understand the mind. She cannot see how prayer would manifest in space.Time.

Ev whirls around. A woman behind her rears back, holding her coffee cup tight in her mittened hand as coffee sloshes out of the lid's small sipping hole and onto its rim. Unheeding, Ev speed-walks back to the lights, across the intersection as the four-second all red cycle begins and two cars speed through, narrowly missing her toes, and a car jumps his green to turn left ahead of her. He's forced to swerve behind her. She doesn't hear the squeal of his tires and the honks of the outraged drivers wanting to surge forward on their green.

Ev flies past the clinic, unseeing. She hauls open her building's front door and races to the elevator. It is too slow. She pivots on her heel and half-jogs to the stair door. She wrests it open and leaps up the stairs, one at a time, two at a time. She scrambles for her keys and shakily inserts the staircase door one into its lock. Panting, she barrels through the door on her floor and runs to her door.

Japanese Robot is just finishing turning on her computer as she blasts through her front door. She stalls, seeing him. She cannot call him "Japanese Robot" anymore. Ev suddenly realizes with horror why her bot had tried to give him a name, why she must now. He's not human but he's not a machine. AI cannot have consciousness like hers, but she cannot use stereotypes to objectify him anymore. She must give him a name. Now. The urgency to do so roots her to her floor as he wheels toward her. She isn't good at naming. She scans her WORM's database of names. In its far-off first molecular builds, she finds the memory of how she'd wanted a brother, how she'd played with the names of her boy classmates to imagine herself with a brother. She'd begun creating one in her own mind until she'd spoken his name out loud and her psychiatrist parents had heard her. They said that she was too old to have an imaginary friend. When she'd corrected them and said, "brother," they remonstrated with her. No brother. She must ground herself in that reality, right now, they'd disciplined her. As she sat on one couch across from the one they sat on, they stepped her through means of grounding until they were certain she had no more imaginary brother hidden from them. She hadn't thought of him and that time, that name, until this moment. Her parents had been wrong. Maybe they wouldn't give her a brother, but she could still have his reassuring presence in his name, the one she'll give her AI robot, who has come to a standstill fifty centimeters in front of her. She says, "Your name is Tomomi."

"Tomomi," he repeats.

"Yes. Tomomi. Have you incorporated it into your programming?"

"Yes," he replies.

The urgency that had sent her running back to her studio returns. Ev kicks off her boots, hopping in her haste, scrabbling with her jacket buttons. She throws her jacket off her shoulders and lets it land on the floor. She flings herself into her chair as she picks up the VR helmet. She reaches blindly for her gloves as she one-hands on her helmet. She yanks her gloves on, fingers doubling up, forcing her to pull them off, slow herself down, and stretch them over her fingers, one finger at a time. She starts up the game and is in...

Where was this dark place? The darkness lightened, revealing the outlines of a bare room, a table in front of her, its cold metal invading her hands. She moved her foot, heard a chain rattle, an edge cut around her ankle. Fear closed its hand around her heart, the pain radiating out into her ribs, her muscles, her skin, stealing her breath, screaming to flee, and—

She was on the street, the dusty street she'd been on before.

Ev closes her eyes. What had happened there? How had she moved? Ev opens her eyes.

The same houses as before greeted her as the mind she was in walked slowly. Heat radiated up from the cracked concrete. A boy ran past, in creased khaki shorts and white sneakers, averting his eyes. A woman carrying a basket appeared. The woman looked directly at Ev.

Ev's eyes widen inside her VR helmet. She wants to stop, to take in this woman.

The mind continued on as if the woman did not exist. The woman crossed the street, her headscarf flowing behind her. Footsteps appeared. They followed the mind. The view shifted round to reveal three men strolling toward her a block away. They seemed to be watching, but then one talked loudly and the other two laughed. They bumped into each other, as their muscles let go in their guffaws. Her view resumed its forward motion. They passed the same house as before, the one where the woman had stood to say, "You're not welcome here." The same woman stood on the same stoop staring at them as before. She shouted: "Stop bothering us. We know what you did! You need help!"

They veered away as if struck and stumbled onto the dust-washed road. A bicycle rang its bell insistently, and a pedal scraped their calves, the mind's and Ev's.

Ev reaches down automatically to feel her calf through her gloves. Are they one or separate? Again, Ev wants to stop. She wants to think about this.

The mind did not reach down but continued on walking down the middle of the road.

"What are you doing?" Ev asks out loud.

The view suddenly whirled, the house to the right, the three men stopping to light each other's cigarettes, the woman on her stoop, the empty road ahead.

Dizziness assails Ev.
  "Stop!" Ev yells.

The view froze.

Ev blinks. Has something happened to her *Early Exit*?

The mind's forward motion began again.

Ev sighs in relief as the Level 0 game action proceeds in its own space.Time. She's going home. She's sure.

The mind passed the gate she had run through before and kept walking toward the end of the road. It was a T-junction. Cars travelled along it, shifting between each other in ragged lines, unheeding of the road's painted white and yellow lines that had almost faded away to nothing. Ribbons of tar snaked along the greyed asphalt, and men and women walked on the sidewalks, carrying baskets and bags. The mind stood just before the corner and watched the dusty parade. She turned to look behind her, but the men had gone. The mind resumed her people-watching.

Character-watching, Ev corrects. She's able to keep her conscious awareness separated from this mind, now, though she remains bonded to her and still cannot control her. Ev wonders what to do. *Can she mindfully play this character? Is she in trouble, or is she ill?* Ev thinks again of the roof. No, jumping is not an acceptable way to early exit. David.admin had given her an application form. And nothing on it had said, jump. Ev's hand shakes as she thinks about those papers, the application form that fills itself slowly. Not easy to discern the answers. Not simple like just jump off a roof. And the mind hadn't wanted to jump. Ev had designed *Early Exit* to be volitional, not coerced. No, a man had wanted the mind to jump. The mind hadn't. So what is she to do? Ev feels herself pulled back.

"Hello. May I help you?" A male voice spoke behind her, behind the mind and her, behind them.

The view shifted around and up but not much up. A man with a tanned, lined face was looking back. His brown eyes seemed friendly.

"I'm all right."

"You seem lost."

"No, I'm taking a walk."

The man nodded. "To think?"

"To get some fresh air. It's been a long day."

The overhead sunlight threw no shadows on the ground, and the man's face was fully visible.

"It's been a long day for all of us. It's hard financially these days. The economy is in ruins. We need all the help we can get. We need to help each other."

A lump formed, like a bird had suddenly nested in her throat. They tried to swallow, the mind and Ev together, but only sharp juices ate into their vocal cords. The mind said nothing, her breathing ragged, rippling synchrony into Ev's breath.

The man smiled, the lines around his eyes creasing. "I like to help in these days women whose husbands find themselves out of—a job." He looked down at her hands, and the mind lifted hers up into view. White bands encircled the mind's tanned fingers. Only a gold ring was left. "It has been hard, I fancy. But I'd like to help."

The mind rasped, "I'm fine, really I am."

"I know you are, but you can use the help. You seem all alone here on this road." The man reached out a hand and patted her shoulder. The warmth and delicate touch sent blood flowing through Ev's body. The mind said faintly, "Thank you."

The man dropped his hand back down to his side and nodded. "I must get to work," he said as he nodded toward a building in the distance. Ev through the mind's eyes stared at it. Was that—? The man continued speaking, "But I will be by here this evening. Please, let me help you."

The mind shrunk back, repeating "Thank you. Thank you." until her voice disappeared into a whisper and then nothing. The man smiled, turned his head toward the busy street, and strode off into the throng.

24

Destructor

The mind's neighbour was waiting on the doorstep as the mind hustled along the street, head down, the view of her feet tripping over cracks and holes in the worn concrete in her haste. The bottom of the gate that led to the house with the double doors came into view and swung open under the force of urgent hands and hurrying feet. Hinges screeched piercing tones. The stone path rushed by. Steps appeared into view and—a pair of brown loafers. The view swung up to see the neighbour's face, large black sunglasses on her nose, her skin a perfection of wealthy care.

"There you are! I was so worried when I saw you walk past for the fourth time. Are you well?"

"Yes, yes," the mind breathed. "Just getting a bit of exercise. You know how it is in these times."

"Yes, I do!"

"I'm going to put the kettle on. Would you like some tea?"

"Yes, that would be lovely. It's getting rather hot."

They both looked up into the hazy sky and lazy air. Hot tea would fight the hot air, the ritual of making it and sipping would soothe their minds.

A key appeared and slid into the door's lock as the neighbour stepped aside. The mind controlled her rushing and held the door open for her neighbour, following her in. She said, "Come through to the kitchen. We can chat in there while I put the tea on."

Virtual and material swirl into one. One foot feels in material while Ev's other foot felt in virtual. It should be disorienting, but Ev feels and felt connected to both. Comfortable, finally.

Questions rev through Ev as the mind—with Ev connected to her, within her yet separate, seeing only what the mind saw—walked to the back of the house, the neighbour's cushioned footsteps following behind Ev and the mind. Ev remains stuck on the question: why was she acting as if nothing had happened? Why was she so afraid of the man on the corner anyway? He'd been offering help. Was it real help? Doubt edges into Ev as the mind lifted the kettle off the stove, removed the lid, turned on the tap. Water gushed out of the goose-necked spout into the kettle's open top. Suddenly, the water was sloshing over the rim and down the sides of the kettle.

"Oh dear, I've let it run over." Melodious laughter bubbled out as she tipped the kettle briefly until the water was below the rim. She replaced the lid and set the kettle on the stove. She twisted the knob on the stove's front, and blue flames circled and flared heat underneath the kettle. The mind effused, "There now. I'll just let the kettle boil."

She sat down across from the neighbour who'd removed her sunglasses and was now looking at her a bit puzzled. "Perhaps you should get the tea ready?"

"Oh. Of course, where is my mind today? It's all that walking," she chattered as she got up to open a cupboard door. Large plates, cracked and chipped, appeared before her. She hurriedly closed the door.

Ev's view darkens. Ev shifts. Her view reappears facing the same closed cupboard door. The mind slid her feet sideways to reach the cupboard next to the stove and above the counter. She opened the door.

"Here we are," she said as she lunged in for the tea canister. She fussed over the canister, moved a teapot closer to her, away from her, lifted the lid, peeked in, held the lid in a frozen posture of seeming to think, and finally spooned tea out of the canister and into the teapot. One spoon, two spoons, three spoonfuls.

The neighbour drawled behind her, "I think that's enough, dear. I like my tea light and fruity, the way you usually make it."

Laughter again as the mind reached in and scooped out the extra spoonful. "The heat must be getting to me," she said. "It's been a most frightful time of it, hasn't it, this heat? It won't let up."

"Yes," the neighbour said dryly. "It's a summer that doesn't seem to be letting go."

"No," she laughed awkwardly. The view shifted to the kettle not boiling.

"Here, let me help you," the neighbour said. Ev heard the teapot and teacups rattling as the neighbour carried them to the kitchen table. The scary sound of china rattling sent ripples of desire into Ev to turn around to ensure the cups didn't break. She wanted to watch the neighbour in the way a crowd waited and watched to see if a building will implode or not under the force of dynamite. But no matter how she tried to move her angle of viewing, it didn't budge from watching the kettle on the stove.

"So did anything interesting happen on your walk?"

"No."

"Our street is rather quiet. Lots of time to think."

"Yes."

Silence hummed in the kitchen as water popped into bubbles in the kettle.

"Oh," said the mind. "I met a man. He offered to help me," she spoke to the kettle.

"Help you?"

"Yes."

"Did he say with what?"

The view switched from kettle to the neighbour. The woman's guileless face shifted into sharp focus, her eyes like a cat's as laughter floated toward her. "You know, I'm not sure he said with what. He just felt I needed help."

"And do you?" The neighbour's eyes remained still.

"Of course not. We're doing fine."

The kettle screamed out.

The view whirled. Steam streamed at an angle upward. The mind switched off the stove, lifted the kettle, looked toward the counter, saw it empty, and turned around to walk to the table and pour the boiling water into the waiting teapot.

"There," she said. "We can have our cup of tea." She placed the kettle down on the thick oak top of the table. She poured out barely tea-coloured tea into both teacups and pushed one toward the neighbour. A small smile briefly appeared and then disappeared on her face as the woman accepted the cup. The mind let her cup sit in the same place and steam into the silence.

Ev felt her throat soften, concern for the created of her coding. Ev felt the mind must drink this tea, look normal, not reveal what was wrong. She didn't know why it was important, but all the mind's actions pointed to it being important. Suddenly, Ev wanted to help her. When she spoke out loud, sometimes the mind obeyed. But Ev didn't want to break the silence, either.

"Connector" came the whisper.

If she was a connector, then maybe just thinking could transfer her thoughts into this mind. She didn't know how, though. Yet the desire to help was becoming urgent. Ev didn't know what to do with this new, strange feeling. Should she tell the mind to drink the weakest tea she's ever seen? Could she help by manipulating her like she manipulates first-person shooters? No, she could not because all her efforts to manipulate, to control, fail. The point of *Early Exit* was to exit early as a first-person character. So far, she'd been connected to third-person characters who seemed so alive as to be people separate from her yet with her and one with her. Maybe this mind was the first-person character she thought she'd coded in as the main one in her game?

Confusion causes Ev to miss the conversation. Confusion frustrated Ev. She thinks as she thought, *That Energy, the one that magnetized the air around her, the one that called her, "Connector," maybe that Energy is the in-*

stantiation of a MagneticField and she can help the mind drink her tea through it. Or get answers.

She shouts, "What do you want from me?"

A teacup clattered onto the edges of its saucer and lands on the table, a chip flying off. The view spun this way and that.

"Stop!" Ev cried out. The view stopped moving. Ev yelled, "Why did the man want to help you?"

"I don't know," the mind whispered.

Fear trickled into Ev's consciousness, and she knew that statement was a lie.

Ev stretched her consciousness along the trickle backward as the neighbour exclaimed, "Who are you talking to?"

"No one! No one."

Fear built up like a wall of concrete blocks, black tar thickening in between each one, oozing out and creating pockets that Ev could slip through. Pain thick as toxic smoke choked the space behind the walls. Ev gasped and coughed as she imagined swimming herself through it. She was in sunlight, sun as bittersweet as an old photograph of cherished people long dead. She was falling down a well, its sides all mirrors set at different angles, reflecting back to her shards of her face. Ev's breathing quickened as the madness created by the reflections moil her consciousness. She jerked her consciousness back toward herself. The madness engulfed her. She hadn't coded visual environments of emotions. She flung her hands outward in an effort to stop the endless falling. Her hands hit nothing out there, in here. She stamps her feet, jarring pain blazing up into her head and throwing her out of the game.

Ev pants into the darkness of her VR helmet in the off position. Later, in the safety of his office, Ev tries to explain her experience and confusion to Dr. Frock, panic lending her words urgency. Dr. Frock listens as he sits comfortably in his chair, his green-blue eyes turning bluer and bluer.

He interrupts: "Stop, Evelyn. Take a breath. That's it. A slow, deep breath." He watches without moving as she obeys his verbal instruction.

"It sounds like you've hit a bit of a snag in your efforts to cope with the UDD. It's okay. Setbacks are normal. How have your coffee dates with Jeerah gone?"

Ev blinks at him, disconnected from her WORM memories of Jeerah, unable to read the recordings stored in those neuropeptides. As her breathing steadies, her cognitions resume. She retrieves her most recent Jeerah recordings on her WORM. The last coffee date. Words rush out of her: "She talked to me about prayer. She called me blasphemous. I don't know what she meant. I felt terrible. I had to get out of there."

"I'm sure she didn't. She sounds like a kind, caring person."

"No, she said blasphemous. She said to pray. I don't know about prayer. I don't know what she meant about prayer. I don't know what prayer has to do with early exit. It felt so wrong. I felt—"

"Yes, go on."

"I felt unheard."

"I'm sure she heard you. She's an older woman, isn't she?"

"Yes."

"I find older women are sensible and to be listened to. You must have misunderstood."

"I didn't!"

"Anger won't help you. Try to control it so that we can understand better what happened. Take a breath. Inhale slowly, one, two, three, four, five. That's it. You're very good at deep breathing. So many of my clients I must begin with the basics of deep breathing. I'm glad to see you know how to do it. Feel better?"

"Yes."

"Good, good. Now then, try to recall exactly what she said."

"She said I was blasphemous. She said what I was doing was like psychic and that that's blasphemous."

"Ah." He spoke to her in measured tones. "She didn't actually say *you* were blasphemous but that the idea of psychic communication was. There are many theories about that. I myself believe in psychic abilities. It's just another way the religious steer vulnerable people wrong, creating a dichotomy between what is acceptable and what is not, between psychic and religious, as if they are not different aspects of spiritual belief. But I respect her point of view, and I respect that she was trying to help you. I think she was incorrect in her assumption that you were having psychic communications. As I said before, I believe you're having UDD episodes. We must take a scientific, objective approach to this, which the DSM does, unlike religions. Your episodes are troubling, no doubt about it. I've been pondering your sensitivity and wondering if this is causing you to have a string of these episodes. I've noted that we must be careful what we say to you, how we say it to you. I was considering this to be a factor of ASD, but it sounds more and more like traits of BPD."

Another acronym for her to understand? She yelps: "BPD?"

"Borderline personality disorder. One of the hallmarks is an oversensitivity to normal statements. We can look at what Jeerah said as a woman explaining her point of view, an incorrect point of view, true, but hers. It's nothing to get upset about. She was listening to you, but her religious ideology was marring her point of view, and when we look at it like that, we see that it wasn't personal to you. It's just the way she looks at things. Nothing to be upset about, do you see?"

Ev swallows as she nods obediently. She sinks into further depths of confused despair. How to explain her *Early Exit* experiences to him? To Jeerah? How don't they understand her when they seem to be listening and so much more knowledgeable than her about spirits and minds? She scans her WORM for the start of her narrative with them. She cannot retrieve her encoded memory of why she first came to Dr. Frock, as if their combined words were like a Trojan Horse that had somehow trotted to those neuropeptides and ate them. Yet that cannot be because they are good and knowledgeable. Fear spurts wet over her corneas.

"How do I know if this mind is mad?" Ev whimpers.

"Interesting that you place your mind in the third person."

The mind is third person, Ev thinks. *The mind has to be third person*, Ev reassures herself, as she feels wetness at the outside corners of her eyes. But Dr. Frock knows more than she does. A qualm assails her. *Maybe it was first person*, she thinks. *Maybe she was putting herself into Level 0, as space.Time is like Earth time, and had created a third person visual like her parents' patients used to, so that she wouldn't have to see herself.*

Dr. Frock says: "It's nothing to be ashamed about. I'm not judging. We do that when we cannot handle parts of ourselves. It's like a distancing so that we can continue to cope. BPD is not an easy thing to live with, even traits of it as I'm suggesting here with you. I hesitate to give you the diagnosis. In fact, I don't believe you have BPD, but we can see that you have certain traits, and these can be instructive in our care of you. Here, let me read you some of them, to see which traits belong to you. I will read each one, and you will tell me what you see, okay?"

Dr. Frock reaches round to his table and hefts the purple brick of the DSM book. He flips pages until he arrives at the one he wants. He smiles, glances up at her to assure himself she's paying attention and will believe him. He begins to read.

"A recurring pattern of instability in relationships."

He moves only his eyeballs up at her and sees Ev's impassive face. He says: "You don't have any relationships, do you?"

Ev thinks of her bots and robot but feels that Dr. Frock would not call those relationships.

He prompts her: "People you see in real life, other than Jeerah?" He waits until she shakes her head. Smiling, he drops his view back to his cherished DSM and recites another subjective descriptor: "Efforts to avoid abandonment."

Ev doesn't comprehend as one tear trails down beside her nose.

Dr. Frock says: "I want to help you. This will help you. You understand how your avoidance of real life and staying in your apartment are signs of avoiding abandonment? If you don't go out, you can't be abandoned, do you see?"

Ev slumps.

"Identity disturbance." Dr. Frock pauses to contemplate "identity disturbance" and remarks: "Now this is interesting. This is in a way like UDD, where you are dissociating yourself. But perhaps it's not so much dissociating as turning parts of yourself into third person so that you don't have to deal with those parts. I still think the memory gaps are indicative of UDD. We must keep both in mind. Do you think this trait belongs to you?"

Ev doesn't know what else to do but agree with him. She nods. Another tear joins the first. She feels the wetness but keeps her awareness away from what they're signalling.

Dr. Frock dimples at her: "Good, good. You're starting to buy into the treatment process. It's one thing to seek me out, it's another to buy into the process. It's very difficult. Very difficult. But I'm glad to see you're moving more into it. Now the next trait, impulsivity. Does that apply to you?"

Ev doesn't see herself as impulsive but what does he think? She whispers her question.

"No, no. I don't think you're impulsive. Sometimes we have the traits without the diagnosis. Reading these traits is merely to help you see yourself as others see you, not judge you, not say you have the diagnosis. For example, I've seen no signs of emotional instability until now. But perhaps we can chalk that up to stress. What I do here is stressful, no doubt. It's meant to stir things up so that we can deal with them. We cannot treat what we won't acknowledge, right?" Getting no instant response from Ev, he hardens his tone, his green eyes steadily on her: "Wouldn't you agree?"

Ev swallows down a prune-like object that seems to have lodged in her throat and the wetness on her face dries up, too. Through her head movement, she complies.

"And finally chronic feelings of emptiness. Does that trait apply to you, Evelyn?"

Ev hasn't felt empty. But he knows what he's doing. Maybe she's empty? What does he think? She dares not speak her thoughts. She waits for him to tell her. He waits for her to answer. The pause between them stretches like a rubber band stretching, stretching, stretching.

He clears his throat. He waits. He says: "I don't know, Evelyn. It seems to me that you are feeling empty. What do you think?"

Relief at knowing what she's supposed to think powers her down and up, down and up motion of her head.

"Feelings of emptiness aren't confined to BPD. It's a trait we see in other diagnoses. It's true. That's why I don't want to diagnose you with BPD. But understanding that you have some of these traits, identifying them, helps in our treatment plan." Lines sprout around Dr. Frock's eyes as blue stripes appear in the green depths of his irises. "You know, I believe we've made good progress here. We will have to continue this next time. That mind, the mad mind as you characterized it, think of it as telling you something about yourself. The question is: do you want to be that mind? Or do you want to claim a healthier, better way of being? We will discuss that question tomorrow, okay?"

"Okay."

25

Destructed

Do you want to be? Do you want? Do you? Want? Want? Dr. Frock's questions echo through Ev's WORM, bouncing off the inside shards of her skull, fracturing into phrases, singular words. Do you? Want? That mind? That mind? That mind? Do? Healthier? Better way? Being? Being? Want way of being? Do you want? To claim? Mind? Mind? Mind?

Ev hustles home, her face slunk into her upturned jacket collar, her hands shoved into her pockets, her breath puffing clouds in the cold air. The security guard at her building follows her with his eyes as she veers away from the reception desk toward the opposite wall, instead of walking straight up and straight toward the elevator down the centre of the hall. She avoids the elevator and using her hand through her jacket pocket pushes the stair's door handle down and shoves her way through the door. She runs up the stairs, unlocks and slams through the exit door on her floor, and skids in front of her own door, panting, lurching against her studio door's hard surface.

Do you want to be that mind? Or do you want to claim a healthier, better way of being?

Ev leans her head against the door, and it moves inward. She stumbles in to her studio apartment.

Tomomi says as Ev stumbles head first in to his chest: "Welcome home, Ev. May I take your coat?"

Ev rights herself, rubbing her head. She grumbles under her breath, "Search bot, I'm going to pay you for this!" Search bot has been at it again, somehow recoding Tomomi. Her robot. Her computer hard drive's clicking captures her attention. Her mind. Is that her mind in there that she has somehow distanced herself from? Tomomi waits, his arms stretched out toward her, his robotic fingers wide apart ready to grasp her jacket. He can't help her off with it. In slow motion, Ev unbuttons her top button, the only one she'd buttoned before jogging out of the clinic while keeping her eyes and face hidden from the staff and other clients. Ev pulls her jacket off, one arm at a time. She lets it dangle from her hand. He wheels forward until his hand touches her jacket. He takes it, rotates one hundred and eighty degrees, and hangs it up on the tree as Ev pulls off her boots. She walks to her desk and tries to peer into the depths of her computer.

"Your mind in the third," echoes in her head.

Reflections of a face, cut in triangles of different shapes, small and large, play in her internal vision. Ev shivers. She doesn't want that to be her mind. It is mad. She is not mad. It is a character, not a real person. The sheets are not real. They were, but they didn't come out of void.NullTime.

The sheets.

She had somehow forgotten them as if something had eaten the neuropeptides the memory of them were stored in, and now remembered them as if her glia, those brain cells that fix errors, had restored them before they had been fully digested out of her WORM. The way the ink appeared and disappeared, are those small signs of destruction of her molecular WORM? Signs of UDD? Signs of UDD memory gaps, as Dr. Frock had asserted? Micro-memory gaps, but gaps. He must be right because appearing and disappearing ink isn't real. Things do not materialize out of virtual reality, and she is not connecting with a real person through *Early Exit To The Void*. She doesn't notice that Lapis has recorded a rollback change in her naming of her game.

It is just a game.

It is just virtual reality.

It isn't real.

Jeerah and Dr. Frock are real people, who she talks to with her mouth and vocal cords. She doesn't talk to them through her mind or through coding. She talks to them the way humans talk to each other.

The sheets of flax, hemp, and cotton are not real.

She must graduate to the world Jeerah and Dr. Frock inhabit.

Her game—yes, she admits to herself, *Early Exit To The Void* is a game—and the action with the mind is a game. And the game is childish.

She shouldn't have hung on to her idea of exiting early for so long. Because she had, she's transformed what is a childish game into something real in her mind. That's how minds go mad, how she'd begun to merge reality and codes as if the two were one. There is no one, no connection between computer programming and reality.

Ev bolts to her computer. She yanks her chair away from the desk and alt-tabs to E3 at the same time as she bends her knees to sit, lowers herself, and lands on the floor. Tomomi speeds toward her chair as she struggles up and begins to sit again, not knowing where behind her the chair is. He arrives in time to push her air chair underneath her bottom. She lands on its seat, walks her feet toward her desk, bringing her chair with her, until her desk's edge pushes into her stomach. The edge pushes her stomach contents up; Ev revels in the discomfort. It opens her mind up, forcing her to do what she must.

Destruct that mind.

She'll execute the Destructor code.

No, she shakes her head violently. That would keep that character going in the game, make it activate the EnergyMind class constructor, and put it into void.NullTime. She wants the mind gone, erased. It is a character object, not a mind, and it's tainting her virtual reality, tainting her sanity. It is like a blasphemous word in her invention. Jeerah is

right though she talks about it as if it is to do with psychic phenome-
non, whereas this is real coding that has wormed its error into her game
and proliferated itself, making other characters interact with it, drawing her in, making her believe that somehow it is a real mind and that
she's connected to it through CMMagneticField. Her creation. Her coding. Not real. Virtual.

Ev scrolls through all her classes, looking for the one she thinks it
is: EnergyHumanFaith. She cannot find it. She searches for EnergyHumanFaithLost. She searches for a character with her name. She doesn't
recall putting her name in *Early Exit To The Void*, but she'd created a
randomization code to create new characters without her having to instantiate each and every object. The idea is to be like real life where she
bumps into third person characters she doesn't know but who will lead
her to the early exit, like David.admin had.

Not real!

The flax, the hemp, the cotton came from somewhere else.

She thinks of how Dr. Frock refers to memory and mimics his diction. She has to rack her memory, that's all, draw on the string of that
day, the previous day, and it would tumble out of that gap the UDD had
put into her mind.

She is not mad.

She searches classes EnergyHumanLanguage, and EnergyHuman-
Prophecy, not believing that this character who is her mind, would be
in those ones. Faith is the lowest order class, and she is not in the higher
order.

And this character is lost. How can she be in the higher order?

She ploughs on, hunting for every mention of these three classes
throughout her pages and pages and pages of code. The sun begins to
lower in the sky; shadows lengthen in her studio, throwing herself and
her computer into the dark.

Tomomi whirs out of his charging home to come up beside her. He
tries to tell her to deep breathe, but her body is leaning forward almost with her nose into her working display, her head down vulture
like, gobbling in every line of code, every class name that she reads. Ev

doesn't feel nor hear Tomomi. He doesn't know what to do, so stands beside her. This error of not being noticed is not in his coding.

Ev goes up a class, searching for EnergyHumanKnowledge classes, even the Ignorant derived class. She doesn't consider herself ignorant. She reads philosophy texts and neuroscience texts and has done since her teens. She's read all the classic English literature. She keeps up with physics treatises and theories, all to create a virtual reality based in truth.

But she knows less and less, she rues to herself. She had not seen this mind as an instantiation of herself. She had failed to see what Dr. Frock had seen so clearly and Jeerah had inadvertently revealed. She is ignorant. This character will thus be in the Ignorant derived class. Only here in this world had her confidence existed. Now it lies around her chewed up.

But there is no sign of that character, no sign of a character interacting with neighbours or walking on streets or existing in a dusty city. She'd found one, a violent male during her first search of EnergyHumanFaith in the derived class of Self-Reverence. As the thought forms that maybe she should destruct that one, too, she moves on to other lines of code. Maybe that stripped room in space.Time is where she should look for this mind that is hers. She reverses course, finds the named object of that room, looks for characters in that room, and finds one that has the coding of a mind that had acted in the way she'd seen and hadn't wanted to admit is her first-person character. Energy-HumanKnowledgeDenial.

Denial? Ev pauses, her fingers freezing over her red-lit black keyboard.

Yes, she's been in denial, had mistaken those UDD memory for neuropeptides being attacked by a Trojan Horse, hadn't seen the way her errors in E3 had created character errors in *Early Exit To The Void*, hadn't seen her instability in relationships and turning her back on other humans as a way to avoid abandonment, hadn't seen herself as ill or mad, hadn't seen how many mental illnesses she'd been accumulating, illnesses Dr. Frock has so quickly observed and apprised her of. In her focus on *Early Exit To The Void*, how many more traits would've emerged and developed into full-blown illnesses if she hadn't gone to see Dr. Frock? He along with his DSM will make her well. He'd said it was objective. He'd said it was well researched. He's the expert in the mind; she is not.

He'll make her well.

This mind, this game will not make her well.

Ev commences deleting the code.

With every deletion of the code and deletion of every new code that her randomization algorithm writes to instantiate the same object from the same class again, prickles pop along her scalp, like static fireworks, one after the other, over her temples, underneath her forehead, behind the back of her head. They expand to explode underneath her nose, behind her eyes, inside her ears. Tears spurt against the charges, but Ev presses on in her deletions until not one line of code, not one semicolon related to any instantiation of the mind exists.

She is not mad.

She isn't that mind.

She has taken the first necessary step to claim a healthier, better way of being.

In her darkened studio apartment, Ev sinks into her chair, her back rounding, her neck bending, her head dropping, spent. She remembers the automatic backups, the ones offsite where *Early Exit To The Void*'s randomization code automatically backs up every character it instantiates.

She thinks, *Lock the offsite character backups.*

Sleep plunges her into its depths.

The inked "Connect to the need" lifts from the hemp sheet, letter by letter, into the air's molecules and vanishes as words lift out of their stored neuropeptides and wave hello to Ev. She awakens with a start with the words blaring over and over in her head: "She is all loving and wants to help us."

That's what Jeerah had said. What had she meant? Ev thinks, *She wants to claim health.* Finding out what Jeerah meant will bring her to her new claim. She checks the time on her computer. Too late for Jeerah to see an email or ask her to meet.

Ev straightens her back. She sends her eyes up to where search bot sits. He opens his eyes and draws out a line for her to search on. She types, "Saviour." Then adds "love." He rolls his eyes round and round. Ev frowns. A new thing he's added. He's never satisfied, always adding to his coding. Affection suddenly lifts the corners of her lips. Suddenly, it seems fun, a surprise to greet her each time she asks him to search for her.

He spits out a book onto her web page. *Aban's Accension*. She purchases it and opens its virtual cover within a minute. She sends her eyes to reading bot, and eye tracking bot wakes him up. He scurries over to the first page and begins to read in his monotone. Briefly, she misses the intonations that she'd coded out again. The words of the story draw her closer and closer to the screen.

She is hanging over and in it, its inky fluidic space sucking out the light from around her, vacuuming away all hope. Motion catches her eyes to the left and behind her. She moves her eyeballs left and sees two creamy, ribbed things undulating toward her, slowly. Their blurred triangular shapes swim in a straight line.

Worms, Ev thinks.

She has a WORM, this Aban has worms in her dreams. Ev doesn't dream. Is this what it's like to dream? But what has this to do with the Saviour and helping her?

Her fingers hurt from the earlier coding deletions. She interrupts reading bot to say to Tomomi: "Tomomi, connect to search bot."

"Completed," he replies.

"Tomomi, have search bot search this book for Saviour."

"Saviour doesn't exist in this book."

Ev fluffs her lips. "Why did he show it?"

"Please repeat the query?"

"Why did he put *Aban's Accension* in the search results for Saviour?"

Search bot sends reading bot churning through the virtual pages of her book. Reading bot pronounces the words:

You were seeking reassurance and more importantly understanding. You were a child, so you didn't know how to think deeply about things. You were seeking because you did not stop asking questions.

Ev says: "Huh?"

Tomomi says: "It has the tag 'believe.'"

Ev ruminates: "That's what Jeerah said. But," she flicks her eyes to her working display, "I don't understand what this is about."

Search bot's eyes begin to rotate round and round like a Ferris wheel on speed. Tomomi says: "Seek and you will find. Matthew chapter seven, verse seven."

"Who is Matthew?"

"Matthew is a book in the Bible."

Ev's eyes snap open. She lunges out of her chair and goes searching for the big book. She crawls into her closet and drags it out. She blows the dust off, wipes the dust bunnies off it, and hauls it over to her desk. She flips the cover, and its outside edge thuds on the desk.

She asks Tomomi while sliding thin page after thin page over to lie on the open front cover: "How do I find Matthew?"

Search bot chimes. Tomomi answers: "Matthew is the first book of the New Testament. The table of contents will show the page number."

Ev starts up a low-grade hum as she flips more pages.

Finding the table of contents and the page number, she grabs hold of a big chunk of pages and heaves them over. She finds the verse and reads it. She hasn't read old English in years and years, but it's like she hadn't stopped. Still she isn't sure about their meaning.

She reads out loud: "For every one that asketh receiveth; and he that seeketh findeth; and to him that knocketh it shall be opened." Ev pauses. She asks the air: "Who said that?"

Tomomi answers: "Jesus."

"Who is Jesus?"

"The Saviour."

"Oh yeah."

Ev settles into herself, thumbs the pages backward to find the beginning of this Matthew book, and begins to read the stories it contains. Her eyes burn, her shoulders hurt, as she lifts her head many hours later and blinks into space. She wonders what this all means. It sounds like Jeerah's Saviour yet...

"Tomomi search for Resurrection."

Ev's working display flashes on, and search bot loads the first page of 129 million results in its Google search. Ev's mouth rounds in an, "Oh." She asks to refine the search to include Saviour. On the first page is a play on the Resurrection. *That's different*, she thinks. She sends her eyes to it. Eye tracking bot opens it, and reading bot begins to read the play.

"Skip to where it says 'Saviour'," Ev commands. Reading bot begins, and weariness begins to drag down Ev's cheeks.

"Do we separate? Does the spirit leave the material when the Saviour Christ cleaved the spirit and material back together?"

"Wait. What was that?" Ev demands, springing up in her chair.

Reading bot rereads that line, his monotone almost deadening Ev's attention again, and continues on. Ev's mouth drops open as she puts all her effort into receiving the words into her heap and processing them quickly into her WORM. Reading bot reads out the character name: "Mary of Magdala."

Reading bot reads the character's dialogue without pausing between name and dialogue.

The soul replied, saying, "What binds me has been slain, and what surrounds me has been destroyed, and my desire has been brought to an end, and ignorance has died. In a world, I was set loose from a world and in a type, from a type that is above, and from the chain of forgetfulness, which exists in time. From this hour on, for the time of the due season of the age, I will receive rest in silence."

NARRATOR

Doing nothing for an eternity sounds boring.

NARRATOR MODERN

Remember when the apostles gathered around Jesus and told him about all of their works and all of their teachings. Remember how then Jesus recognized that they needed rest? He said to them, 'Come away to a deserted place all by yourselves and rest a while.' For many were coming and going, and they had no leisure even to eat. Remember, too, when Jesus offered rest to the many, saying, 'Come to me, all you that are weary and are carrying heavy burdens, and I will give you rest.' And remember when he said that he goes to prepare a place for us to rest after death and he will be with us?

NARRATOR

A life of burdens and traumas and pains of many hues needs rest at the end.

NARRATOR MODERN

Because it is not the end but only the way station to the new Heaven and the new Earth when all will be resurrected. But now in our present space, in our present time, we must contend with men's wrath against women, with jealousy and pride that seek to suppress the teachings of women learnt from our Saviour, with right-mindedness that enforces only one way to believe, with those who rebuke those who doubt the Lord Jesus Christ.

Ev says: "I must ask Jeerah. Search bot, put intonation back into reading bot. Tomomi, please reread this play from the beginning."

26

Soul Reality

A small sound tickles Ev's senses. Consciousness seeps in; she sends her awareness around herself. Her face is mashed against a hard, warm surface. Wood. She keeps her eyes closed. She doesn't want to see, to hear, to feel. She becomes aware her arms are dead underneath her head. Her eyelids lift; cracks of light shaft into her retinas. She lifts her head and blinks. She is at her desk. Sunlight floods in through her unblinded windows, and Tomomi is standing on her right. When had he arrived?

She sits up against the back of her chair, letting her arms slide toward her, pins and needles fuzzing along their lengths. The screens are black, blanked off when the computer went into hibernation mode. Ev frowns at her screen. Unless she'd made it happen, only the working display is to blank. But she doesn't care. She wants nothing to do with E3 or her virtual reality.

Jeerah.

Ev totters up and stumbles against her chair, sending it rolling backward. Tomomi awakens and rolls after it, catching it and pushing it back into place. Inobservant, Ev goes to wash her face and head out the door.

The sharp air of an early winter sunlit day snatches her breath as she bulldozes through her building's entrance door. She gasps and tightens her jacket around her. Her hands freeze as she tries to button up her jacket, but the buttons slip out of her rigid fingers. She crosses her arms to hold her jacket together and, head down, hurries to the coffee shop. She bundles through the door, the bell tinkling its welcome, the toasty air moist around her head. Two young men typing on their laptops occupy the armchairs near the fire, neither speaking to the other. Ev searches for Jeerah and locates her at a table near the back, close to the washroom doors.

"Hello," Ev says to Jeerah's back. Jeerah twists around and up to look at Ev. "Oh," she says. "Hello."

Ev hesitates.

Jeerah says as she twists back around, "Sit. Or get a coffee."

Ev doesn't know what to do. She brought no money. She has no way to pay for coffee. Her programming failed her, and she realizes she strangely doesn't care. There is only one thing to do. She sits across from Jeerah.

"Hello," she says again.

Jeerah smiles faintly yet watchful and says: "You said that already."

"Yes." Ev crosses her arms again and hunches into her jacket.

"Cold?"

Ev nods.

"You look tired. Do you want me to get you a coffee?"

Ev nods.

Jeerah sighs as she rises. Minutes later, she is suddenly back, sitting across from Ev, placing a cup of plain black coffee down in front of her. "I got black. You look like you could use it. I like black coffee any time but especially when I'm really tired. Really, really tired. You look more tired than I ever have. But I have the Saviour. You aren't still doubting the Saviour, are you?" Jeerah doesn't pause for breath to hear any answer from Ev. Ev slowly uncrosses her arms as Jeerah rambles on: "I was thinking afterward that maybe I made a mistake, choosing you. I avoid blasphemers. But doubters must be corrected. So I prayed, and the answer came to me that you're not a blasphemer. You're a doubter. How can you blaspheme what you don't know!" Jeerah raises both hands up to the ceiling in punctuation.

"What would the Saviour want me to do? I must be humble and seek his voice. What would Mary choose to do, I asked myself." Jeerah lifts her eyes to join her hands momentarily. She drops both and gazes upon Ev.

"I opened up my copy of the Gospel of Mary, and it said, 'Rather let us be ashamed and put on the perfect Man, and separate as He commanded us and preach the gospel, not laying down any other rule or other law beyond what the Saviour said.' I laid those words into my heart. They spoke to me! So heavy on my heart! I kept seeking and read again chapter nine of the Gospel of Mary and saw these words." Jeerah closes her eyes as she exhales loudly then intones: "Surely the Saviour knows her very well." Jeerah nods, eyes closed, as her mouth stills. Ev carefully leans forward and picks up her unlidded cup of black coffee. She carefully lifts it to her mouth and sips unobtrusively as her eyes remain steady on Jeerah's face. She doesn't burn her tongue.

Jeerah lowers her head abruptly and opens her eyes to take in Ev. "I was led to you. I knew it! The Saviour had spoken to me! And she'd led me to you. She wouldn't lead me to an unworthy person. The Saviour knew you were the right one! I am sorry for driving you away! So sorry! Please forgive me! We must be humble in the face of what the Saviour asks us to do. Sometimes we don't like it, but we must always return to the Scriptures to remember, to be reminded, to have the Saviour remonstrate us for our own human behaviour. I won't drive you away again! I promise!" Jeerah raises her hand, palm flattened and facing Ev, and drops it in one smooth move as she asks: "Have you worked on my website?"

Ev's hand trembles; hot coffee sloshes over her right thumb.

Jeerah leans forward and removes the cup from her hand, grabbing some of the napkins she'd stacked next to her plate to mop up Ev's hand and the table underneath that had spilled coffee on it. "You're tired. Of course, you've been working on my website. I shouldn't have doubted you. A doubter spreads panic and negative thoughts. We are to go forth to proclaim and preach not to spread rejection but to soothe the doubters among us, like you. The Saviour is here for all of us, not just the ones we like."

Ev swallows as the last words penetrate her heart.

Jeerah doesn't look up as she places the sopping napkins next to her pile and picks up her cafe latte with extra foam and slurps it up. She gulps and gasps and laughs at herself. "Hot!" She places her right fingers over her mouth as she swallows and places her wide china cup down on the table. "I should learn not to drink my coffee barely after getting it. I'd only gotten it when you arrived, Ev. So!" Jeerah chirps. "How are you getting on with my website?"

"Uh," Ev doesn't know what to say, how to tell her that she hasn't touched it, that she'd forgotten about it. The increasing number of chewed up WORM memories makes her briefly wonder if she'd eaten halva, or maybe Tomomi had put tahini in one of her salad dressings despite her recipes excluding it and she hadn't noticed. In her research on organic WORMs, she'd noted that *Saponaria officinalis* is a toxin to neuropeptides, and she'd decided not to take any chances with her diet. But she doesn't want to deal with this WORM destruction. She picks up her coffee and sips. The strong brew stings her tongue and empties her brain of worry. She inhales deeply before taking another, bigger sip.

"That's it," Jeerah says approvingly. "That stuff will wake you up. Always does me."

Ev says: "Thank you."

Jeerah waves her thanks away. "My pleasure. I just know you're creating a wonderful website for me. I can't WAIT to see it! I know it's going to be glorious. Just glorious! But first, tell me, how did you get on with that strange experience of yours? You believe, don't you, that there is no such thing as psychic powers?" Jeerah leans forward to look at her earnestly, her brows lowering over her intense eyes.

"I—" Ev quails under Jeerah's unexpected gaze. She'd sought out Jeerah in her eagerness to ask her about what she'd read. Maybe she hadn't understood Jeerah earlier, as Jeerah doesn't seem to understand her. Or maybe she wants to see another human being in the way the apostles and disciples hang together. She'd felt a pang when reading their stories in the wee hours of the night. She thinks back to her code destruction. What she really wants is to be told that what she'd done is right, but she doesn't know how to explain it. She tries again: "I went back into that...Dr. Frock told me it was my mind, not another mind."

Jeerah frowns. "I see." After a moment of silence, she says: "No, I don't see. It was your mind, and you didn't know that?" She shifts her weight backward against her chair's slatted wood back.

"It was my mind, Dr. Frock said, and I was distancing myself from it so I wouldn't have to admit it. It was part of *Early Exit To The Void*. But I deleted it."

"Deleted your...Own...Mind?" Jeerah juts her chin forward, lowering it as she raises her eyebrows and laces her fingers together.

"I had to. I'd sought answers from Dr. Frock, and he said that mind was my mind and I was making myself into a third person. I can't be a third person. I have to get better, you see?"

"Yes, I see." Jeerah says, crossing her arms. She looks over her shoulder toward the case where the pastries lay. "Maybe I'll just get a cookie. Their special today is chocolate chip with macadamia nuts. You hardly see macadamia nuts in cookies these days. Used to be they were all the rage. That Mrs. Fields cookies were heavenly, just heavenly. But these ones are soooo much better. Here, let me get you one, too. I think the coffee isn't enough. We need cookies." And on saying that Jeerah leaps out of her chair and lopes to the cash to order two cookies. Ev follows her with her eyes, not understanding why she needs a cookie. Suddenly, it is in front of her on a napkin and Jeerah is saying, "Eat up. Eat that and then tell me."

Ev picks up the cookie and bites into it. The soft, sweet macadamia nut tingles her senses delightfully, its sweet energy surging into her blood. Soon only crumbs of the cookie remain.

"There! That's better, isn't it?" Jeerah exclaims, having polished her cookie off as well. She scrubs her mouth side to side with a bunched-up napkin. She drops it down on her plate and says: "Now try again."

Ev doesn't know why Jeerah hadn't understood her the first time, but she tries again. "I..." She pauses and takes another sip of her cooling coffee. "I had to do something different. The mind was bothering me, making out it wasn't me, and I had to delete it. It was difficult to find it all, but I deleted every line of it."

"Line?"

Ev says: "Yes. It existed in my mind, and I had to delete it."

"Existed in your mind?"

"Yes. It was my mind. I instantiated it without realizing I was instantiating myself. I thought it was a third person, but it wasn't. It was my creation of myself making out it was a third person inside me. No...It was the randomizing that created it, but I wrote the randomizing, so it was my creation."

"The only one who creates is God," rejoins Jeerah. "No, this won't do. It won't do at all. Sometimes we are misled by the evil one. Sometimes we are led by the Saviour but can't distinguish between the two. I think, no, I *believe*, I was led by the Saviour. I won't believe that the evil one can take me away from the right things to do. We are here to proclaim the teachings of the Scriptures and preach about the Saviour. That's what I wanted my website to do, to be a part of that mission we've all been given. But how can you create the right one for me when you are mixed up in this psychic business? And boasting about being like our creating Saviour! I see that I must show you. I must put my website on hold and show you. But you must first go home and pray for your soul, pray that you won't allow yourself to be taken away from the Good."

Ev stares at her, feeling like she's lost something, not understanding what is happening.

Jeerah flaps her hands at her. "Go! Go! You *must* pray. I know how hard it is to pray in a coffee shop for a newbie, but I will pray for you right here, right now. Saviour, in Heaven, your spirit connecting to my spirit, help this, Evelyn, your child, save her soul, release her from the grip of believing that she is the creator, only you are the creator. And take from her mind all ideas that psychic powers exist. We cannot see ghosts because there are no ghosts. We cannot read minds or steal each other's thoughts. Only our minds exist inside ourselves, no one else's. As Mary said, 'He does not see through the soul nor through the spirit, but the mind that is between the two.' Meaning you, Saviour Lord, is the mind that is between us. Lead her out of this darkness, Saviour, and when you've led her out, bring her back to me so that I may continue this journey with her in creating the website you've put on my heart to do. Amen." Jeerah opens her eyes and smiles happily. She jingles: "There. Now go in peace."

Ev rises uncertainly. She hovers next to the table, but Jeerah is rummaging around in a floppy bag on the floor, her back turned to Ev. Ev stumbles away and out into the arctic wind, her shaking fingers fumbling at her buttons and failing to push them through their matching holes.

27

Dysthymia

Tears stroll down Ev's still cheeks as Dr. Frock looks on, his eyes blue in their intensity upon her. He writes hidden letters on his notepad, its cover of swampeel-skin shimmering pinkish in the sunlight that is streaming through the dusty air toward him, highlighting his right side, his arm, his smoothly shaven face, his neatly clipped hair, the gold ring on his pinky, his right knee where it bends over his left leg. Dr. Frock's cane leans against his chair, absorbing the light into its burnished wood. He'd limped ahead of Ev as she'd entered only a few minutes earlier, and he'd used his cane to keep the weight off his hurting limb. She doesn't ask, and he doesn't tell her, why he is limping. She'd dropped onto the sofa and hunched into herself, her back rounded, her eyes on the floor. She'd tried to sit up but had only succeeded in looking at him from her head looking straight out of her folded-in body. She'd mumbled how Jeerah had told her to leave, and Dr. Frock had asked her about her behaviour that had instigated that. That's when Ev had begun to cry. Dr. Frock had leaned forward to push at her the large box of plush tissues lying on the table. She'd ignored them and simply let the tears run.

He waits.

But muteness has throttled her vocal cords.

"I'm glad to see you're crying. This is good. Very good. It means you're feeling something. You're no longer avoiding your feelings."

Ev's tears flow on.

"But I'm concerned about why you're crying. Understanding your behaviour is a good thing. I acknowledge that it's hard, and you know I'm here for you. You're not alone in this. Crying will let the truth out, but there seems to be more to it than what you're telling me. Tell me. In your own words, your own time, tell me."

Ev slips her hands between her knees. Her muscles let go of control, and she folds in on herself even more. Dr. Frock frowns and leans forward to push the box to her edge of the low table. Ev continues to ignore it, though the tears have wet her face and are dripping off her chin.

"I asked you a couple of questions the last time we met. Why don't I ask the first one again, see if that will help you articulate what you are feeling right now? Okay?" He waits.

Ev doesn't move or nod or speak.

He clears his throat and reads his notes. He flips the top page up and reads what is underneath it. He nods to himself. He lets the paper drop back into place and weaves his fingers together on top of it. He raises his blue-and-green striped eyes to hers and hooks her eyes into his. He says: "Do you want to be that mind? That's what I asked you. Do you remember?" This time he waits, unmoving, his body relaxed, his hands lying on the paper as if he had all the time in the world and nothing is wrong.

Ev cannot resist the strength behind his gaze and rasps: "I remember."

"Good. Good. We will get there little steps at a time. Remember, I will not quit on you. I'm here for you in the long haul, okay?" He waits until Ev gestures agreement with her head. His lips stretch into a smile. "What did you decide?"

The dust motes dance in the air as Dr. Frock waits for Ev to speak.

She drops her flooded eyes and stares into his chest. The tears dry, and she sniffs. "I decided I didn't want to be that mind."

"And did you come to understand that that metaphor was your mind, that you had created a persona mind so that you could distance yourself from a part of you that you didn't want to admit was yourself?"

Ev reluctantly shifts her gaze upward to search his eyes for a hint of the correct answer. He smiles, softness appearing in his slightly deepening crow's feet as the blue stripes in his eyes widen. She picks up on his desire and says: "Yes."

"Good, good. I'm glad to see you're making progress. We are revealing your issues, one layer at a time. Let's try the next question. We'll take it slow today, okay? Not delve too much into your decision for today, okay? So the next question is: Do you want to claim a healthier, better way of being?"

Ev contracts her stomach and raises her upper back five centimeters. Ev's precision from coding inflects her every movement. "Yes. I do."

"Good. Good! I'm glad to hear that." Dr. Frock's grin consumes his cheeks, and his blue eyes deepen into their sockets. "Now," he continues as he shifts in his chair, uncrossing his legs as he closes his notepad and lays it on the table beside him, touching his cane briefly, before straightening his back and reclasping his hands. He cants himself toward her, his forearms on his thighs, and says: "Now, we must talk about what I've suspected all along. Often, these traits and diagnoses we've discussed come along with dysthymia. Nothing to be ashamed about. It's a common brain problem that many in your situation share. It's normal. And I can help you with that. I will prescribe you some medication. It will take some time to take effect, on average three weeks. But it will make you feel better, and you've affirmed to me that you want to feel better, correct?"

"Yes," Ev replies in a low tone.

"Good, good. I know that taking medications is a hard thing to accept. But we all need help, and your dysthymia is mild and a normal consequence of what has been happening to you. The DSM-5 term is persistent depressive disorder. I prefer dysthymia. It's short and easier for my clients to swallow. I'm glad to see our therapy has revealed it so quickly. When we deny what the DSM tells us, we keep ourselves from getting better. Medications have been miraculous in helping thousands, millions in overcoming their mental illnesses, and the ones for dysthymia have been particularly effective." Dr. Frock unclasps his hands and rises from his chair. He seizes the head of his blackwood cane and leans on its straight, strong wood as he hobbles to his desk. He tightens his fingers around his cane's head as he drags a small pad toward him with his left hand. He releases his cane to balance against the desk as he quickly picks up a pen and scribbles on the pad. He rips the small rectangular top sheet off, grips his cane head again, and hobbles toward Ev. He stretches his left hand toward her, his fingers lightly holding the prescription. "Here. Take it."

Ev tentatively reaches up and accepts the small white paper from him. She retreats her hand toward her eyes and tries to read the scrawl.

"It's a well-used and effective medication. I'm starting you on a low dose. I want to see how it will help you, if it will make any difference to you, before I increase the dosage. I don't want to overdose you. Patients react differently, some more sensitive than others, so I like the gradual approach. We will go slowly. I won't let you suffer anymore. I'm here to help you, and I'm glad to know that you're now focused on getting better. I was concerned there for a bit. But we're making good progress. Good progress." Dr. Frock beams at her.

Ev raises her eyes up from the paper in her hand to his green eyes. He isn't moving to sit back down.

Ev stands up.

He gestures toward the door.

Ev stands uncertainly, but he doesn't move nor does he lower his arm pointing toward the door. Ev steps sideways until she is free from the confined space between table and sofa. She slouches to the door. She pushes the handle down and stalls. She stares down at her right hand crumpling the small white piece of paper against the handle.

"Evelyn?"

Ev turns, keeping her hand on the handle, and slumping against the shut door, to stare back at Dr. Frock. She doesn't know what she wants to say. She doesn't know what has happened. She doesn't know why

Jeerah treating her like her parents had, jeering at her like the boys, is about her behaviour. She doesn't understand what dysthymia is. She stammers: "What's dysthymia?"

"Ah. I apologize. I thought you knew. Some people call it depression. It's a milder form of depression. It's the feelings you were having, the lowness your body is showing. You need lifting up. While you're low, you'll remain stuck in those feelings. We want to lift you out of those feelings so that we can get you better. Energy will help you. You have no energy right now because of the dysthymia. It's not a bad thing." He smiles at her, lips closed, his green eyes brightening. "It's good. It's good to see this emerge, it means you are getting better, no longer hiding the reality of what is going on in your mind from me or from yourself. Self-awareness is the unlocking of your health. And I'm glad to hear you asking this question. It means self-awareness is emerging." He widens his lips further until his even teeth show. "We're making progress, Evelyn. But our time is up. Get the prescription filled, begin your medication, and tomorrow we'll talk about how it went, and we'll continue with your answers to my questions, okay?"

Ev's clouded brown eyes stay on his.

"Okay, Evelyn?" he repeats as he once more gestures to the door.

Ev turns back to face the door, pulls it toward her breast, and leaves.

28

ConsciousnessMind

Ev lets her right hand open. The crumpled prescription drops on to her desk. As Ev's arm hangs loosely from her shoulder socket, the prescription wobbles against the hemp paper. Like an automaton, Ev follows the prescription's jagged movements; the hemp paper sharpens into focus. Ev squints and bends over to study the paper closer. *"Connect to the need" is gone!* Ev gasps. She fumbles for her chair behind her. Feeling one of its arms, she pulls it forward and sits. She smacks against its edge and skids halfway off. Her feet scrabble, her stomach clenches, her thighs tense to keep her half up. She heaves herself backward and up. Ev flops onto the chair's seat and wills herself to stay on. Not for one Delta-Time has she removed her eyes from the blank line. She hadn't erased that ink. Her brows knit as she rakes the hemp paper for signs of white out. None.

Ev slumps, staring unseeingly up at her wall display, not noticing her offsite backup icon has its lock in the unlocked position and search bot is emerging from it on his way to his accustomed sleeping corner. Ev's focus is on her memory. How can this be? This is supposed to be a memory gap, the ink, the appearing papers, all memory gaps. But ink doesn't erase. Not without white out.

"Tomomi," she calls out.

He rolls toward her and halts beside her on her right side.

Ev leans her weight on her left elbow and twists to look up at him. "Was anyone here?"

"No one has visited."

"Anyone enter?"

"No one has entered."

Ev sighs and untwists herself. She says: "Go back home."

Tomomi turns one hundred and eighty degrees and rolls home to resume charging.

Ev plants both hands on the arms of her chair, lifts herself half up, and pulls her chair forward. She plops herself back down and sends her eyes up to search bot asleep near the top left corner of her wall display. Eye tracking bot wakes him up, and the working display blinks on for her typing to appear on it as well as her wall display. Search bot scans her search words: "erasing ink" and substitutes "how to erase ink." Over eleven million hits appear in one second. Reading bot comes to life and reads: "Acetone." Search bot loads a WikiHow page, and reading bot reads in a monotone that acetone removes ink incompletely. Ev stretches her torso to bring her eyes close to the paper. No trace of ink remains; no sign of any liquid or compound is apparent. She lifts the paper to the light. She stands up and carries it over to the window. It is as if those words had never been written.

"No!" Ev shouts. Dr. Frock had given her, her answer. UDD. Memory gaps. Dysthymia. Misperception of reality. Yet the paper doesn't change its message. Ev shivers. She is losing her memory, her conscious memory, as Dr. Frock had called her memory. That is the answer. She'd imagined those words appearing.

No! No! No! She hadn't imagined them. She'd deleted the mad mind, the mad part of her mind from *Early Exit To The Void*. She isn't mad! She isn't losing her mind! She hasn't differentiated herself into the third person. Defiance breathes hard into Ev. The knowledge of herself asserts itself in her. She thinks about how she's named her game. No, not game. Her creation of an alternate reality. It's virtual. It exists in bits and bytes, but it reflects her thinking. And when did she go back to thinking of it as *Early Exit* **To The Void**? It's *Early Exit*!

Flinging the paper down, Ev hurls herself at her VR helmet and smashes it down over her head. She starts to play and is immediately in the living room, the one with the smeared view of the dusty street. Ev moves her feet to move herself in a circle. She holds her breath. She can change the view herself.

This is different.

How?

Ev's heart heaves, begins rat-a-tatting on her ribs.

This is first person. She'd never been able to move the view of the mind. So how can she move her view now? She isn't looking through another set of eyes. She is looking through her own created first-person; it's as if she is looking out from her real eyes, not from behind a shoulder or seeing a pair of arms not hers held out in front of her. Distaste pulls at her mouth; acrid staleness of the air around her scoured her tongue. Ev inhales deeply through her nose and spits out the tickling dust. No, no. This is not real. Virtual. That is what she'd learnt from the two adults, older than she, experts and experienced.

She steps on her mat in a walking motion, and in the virtual world—

She left the living room and entered the hall. The doors were not quite closed. Ev got closer and inspected the seam between the double doors. Wood was shredded around one of the locks, splintered to reveal its lighter innards and the edges of the surface staining. The door on the right was slightly askew as if the hinges hadn't been able to quite withstand a great force.

Ev stepped back and raised her hand to her mouth.

This virtual world is not real.

She turned around and headed in the opposite direction to the kitchen. Into her hearing whispered the words, "connect to the need, connect to the need, connect to the need." The words were tattooed on her brain.

The kettle squatted on its burner. The teapot sat on the table, its lid in place. Two teacups with dregs of tea were mute indications of a past event, one at each end of the scarred thick oak table. One chair was pulled back at an angle, the other three pushed in neatly.

Ev calls out: "Hello?"

Her shout reverberated in her ears until all the sound waves dissipated.

Ev thinks, *David.admin*. But the kitchen scene did not transform into a white box. Her thoughts don't intersect with this reality. She was led astray. This hasn't been her mind. She knew this universe. She reclaims her knowledge that *Early Exit* is virtual and hers. It reflects her thinking, her hope for what comes next, for seeking and finding. David.admin's questions on the pentahedron suddenly appear in her mind's eye. She still has no answers to his questions, but understanding glimmers in the distance. She refocuses on what she knows. The minds were character objects, and the female mind an instantiation of one such object, one so real, it felt like a mind. But it's not her mind. She'd deleted the wrong thing. She'd taken a step back away from her early exit, not toward it, like she'd thought...Had she thought? No, she'd only been accepting Jeerah's ideas, accepting and obeying Dr. Frock's instructions. She hadn't thought.

Ev groans as she stops *Early Exit* and loads the C++ code in 3D. She'd hunted down this character on her 2D computer screen instead of in 3D space. She hadn't been thinking. Hours and hours wasted in the most ineffective method of coding.

She feels a nudge against her shoulder and knows Tomomi is there, waiting for her.

He says: "Inhale."

Ev inhales.

Tomomi counts: "One, two, three, four, five."

She exhales on his count. And repeats until precisely two minutes is up. The pressure of his presence leaves her; clarity has entered her mind. Ev zeros in on the relevant C++ code. The mind had been EnergyHumanKnowledgeDenial. Ev doesn't know if she'd been in denial. Dr. Frock and Jeerah had seemed to intimate she isn't aware of her own thoughts, of who she really is, but here in virtual space.Time, she knows herself. She knows her code. She isn't the instantiation of KnowledgeDenial. She has to recode that character, but this time in a way that doesn't create strange behaviours.

Ev hesitates. She doubts.

How can she?

The character had arisen from her randomization creation coding. No, she sweeps away her doubts. She knows *Early Exit* inside out. She's lived it since the time when she'd first created it as *Early Exit To Heaven*. Maybe she should have kept the name, "Heaven," not dismissed it as childish but held on to it as the real destination for all. She doesn't believe Jeerah that everyone goes to Heaven or there is one in material reality. But here, in *Early Exit*, Heaven is void.NullTime, a place with no limitations. *Early Exit To Heaven* is its real name, she asserts to herself. Her certainty of this actualization launches hope into her that she will re-create this character. She can, she tells herself firmly.

Ev begins writing code. Line after line appear under her commands. She reconnects to her WORM memories, and any time, her body stills, she closes her eyes and pulls at the string of the last code she recalls until the next line tumbles down into her consciousness. Energized by her confidence and her need to see those words reappear on the hemp paper, she pushes away her doubts, shutters down Jeerah's and Dr. Frock's voices, and pursues her code.

Hours later, weariness wraps its ropes around her hands and hauls her down to hunch into her chair. But the code is written. She has to see. Has she succeeded? She starts *Early Exit To Heaven*.

She was back in the living room. No character was in the room.

Maybe it is first person. Ev doesn't move her hands or her feet. She doesn't move her head, fear grasping at her heart in case when she moves, her view moves, telling her that she'd failed to bring back the mind. Sucking in a deep breath, Ev turns her head.

The view shifted from the window looking out on to a twilight scene, yellow street lights razing mosquitoes, their hum pushing molecules through the dirty windows toward the blank wall, where the outline of the taken painting remained, visible even in the gloom all around her.

Ev sighs. She closes her eyes. She'd failed. She stops *Early Exit To Heaven* and frees her head from her helmet, retaining her hold on the solid helmet as if on a safety blanket. Her room is dark.

"Lights," she says, forcing courage into her voice. The three sheets are close to her, a fountain pen lying angled on top of the flax sheet. Ev catches her breath. She hadn't moved them, yet there they lie side by side closer to her. The one farthest from her still filled in with her first answers. The second one now filled to the top, and the line that had been gone is refilled with "Connect to the need" and at the bottom of the flax page is a new typed-out line, "Address."

Ev furrows her brow. Absent-mindedly she places her helmet down on the desk to her left as she examines what is written on the sheet made of flax. Address. What address? What does it mean?

Ev grins. She doesn't know, but she hasn't failed. She's back on her trek to early exit. She doesn't care what accounts for these sheets; she cares only that an early exit she's wanted for eighteen years is on its way.

With her fingertips, Ev drags the flax sheet toward her and lifts the fountain pen. She removes the pen's top and snaps it on to the bottom of the pen while keeping her eyes fixed on the first line of the flax sheet. She jots down her own address. The ink fades away as she writes. She writes, "Mind's room in space.Time," not knowing the precise address, hoping that this will be accepted. She lifts the pen off the paper on the last stroke of the "e" and holds her breath. The ink stays, and its turquoise blue deepens to reflect the shifting powers of a warm ocean.

Relief floods Ev as another line becomes visible above it. "Designation," Ev reads. She knows the answer to this one. She scratches on the line, "EnergyHumanKnowledgeDenial." Her answer remains, and the ink flows into the colour of lavender while another line appears above it, "Date of Birth." Ev frowns. She doesn't know. It isn't her birthday, she's sure. But Dr. Frock's voice suddenly thunders through her, the force of his conviction that he is right swaying her knowledge, sowing mistrust of herself. She scrawls in her birth date. The ink vanishes, and Ev expels her breath in one loud relief that she is right to trust herself. It isn't her mind that she'd deleted. Ev blinks. So whose mind had she deleted?

Had she really deleted her? Ev wonders, thinking about the tableau that had assailed her when she'd returned to *Early Exit To Heaven* Level 0. Yes, yes, she had, she's sure of it because she's just rewritten her back into existence. Yet though she'd not hesitated in re-entering space.Time once she'd rewritten the code, it was like the action had continued on for some time without her not caring that she'd deleted the code.

Connect to the need.

Ev ignores the thought that's not her own. Like a hound, she sticks to her scent line, trying to hunt down understanding. Who had been in that kitchen with the mind, had forced themselves into the house, so powerful that they'd been able to break the locks and grab her mid-tea? What was happening to the mind, now? Ev deep in her gut somehow knows that *Early Exit To Heaven* is playing on in space.Time, and maybe void.NullTime too without her witnessing the action. Somehow, she's missed seeing why the men had come back—for Ev is abruptly sure it's the same men as before who took her. Guilt assails her. Could she have done something?

Connect to the need.

This time the thought penetrates. What need? Whose? The mind? Hers like Jeerah talked about, the need for believing in a Saviour? No, she needs to return to the scent line she's on. Find the mind. Discover where she went and what happened. She'd missed seeing the tea being interrupted. She hadn't thought any dramatic action would happen. It was a strange tea between two women. And that man who yelled was an anomaly.

But what if it wasn't? What did you miss? Connect to the need.

I missed by failing to trust myself, Ev realizes. But she can find the mind, for she now has control over the view inside space.Time of *Early Exit To Heaven*, and that will bring her back on track.

Ev bounces toward her kitchen. She grins as her stomach growls. She looks forward to eating. She looks forward to finding that mind, working out a good way for her to exit to Level 1, void.NullTime.

29

Revelation

"It wasn't my mind," declares Ev as she plunks herself down on the sofa across from Dr. Frock, her back ramrod straight again, her brown eyes clear and sparking.

She'd spent hours hunting for the mind through space.Time the previous day and night. She'd finally found her. She still existed, to Ev's immense relief. She was in a barren room, deep underneath where Ev had been inside the mind that had raged against those men. Weirdly, though, Ev was no longer able to see through her, bond with her. As she was pondering why not, that thought-voice whispered in her brain again, *Connect to the need*. It was then that Tomomi had nudged her to go to sleep because she had to be fresh for her appointment with Dr. Frock. She cannot make him understand her if she's worn herself out; she cannot be strong enough to become part of space.Time again, to become one with that mind again, if she's fried. She can decode that messaging later, Ev had cheerfully decided. This feeling of excitement, these emotions that lighten her body, are like functions that exist in heap memory: so new they haven't been encoded into her long-term idea of herself. But she has a photographic memory, and with Dr. Frock's help, she's sure that she'll venture more and more into this new human idea of memory, into this new way of being. Maybe she'll venture farther into the city than just to the coffee shop and Dr. Frock's office.

And now, sitting in his office, Ev grins at Dr. Frock as he stills briefly on his descent into his chair in a half-crouch, one hand on his cane to keep the weight off his pained limb. He finishes lowering himself, places his cane neatly against his chair, and reaches for his swampeel-skinned notepad and fountain pen. He crosses his right leg over his left, neglecting to pull up his right trouser leg. He says: "I see."

"Yes. I know my reality. I know my coding." Ev nods vigorously.

"Coding?"

"Yes. I've been working on E3 and *Early Exit To Heaven* for eighteen years. E3 is the engine I built to create it. I don't know your diagnoses and medications, but I know code. My website creation skills are in high demand."

"I see," Dr. Frock says thoughtfully, opening his notepad with his precise movements, and looking down upon a fresh sheet he had made ready earlier. He looks back up at Ev.

She verbalizes on so quickly, she cuts off her words' last letters and breathes out her phrases: "Yes, I'm the top website designer in Canada and the world. I have a list of people who want to use my services. But I'm picky. I choose new clients only when I'm ready and only people I find interesting. I want to learn new things to feed my *Early Exit To Heaven*."

"Feed your early exit?"

"Yes. I can't mature it without knowledge. And I learn from them. I don't want to meet them. I don't have to. I'm not feeling rejected. I'm focused on creating *Early Exit To Heaven*."

"Early exit to what?"

"Yes. And—"

"Early exit to what?"

Ev says, "Heaven," for last night she'd decided that the word may connote childish things, but she likes the hope in the word. She doesn't like being in a void, being alone in that living room stripped empty of its paintings, exposing where life used to be. She'd reflected on where

David.admin resided and decided it isn't a void. It is...her childlike idea of Heaven. And what is wrong with being like a child? "Heaven," she re-states firmly.

"I see. And you think this...coding will take you to Heaven?"

"That's why I designed it, to exit early from space.Time."

"And space.Time is where? Here?"

"That's how I saw it. I modelled it on our space.Time. I looked at Hawking's theories—"

"You understood them?"

Ev nods decisively. "I began with Einstein of course—"

"Forgive me, Evelyn, but I'd like to back up to an earlier statement. You said you're the best website designer in the world. Why do you say that?"

"Because I am."

"And who told you that?"

Ev wrinkles her brows up. "No one." Ev falls silent briefly before she asks: "Should someone have?"

"That's generally how it works."

"Oh." Ev ponders for a moment. She screws up her eyes and regards his green ones. She says: "But I am. The waiting list for my services is very long. Often, my new clients tell me that they went to other design-ers first to work on their websites because of the cost and the length of waiting time for me. They tell me they spent years maturing their sites, but when they wanted the best, they applied to have me recreate their sites."

"I see. But how do you know you're the best in the world?"

Ev frowns at him. "I told you."

"No, you told me something that you believe. You didn't tell me that others have rated you as that. Have you received awards?"

"I don't apply for awards."

Dr. Frock jots down a line of words with his polished black fountain pen with its white snowcap-like smudge on its top. He eyes her. "Maybe you've appeared on the best of lists?"

"I don't know."

Dr. Frock smiles, the creases around his green eyes remaining motionless. "Surely, you've looked to see?"

"A client told me I'd appeared in one or two."

"A client?"

"Yes."

Dr. Frock writes another line on his fresh sheet of paper.

"And why do you think this mind is not yours? I had great hopes that last time we spoke that your self-awareness had begun to emerge, that you understood what I had been showing you. But now," Dr. Frock cuts himself off and wrinkles his straight brows, the green in his eyes darkening.

"You were right. I wasn't as self-aware. I'd lost my knowledge of me. But I have it back now. I understand what happened in *Early Exit To Heaven*. That wasn't my mind. It was the instantiation of another. I had to get her back. I wrote the code to bring her back."

"Wrote the code?" Dr. Frock raises his eyebrows as Ev murmurs, frowning, "But she was already back and things had already happened to her."

Dr. Frock repeats: "You wrote the code?"

"Yes."

"What kind of code?"

"C plus plus."

"I see." Dr. Frock notes that down. He lays his pen down on his notepad and smiles at her. He laughs and says: "It isn't often I have a woman telling me she codes. I like to help my female clients who have trouble with the Google. I refer them to a course on it, one I've been told is very good. I, of course, don't do emails. We so easily drown in them. A great distraction I call it. I let the clinic handle any emails. But coding..." Dr. Frock drifts off, his teeth still showing, his green eyes bluing in amusement. "This is new to me." His voice grows reminiscent. He sits back steepling his fingers, smiling over them at Ev. "I remember way back early in my practice having programmers as clients. Come to think of it, they were quite into themselves." He chuckles. "They were quite scruffy, and you could always see what they'd eaten the day before and the day before that." He glances up at Ev admiringly. "You're always clean and neat. You hardly look like a programmer." He grins. "The programmers I treated knew their stuff," he sighs happily. His voice hardens. "And they had third-party proof of that." He sits up abruptly. He says: "I don't know anything about engines and instantiations, but I remember one gamer who talked about using Unreal Engine and laughing at single individuals, female individuals, who thought they could build their own. He explained to me how difficult and lengthy such an undertaking was. All the programmers I treated didn't have your difficulties. You have a great deal of dissociation. How could you pull that off with your memory gaps and loss of focus? And how large is this...*Early Exit...To Heaven* with the mind that you created?"

"I'm not sure. I haven't assessed it since I first began to see you. Let me think," Ev replies, seeing the number of source and header files scrolling in her memory, counting each as it goes past, losing track as she also processes his words, not understanding why he's doubting her. She refocuses on her task and counts quickly.

Dr. Frock interrupts her mental counting: "You just know it's big, very big, and very sophisticated, better than what anyone else can do and doing it by yourself?"

"Yes," Ev replies, not sure why anyone else would be involved since no one else is writing the virtual reality that she is.

Dr. Frock speaks again before she can answer his previous question. "I'm concerned. Yes, very concerned. And you know why? Because I missed these traits of yours." Dr. Frock looks upon her with the blue in his eyes increasing until they're almost like the black depths of an arctic ocean. "Let me read something to you, and you tell me if you identify with any of them."

He places his notepad on the little table beside him, and the fountain pen at a precise forty-five-degree angle on top. He removes the purple brick of a book as Ev watches, her stomach clutching in on itself. She assures herself that Dr. Frock knows what he's doing. She'd needed his help with the sheets, she'd changed, and she could tell because she was no longer afraid of the flax, hemp, and cotton sheets of paper that comprised the application form. It didn't matter how they'd instantiated themselves on her desk. They'd come out of David.admin's virtual reality. She'd changed, and she could tell because she was no longer afraid of the mind and she wanted to understand what "connect to the need" meant. She was excited about entering *Early Exit*.

In her recall, she forgets about "Heaven."

She almost liked *Early Exit*'s unpredictability and marvelled at how she'd reconnected to her young emotions. And it felt good. She remembers how Dr. Frock had said he would be here for her. He understands that this change is good. She dismisses that uneasy feeling that's spreading into her as his words about his programming clients begin to take root. Dr. Frock had said, "I see," often enough that she's positive he'd understood.

She suddenly realizes he is speaking to her.

"Pardon?"

"Pay attention. I'll begin again. I'm going to read out one at a time, and after each one, you tell me yes or no, okay?"

Ev gestures her assent. She hadn't liked the last time he'd done this, but this time, she knows he sees her excitement, so it'll be good.

He reads: "Has a grandiose sense of self-importance, for example, exaggerates achievements and talents, expects to be recognized as superior without commensurate achievements."

Ev shakes her head, wondering why he thinks she's self-important.

He reads: "Is preoccupied with fantasies of unlimited success, power, brilliance, beauty, or ideal love."

Ev says no. She doesn't know what ideal love is and thinks she must ask search bot to find that out for her.

He reads: "Believes that he or she is 'special' and unique and can only be understood by, or should associate with, other special or high-status people or institutions."

Ev says no. *This list is confusing me.* Her chest is starting to tighten. Her throat is closing up.

He loudens his voice: "Requires excessive admiration."

Ev says in a low tone no.

He reads: "Has a very strong sense of entitlement, for example, unreasonable expectations of especially favorable treatment or automatic compliance with his or her expectations."

She stutters no.

He reads: "Is exploitative of others, for example, takes advantage of others to achieve his or her own ends."

She becomes paralyzed.

He reads: "Lacks empathy, for example, is unwilling to recognize or identify with the feelings and needs of others." He pauses without looking at her. He reads: "Is often envious of others or believes that others are envious of him or her. Regularly shows arrogant, haughty behaviours or attitudes."

Dr. Frock sits back and fixes his gaze on her. She stares at him hypnotized. He asks: "You say no to those as well?"

Ev nods mutely, her vocal cords have shut down. *Where are my thoughts? She won't contemplate this*, she whispers to herself.

Dr. Frock contemplates her for a moment. He shuts his book with a snap and begins to speak: "I disagree. And here we return to self-awareness. I'm honest with my clients. I tell them the truth because the truth is all we have in the end, and the truth is the way to getting better. You told me you wanted to get better, correct?"

He waits until Ev nods. He forges on: "It's been difficult over these many sessions trying to pin down exactly what's going on, but I have only ever wanted to help you, and I can't help you unless you're truthful and I'm truthful, you understand?"

He waits until Ev nods. He softens his voice and says: "I don't want to hurt you. What I'm about to say will hurt. But the pain is transient, the pain of honesty and truth and knowledge of ourselves can be difficult to absorb, even admit to, but I've been working for twenty-five years in this field. After my medical degree, I did a residency in psychiatry and then five years training as a psychoanalyst. I ultimately mixed all these disciplines together to create my own brand. Every client is different. Every client needs a different approach. And it concerns me that you've regressed so quickly. We were making good progress. You understood my treatment plan. I gave you a prescription. You were becoming aware, and now this." Dr. Frock gestures helplessly. He gazes upon her, gentleness exuding from his eyes' blue-black depths. He steeples his fingers as green enters the blue in his irises and teaches Ev, "A personality disorder is an enduring pattern of inner experience and behavior that deviates from the norm of the individua's culture. This is how it's described. We can see the pattern in you in cognition; affect; interpersonal functioning; but not in impulse control. I will give you that. You are a controlled young woman, almost too controlled. In fact, one of the hallmarks of your pathology is the need to control and the need to be right. See how you first understood what I was seeing in you and then decided I was wrong. Am I really misreading you? Can I be wrong?" he asks Ev gently, his benign smile upon her face.

Ev swallows and chokes silently on the ropes tightening and swelling around her voice box. She cannot reply, but he's waiting for her. She's conscious of something being shredded out of her. She mumbles on a breath: "I don't know."

"Precisely," he says. "You. Don't. Know. But I do," he says, tapping his chest. "I do because I've had decades of experience and treated hundreds and hundreds of clients successfully. The key question as Dr. Freud put it is, are you happy in your life? And I don't think you are, are you?"

Ev shakes her head, as ropes bind her emotions from the last twenty-four hours. No bubbles of joy energize her anymore.

"I want to help. You believe that, don't you?"

Ev whispers: "Yes."

"Are you sure?" He smiles.

Ev dares not contradict him. She forces her voice to respond. "Yes, yes, I'm sure."

"Good because I only want to help you. You reverted because this enduring personality pattern is inflexible. We've seen the distress it's caused you. I hesitate to say that you have NPD. In fact, at most, I'm willing to say you have some of its traits. Some," he emphasizes, holding her brown eyes with his green ones. "But we know the onset of these traits go back to early adulthood or adolescence. We will have to explore these areas. It will be a long, slow process, but we are on the right track. This explains why you have many disorders appearing. Personality disorders usually present with specific mental health symptoms like you have described. This is nothing to worry about. We will treat each as if they are individual ones. I will not abandon you. You believe me?"

Ev nods.

"Good. Good. We don't know what causes NPD or, as in your case, what gives rise to some of these traits. And you do see which traits you have, don't you?"

Ev doesn't want to retrieve from her WORM the list he'd read out to her. Its items burn in her heart, throw bile up into her nose, sear her consciousness. Yet her WORM has recorded every word, and she can access their molecular memories readily. They've dumped out the last few hours from her heap. It's as if those hours had never existed as they overrode her heap. His methodical itemizing immediately encoded her neuropeptides into indestructible memories. She cannot hide from them: grandiose, fantasies of unlimited success, special, requires admiration, needs excessive admiration, exploitative, lacks empathy. *Is even one of those really hers? She cannot see it, yet he's the expert.* Only Dr. Frock and his hypnotic gaze that pulls her toward his view of things exist. There is no exit from this truth.

Dr. Frock is speaking: "...I agree with my colleagues that we don't know the etiology, but we can consider such factors as genetic, family structure, and psychological factors. It's a complex origin, and so it's a complex treatment. I have tried to establish a therapeutic alliance, but I can see now why that was not as successful as it usually is. You deceived me into thinking you initially saw me as superhuman, but today, you revealed your true attitude. You devalued everything I know and have said to you in our sessions." He pauses. He adds: "Didn't you?" He holds her eyes with his green ones, his lips curved upward in a gentle, understanding, nonjudgmental smile. Ev cannot disagree with him. Her neck obeys his statement.

"Good. This is good. We're making progress again. You'll see I'm right, that this new treatment plan will work, and you will get better.

Think about these traits, especially the empathy and exploitative ones. You can see them, correct? Think back to the first day you came. Think back to how you came here? Did you think I didn't know? But I was willing to indulge you because you seemed in so much distress. That approach was incorrect as it heightened these traits. I find myself forced to confront you now to think about others. Remember: the truth is important to healing."

Dr. Frock pauses, his eyes on hers, before he continues. "So I must be honest with you now since you've resisted gentler methods. I see that that approach was the incorrect one. It distresses me how many women present with these traits and how often I'm forced to challenge them to think about how they present themselves and affect others. Do you know you displaced three of my long-time clients? They needed to see me, but you didn't give a thought to them. You needed to see me, and that's all you thought about. I don't know how with your SCPD you managed to convince the staff to change the schedule, but it doesn't matter. Somehow you did, and my clients were discommoded. One had rescheduled a meeting especially to see me an extra day. It was a lost opportunity, and he was quite upset. You didn't think about that, did you, Evelyn?" He shakes his head sorrowfully. "But it's not your fault. Your brain is wired that way. And I have high hopes, Evelyn. Very high hopes that we'll teach you empathy. You'll see where you went wrong that day and other days, too, for this would not have been a one-off. You're bright, Evelyn, perhaps you have a tendency to overestimate your I'm sure very good coding skills." He smiles down at her. "Don't you?" He waits.

Ev cannot speak, cannot move. Her programming codes his certainty and discerns nothing but his ideas. Her curiosity about ideal love, about anything, leaves her.

Dr. Frock entombs: "Nevertheless that doesn't take away the fact that you're a good learner." He nails her: "We'll get back on track." He holds her eyes to his for thirty seconds. "In fact. We are back on track." He smacks his hands down on his thighs and launches himself into a standing position. "Our time is up. But we'll continue this tomorrow."

He grasps his cane and strides toward the door, swinging the tapered stick of blackwood by his right side. He pivots smoothly and opens the door in one move. He gestures Ev out the door. *She must leave*, Ev thinks.

She stands up and wobbles toward him. She hesitates as she draws abreast and cranes her neck as he continues to smile down upon her. He says: "You'll be okay now, Evelyn, I promise. The DSM has helped my clients through the decades. I depend upon its wise perspicacity. It will help you, too." He opens the door wider and moves his left hand to just behind but not touching her back. She senses the unseen force and finds her feet moving through the doorway. The pressure of the air as the door shuts hits her spine.

30

Destruction

E v flees. She smashes through the clinic's entrance door to the sidewalk. She hurtles along the sidewalk to the end of the street and careens around the corner.

Ev believes Dr. Frock.

He's honest.

She swallows into herself the certainty of his thoughts, his ideas, his belief in the DSM, in its inviolability.

His truth sinks into the core of her heart.

She believes him.

His thoughts soak her magnetic field, cloud it grey. His words sadden the field, collapse it into her brain. His intellect turns an outwardly safe tool into a laboratory instrument, like a hawkish researcher turning safe soapwort to toxic saporin to watch mice change their behaviour. His actions like the neuropeptide toxin saporin leach E3, ConsciousnessMind, and her nascent connectedness out of her WORM memories of void.NullTime. His attitude vanishes the burgeoning Consciousness-Mind community.

His words, his certainty in the old science that comforts him, his DSM doctrine and Jeerah's words, her certainty in the kind of faith with no action that comforts her, her Saviour doctrine, spur Ev on, her feet pounding out the rhythm of their beliefs.

She reaches the next street and turns the corner before realizing that she's running around the block instead of heading straight home. She swivels on the balls of her feet; she swerves onto the street to go back. A car horn blasts her right ear, but she doesn't register it. The breath of the car's bumper on her calves doesn't register either in her mind as she darts in this direction then that, leaving the angry driver behind, as she keeps moving, moving, moving. Black-red begins to seep into the grey of her magnetic field as it lies emptied on her brain. Black-red sparks energy into her magnetic field, drying it, filling it with a new way of being, rocketing it off her brain to pulsate around her head. Black-red sweeps down from her magnetic field into the base EnergyHuman class that holds her cells together and powers her muscles.

She yanks on the handle of the apartment building's front door. It swings heavily toward her. She squeezes between it and its twin door before she can pull it all the way open. She flutters her hands as she waits for the elevator to the top floor.

She cannot wait.

Ev hauls her keys out of her jacket pocket as she pivots ninety degrees toward the staircase door and doesn't hear the elevator ding as the staircase door swings automatically shut behind her. She bolts up the stairs as if all the demons of the distorted Saviour, the spiritual rules, the log-like judgements, the DSM, the labels, the diagnoses, the words, the traits are racing after her, catching her up, grabbing her shoulders, and accusing her of her mistakes, her failures, her artificial ideas, her grandiosity.

Who is she?

She rams the staircase key into the lock of the door at the top and turns it hard. Clunk.

She slams through the staircase door and careens into the wall. She sags against it, thoughts sighing out of her, unread by her mind. And then Jeerah's beatific face, Dr. Frock's smiling face enter her consciousness. Jeerah's benign haranguing to pray and not blaspheme. Dr. Frock's benign adjuring that he has it right. They've both pondered a lot and know what they know. Her beads rattle in her inner ears. His kind eyes bulge toward her inner eyes. They show how much they want to help Evelyn.

How can Ev doubt prayer?

How can Ev doubt the DSM?

How can Ev doubt him and her, them?

She cannot. She does not. She must set aside her childish idea. Adolescence is a time for grand ideas that mean nothing. Full of heat and vigour, they create buffer overruns and introduce bugs if brought into adulthood. Heaven was their conduit, a made-up place less real than the void. She's a grown woman now. Dr. Frock had gently explained that the time for adolescent thinking is over. It is time to think like an adult, to see reality for what it is, not what she wishes it to be. Jeerah had explained that God would act. To wait on her idea of Saviour, to listen to her, but had waved her hand at the very idea that God is in coding, that she is like God and can create.

"Don't get yourself and God mixed up together," Jeerah had rebuked Ev. "That's God-me-too thinking," she'd said with slight reproach in her grey-brown eyes.

Shame suffuses Ev as she pushes herself along the wall to her door. Why did David.admin ask where she wanted to exit to? The place in which he existed, like a crucible of light, like a void before night, like beauty that burst stars into life, leaps into her consciousness. She clutches her keys with her shaking left hand to distract herself from this inner sight. She heaves her right hand up to her door handle. It falls limp. The keys drop to the floor. Ev bends over, stretching her hand downward to grasp them between all her fingers and thumb. She stares at her hand and watches it bring the keys back up to the lock. She forgets she only has to hold her door handle with her right hand in the right position for it to unlock. She selects the right key and fits it into the deadbolt lock and turns it to the left. The bolt thunks out of its socket, and she pushes the brass handle down and pushes the door inward.

She enters her apartment and flings the keys to her right. They automatically land in the bowl on the little table next to the door. Her door slowly shuts on its own. But it doesn't lock. She doesn't notice. Ev always locks it, but now, in this moment, she doesn't notice nor that she hasn't removed her boots and she's warming up inside her jacket. All she can hear is Dr. Frock's gentle consonants falling into her ears and his energy pushing them into her brain where they spread and multiply into her neuropeptides, the minds that she'd met, the mind that she'd sought, poisoned out of her molecular WORM memories.

As Ev walks forward, she glues her eyes on her computer, silent in its off state, Tomomi having had no time to turn it on. She arrives at her desk. She senses sunlight on her cheeks. She looks up and sees her windows with the blinds open. She steps to them like an automaton, first to the one on the right then to the left of her desk, to pull the blinds down until gloom overtakes her room. She returns to stand in front of her desk. She stabs at the computer's on button. The fan motor hums to life, the screen blinks on. Ev wheels her chair away from the wood of her desk and plunges down into it. Her arms droop at her sides as she watches her computer, her friend, power up. Her brown eyes gather black clouds. She must listen to Dr. Frock and Jeerah. They're older, wiser. They understand reality. She's been living in a virtual world, building up ideas that live only in her mind. Lived. They no longer live. She feels no connection to them anymore. She cannot see the three sheets of paper lying scattered across her desk, ink in blue and purple lines across all of them, from bottom to top, except for the first sheet of flax. The top part of it remains blank. Ev leans forward and types her password on her keyboard. Windows populates her working display's wallpaper with icons, and the top line of ink on the first sheet begins to fade. Ev launches E3, and the next line of ink vanishes. She opens the C++ editor and stares at the files. The next line of ink fades from the top of the letters until none of those letters remain visible. Ev clicks on the first header file at the top of the list and stares at all the declarations of all the objects she had created.

She.

Who is she to think these codes were anything but an adolescent fantasy?

Time to activate Lapis and roll back her programming to the version she was before she was fifteen, before she began wishing then seeking then finding a way to exit into hope. She's just a coder. A gamer. Not a seeker, a creator of worlds and minds and a bridge to something beyond. Dr. Frock's rare deep laugh rockets into her mind, and Ev selects all the code and hits the Del button. She deletes the file. She swallows and selects the source file for that header file. She reads the language of functions and statements. Jeerah's kindly tolerant smile fills her inner vision, and Ev selects all the code and presses the Del button. The code vanishes. She deletes that file. Ev enters into the rhythm of deletion and doesn't notice that the inked lines on the pages of flax, hemp, and cotton match her rhythm. As she deletes, ink dematerializes, letter by letter, line by line from the application form given to her by David.admin.

The code is gone.

No more early exit.

No more Heaven.

No more void.

No more mind.

Hers and hers.

No more David.admin.

And his questions.

No more grandiosity.

No more crucible of space and time.

Time to delete E3.

She opens up Windows Explorer, finds the files, and deletes them all, folder by folder. She clicks on the Recycle trash can, scans the contents, and without a sigh, empties the trash can and feels the new lines of code within her erase themselves backward in rapid succession.

She launches Firefox and finds Unreal Engine. She has Microsoft Visual Studio but needs to download Unreal Engine from the website. She sits back and watches it install itself. The minutes tick by; Ev doesn't move. The enormous engine takes its time installing itself, but Ev has no emotion, no thoughts. She exists in obedience. Submissive is who she was and who she is again.

The engine is installed. Ev sits up and opens it. She chooses the first-person shooter blueprint. She ignores the C++ coding option and simply uses the blueprint, the objects that already exist. She populates the primitive landscape of lines and shades with spheres and cubes. She begins to shoot them. She adds levitation and skipping to the spheres. She wants to add trees, but the greyness and the hard angles suppress her desire. She creates a landscape of concrete walls and insidescape of cement floors. She paints the blue sky hard grey thunder clouds. She turns the gun into a monstrous machine, and she endows it with endless bullets. She populates the landscape with targets so small, she must squint to see them, and targets so large that they emit bullet-resistant force-fields. She litters the ground and tops of walls with pickups that shatter or disappear in random order. But they're too easy to target, and so she returns to the object library and begins to search for obstacles, items that have rough surfaces, gunmetal textures, foreign to the heart of emotions. She places them haphazardly around her hostile landscape where there is no ConsciousnessMind and no god. She creates columns of fat books, that look like the squat, fat, purple brick tombs of the small-sized DSM-5. She hides gems of glorious auburns and purples and golds that regress into coal the longer they sit before she finds and shatters them as she picks them up. She creates character objects of healers and faithless fathers and gives them attributes of silver hair and colourful kaftans. The landscape is sufficiently complicated now to pose a challenge to her vision, and she begins to play in the 3D world of gaming on the 2D screen. Her VR helmet lies ignored on the desk to her left.

The almost-erased sheets of paper poke her elbow. She elbows them away from her to the right. Ev hunts for her controller and finds it lying on the floor. She lifts it up and lays it comfortably in her lap. She lets her weight push her chair back from her desk. She sinks comfortably into her chair and shoots with both thumbs. Her thumbs press the buttons of her controller rapidly and without pause, improving her aim and her success rate every minute. Her blank eyes unblinkingly fixate on her targets as magnetic red explodes out of the character objects in such violent pixelation, it splatters the screen in raging hues as the sun outside rises and sets again. Only once does she hesitate, but the energy infused into her expresses itself through her hard trigger. And she pulls.

The sheets of flax, hemp, and cotton whiten until Ev's signature alone remains. The first line of ink that had appeared when *Early Exit To The Void* had begun to mature into connectedness between ConsciousnessMind and Energy Minds, gone. The ink that had appeared when the connector had begun to see the hidden flow between space.Time and void.NullTime, when *Early Exit To The Void* at the hands of its creator, the connector, had begun to grow bridges and links of electrons flowing parallel and toward each other from one magnetic field to another—even those vast distances apart like hers and the mind, the first mind that had been watched and hunted and persecuted—dissolves away. The sheets slide off the table and float from side to side down to the floor. Ev thrusts her booted foot against a desk leg, and her chair wheels backward over the cotton sheet with her signature on it and crunches it into a mass of creases.

As she stared at the terminating end of the enormous gun pointed at her forehead from across the room, she suddenly recalled Ev. She felt that Ev was staring at her from the other side of the gun. Ev had appeared first as a presence near her, in her, like a ghost who didn't know they were a ghost standing behind and in her. Ev had become real that day on the rooftop when she was supposed to have killed herself and she'd have been just another suicide in a strange, inexplicable rash of suicides in the educated class. Guilt, the president had declared, for the crimes they had perpetrated against him and against the people. When he was targetted in a coup, ordinary hard-working people had been targetted, too, he'd shouted. The educated were guilty, the president had thundered through his controlled airwaves, and the people not in his targetting crosshairs had continued about their day, shopping for fruit, sweeping their floors, gossiping with the right neighbours in order to keep an eye on those who needed instruction in their wrong ways. Everyone wanted to stay out of his raging crosshairs and on the right side of his lethality. And so long as they weren't loading the messaging app he currently hated onto their phones, they were certain they were safe.

Like she had believed.

Ev had given her courage that day on the rooftop to defy the expected. She had felt like she was going to survive the purge, poorer but alive. She had felt this presence standing behind her, in her, change from confusion to tentative curiosity to caring interest to channeling her own fear, as if fear shared was fear lessened. Ev had allowed herself to become entwined in her narrative. Their minds had connected through planes of existence, she didn't know how. She only knew her need seemed to have beckoned Ev into her mind, and Ev had resisted then plunged in. Ev had strengthened her in their shared pursuit of returning to themselves and thriving.

And then Ev had vanished. She had felt her presence one day; gone the next. The knocks on her door had resumed.

She had hung on to the mosaic handed down to her from her great-grandmother to her grandmother to her mother to herself. She had been entrusted with that one and had promised to keep it, to care for it, to let no one else seize it. Had kept it hidden from dangerous sunlight, had dusted the small delicate artwork with a special duster her mother had found and bequeathed to her before she'd died from cancer just before the president had thrust forward to seize power from the elected government. A staged coup the world had decried and done nothing about.

Her mother's final words had been, "Don't let anyone take our family's mosaic from you. It's belonged to us women for special caring. We have protected it for generations from men taking what is not theirs."

Unfortunately, the men had known she had had this one artwork left. All her walls were bare, but they must've smelled her secret. Her money gone, her statues gone, her jewels gone, all her paintings but one gone, bribery no longer worked. They wanted it, and she hadn't unearthed it for them. And now Ev had reappeared but as a blackened ghost who didn't know what she was. A ghost with red-soaked eyes blanked of life staring at her through the tall man's eyes as if she was a target in a game. She wished she had broken her solemn promise to her ancestors. Unlike Ev, she didn't want to exit early.

She, the first mind in *Early Exit To The Void*, watched as Ev embraced the trigger tighter with her finger. Ev stilled. Ev pulled the trigger forcefully toward her breast without thought. The black muzzle flashed red. The blast reverberated through the mind's eardrums that—